P9-DOC-280

Withdrawn from
the collection of
Handley Regional Library

Best Intentions

Best Intentions

A NOVEL BY

Kate Lehrer

LITTLE, BROWN AND COMPANY
Boston   Toronto

THE HANDLEY LIBRARY

FICTION
Lehrer
9/87
c. 1

COPYRIGHT © 1987 BY KATE LEHRER
ALL RIGHTS RESERVED. NO PART OF THIS BOOK MAY BE REPRODUCED
IN ANY FORM OR BY ANY ELECTRONIC OR MECHANICAL MEANS,
INCLUDING INFORMATION STORAGE AND RETRIEVAL SYSTEMS, WITH-
OUT PERMISSION IN WRITING FROM THE PUBLISHER, EXCEPT BY A
REVIEWER WHO MAY QUOTE BRIEF PASSAGES IN A REVIEW.

FIRST EDITION

Library of Congress Cataloging-in-Publication Data
Lehrer, Kate, 1939–
Best intentions.

I. Title.
PS3562.E442B4   1987   813'.54   86-27496
ISBN 0-316-51973-1

RRD IN

Designed by Patricia Dunbar

Published simultaneously in Canada
by Little, Brown & Company (Canada) Limited

PRINTED IN THE UNITED STATES OF AMERICA

For Jamie, Amanda, and two Lucys

The characters and events in this novel are fictitious. Any similarity to real persons, living or dead, is coincidental and not intended by the author.

Best Intentions

1

OVER AND OVER again I tell myself the story of Sarah. I have a lot of facts, and I claim them. I do not claim objectivity. Still, I cut her out carefully, as I might a paper doll, measuring all the angles, clipping around the elbows and tabs just so. I am not always successful. She obscures conclusions.

As a student of proportion, I try to understand the precise balance of our pulls — competing in soccer games or love, squabbling over first in line or backseat car space, struggling for the gold star and for the hand to tuck us safely in bed; and I wonder how much skewing our fragile accommodations can take before the fairy godmother goes away forever.

Until Leslie died, I lived my life on the surfaces, not wanting to reckon with mortality. I thrived on clutter, and Sarah was a plentiful provider, though she herself was never so deceived or distracted by it. Or maybe not. Maybe — right up until that day — Sarah also was caught in the awesome foolishness of daily endeavors.

Last year in September my life glistened with promises. For three years I had worked for Sarah Corbin Adams, the luminary of American journalism. She had taken me, a twenty-five-year-old woman just out of Arkansas, and taught me about the news business and about myself — to test and stretch and win. She was magic for me. I sucked in her imagination and drew on it so deeply that it came out as my own possibility.

A possibility I was now ready, almost ready, to assert, I told myself that autumn day and filled up with expectation at plunging into another adventure. Soon I would slant my life away from Sarah's, make my debut. Along with knowledge, I had acquired opportunities and planned to use them.

With my car window down, I could hear chants from a demonstration in the next block; the clatter of a helicopter overhead; the crying of a baby in the small park, still half-filled with afternoon strollers lolling on benches, prolonging the day. Bikers and joggers, wearing shorts, T-shirts, and frowns, were out in profusion. It was one of those early September days that Washington reserves for its own in the lull between the summer crowds and the holiday pilgrims. A delicious place to live, I told myself and pulled in front of Sarah's.

I walked around to the side gate of the house, which resembled a townhouse in its height and skinny front but was separated from its neighbors by a pencil of lawn on either side and a deep slope of stone terrace and flower beds behind. This afternoon Sarah and I had transformed the back into an enchanted golden-autumn garden. Pots of mums and containers bursting with marigolds and daisies and zinnias were plopped everywhere, supplementing late-blooming sunflowers and day lilies. The afternoon sun picked up the gleam of brass bowls and candleholders atop gold tablecloths, and it highlighted the flecks of iridescent yellows beginning to appear on the old elm's leaves and a patch of yellow-spotted ivy. Even a yellow butterfly kept company with the flowers.

The party was for Sarah's daughter, Leslie, on her seventeenth birthday. Sarah loved the grand gesture, and this one was especially important. This one was to do nothing less than heal the rupture between her and Leslie, a hard premise for a party. She wouldn't be satisfied with less. She was used to working miracles.

Though, if this miracle did come off, I was partially responsible. My day had been taken up with this party. First calling Mr. Bowman about the wine and Jackson's about the flowers, both because of mix-ups. Then came the questions from the caterers — when to expect Leslie? when to serve the cake? where to set up the keg? the bar? Should drinks be passed also? (No. Sarah preferred guests get their own, thus an excuse to end conversations and move on.) And one last check to take care of smudges on the windowpanes and leaves in the swimming pool.

During most of this, Sarah was working on a column. In the middle of the morning she'd received an unexpected phone call from Australia's prime minister — an exclusive response to a charge made against him by a guest on her television program — and she was revising her column for tomorrow's paper.

"You're here!" Madge Hudson-Marsh, a good friend of Sarah's, called and sailed over to me. While I was home getting dressed, she had come and was now greeting the arriving teenagers. "Isn't Sarah ever going to finish up in there? Can't you hurry her along? I crept to her study door but was afraid to interrupt with that typewriter clicking away. She should get herself a word processor. Cut her work time in half." She brushed a wisp of black hair from her face and held out her hand.

"How lovely to see you," she said. "I've been put temporarily in charge, but Sarah Adams is entirely too picky for me to assume this burden alone. I'm going to be a wreck," she finished, not looking in the slightest perturbed.

Madge had been talking to this country's royalty all her life and always made the remarkable assumption that whoever she chose to talk with would be nothing other than delighted. They usually were. A succulent fifty, she retained all the presence of an early blossomed beauty. The mother of two children in their late twenties, and long ago divorced, she had made a life of parties and travel and special projects, but nothing that built on anything.

"But just look what she's done for Leslie! This garden belongs in a fairy tale. I'm sure this is the most exquisite seventeenth-birthday party ever."

"I expect so," I answered. Because of me, damn it. Once more I had worked my butt off to have Sarah get all the credit. Another reason to move on. Others could spend their lifetimes in self-effacement, but that wasn't for me. "We've worked hard enough on it."

"I'm sure you have," she responded, understanding immediately. "And the results are splendid. Sarah is lucky to have someone like you around."

"I wasn't fishing for compliments," I said and smiled; "at least, I don't think I was." My resentment disappeared. At any rate, no need to take it out on Madge.

"But you deserve compliments," she said. "You should be praised for what you've wrought. Now if Leslie can appreciate the effort you and her mother have gone to."

"Do you think she will? If she weren't so shy, I'd feel better about it." From the beginning these doubts had been in the back of my mind. Leslie usually hated any attention called to herself. When the idea for the party first came up, I had said all this to Sarah, but she was undeterred. "She'll love it," Sarah had answered. "She'll be bowled over." But getting bowled over wasn't the same as loving it, I thought, watching Leslie's friends drift through the yard; and Madge's reassurance was less than wholehearted.

As they waited for Leslie, groups of teenagers, talking in hushed tones and drinking beer and Cokes in paper cups, stood around the swimming pool and competed with palms and ferns and tubs of more yellow chrysanthemums for space. First-hour party awkwardness was still upon them. The pool was actually a part of the house, but in summer (and now) Sarah removed the roof and the glass panels from three sides, leaving only the brick wall the length of the pool and a skeletal steel structure to remind you of its indoor use.

Among all the faces around the pool I was glad to see Billy Long's. When Billy waved, I blew him a kiss — not that I knew him so well, though he and Leslie had been friends since kindergarten. He was just that kind of friendly, easy person with his grinning mouth too large for his face and his arms too long for his pudgy body.

Leslie's best friend, Page Tuttle, came toward me, and I walked to meet her. She would be her usual unpleasant self, for she linked me to Sarah, who disliked Page as much as Page distrusted us.

6

"Up to any good these days, Page?" I asked with what I hoped approached civility.

"Leslie's going to die when she sees who her mother has invited to this party," she said with a certain amount of glee.

"What do you mean?" I asked.

"I mean half these people are the nerds of the world as far as Leslie is concerned. She's avoided them like the plague ever since Miss Tripman's dancing class, and that was in the eighth grade."

"I missed the Miss Tripman's phase," I said.

"You must know about it. We're all sent there to become ladies and gentlemen. Only my mother didn't make me go. She said even in her day it was a pain. She stopped going when she found out her brother slipped another boy money to dance with her. She knew other brothers did it, but she was having no part of that gentlemanly scene again, and lucky for me. Sarah made Leslie do it, anyway. Leslie hated it and hated those grodies who got off on it. So she's just going to love having them all here."

"Maybe if you don't remind her, she won't notice them," I said and walked off. Earlier I had suggested that we consult Page, but Sarah wasn't about to. She knew exactly what she was doing, or thought she did.

Just inside the doorway I bumped into Jack Kelman, an old boyfriend of Leslie's. "How ya doing?" he said, smiling down at me. Looking up in his open, broad face, I wished him twelve years older or myself younger.

"Fine. I'm glad to see you," I said. *What are you doing here?* I wanted to ask, but, of course, I knew exactly what he was doing here: Sarah was aiming for a rematch. Two years ago Sarah had decided this good-looking, straight-A jock was too dangerous for a vulnerable girl like Leslie and became convinced that he saw her daughter as an easy mark. Other than passing her concerns on to Leslie, she hadn't interfered — the fling had passed quickly enough. Now she probably viewed him as a white knight compared to Rich Sanford, Leslie's current flame.

"Mrs. Adams asked me herself," he said. "Which goes to show

you never know." He punched me lightly on the arm and walked away.

But I did know. Sarah was desperate to get rid of Rich Sanford, the cause of a lot of the recent trouble between her and Leslie. He had dropped out of high school, partly because of drug problems, and was now playing (very poorly, I understood) in a punk rock band. Several months ago Sarah had found out Leslie was seeing him and had gone into a rage, forbidding Leslie even to talk to him. Since then there had been tears and cross-examinations and denials, but Sanford hadn't turned up again, and Sarah had almost convinced herself that it was over.

Sarah had organized Leslie's crowd to show up for the surprise. Family friends were to come later, but already they were beginning to trickle in. I watched a four-piece band called Phobia set up in a corner of the garden. They were to alternate with another that catered more to the adults. I was apprehensive about both, for Sarah had left the music to me.

More and more often I wondered what it would be like to give up the role of nursemaid and chief bottle-washer for the Adamses. Not that I wasn't grateful. I remembered how, discouraged and ready to go back to Arkansas, I had walked into Sarah's office with no references and no connections and how Sarah, on the basis of a thirty-minute conversation, had given me the job as her assistant.

I'd taken my own chance that day — a calculated guess that she'd want somebody tough-minded. My interview was only part of it. Sarah, wanting to please in that way of public personalities, as if to atone for success or mollify fate or prove once more an ability to charm, was challenged and intrigued by what she came to call my "puritanical hang-up," a subtle withholding of approval until I registered the sureness of a situation or person. On my part, the attitude was real enough, but like any good Puritan, I knew how to use it.

The time had come for me to take another chance. I needed to keep reminding myself, for leaving Sarah would never be easy. She filled my whole life. Another reason to leave, if I was honest with myself.

The music, I decided, would be just fine. So what if it wasn't perfect. I had to stop putting myself in Sarah's place. Separation had to begin somewhere.

And now Madge reappeared, shushing everyone. Leslie was pulling up in front, she said. Everyone quieted down, all eyes on Madge (Sarah, still inside, would make her own later entrance), and waited for the signal to share one of the few common rituals left to us. I was excited, too, though I didn't like Leslie very much anymore. Sullen, hostile, she had begun to withdraw from me as she had withdrawn from Sarah. She had no sense of how privileged she was or of the effort expended to attain that privilege.

Before Leslie was a year old, Sarah's husband had left the two of them. I didn't know why. Sarah never talked about him, nor did anyone else. Sarah had gone to work as a junior copy editor on the rewrite desk of a weekly magazine. Within a year, she was writing stories and convincing them to give her space to cover legislative committees and regulatory agencies, the great uncovered in Washington. Because it was tedious, hard work that most reporters weren't willing to do, she established herself as a true authority on how the government actually functions. She used that knowledge eventually to produce columns, books, radio shows, TV shows, lectures. She could decode the jargon and connect it to people's lives.

Her reputation grew out of her hard work; her fame grew from the hard work and her personality. For the last seven years she had hosted a weekly television show called "Sarah Adams' Spotlight," in which she focused on a guest who was in the news or whose policies were in the news. Along with the interview, she would run film clips, possibly bring in panelists for discussion, and give always her own personal commentary on the person and the policies.

The personal commentary made the difference. When she began, no one understood just how much difference. The network had felt pleased with itself for putting on a show of quality in prime time. (Not a completely altruistic move: they were up against what had appeared to be an unbeatable winner, and this was an inexpensive alternative.) They never dreamed it would become a hit and beat out the other shows in its time period, and all because of Sarah's personal style. She was honest with the audience about her own reactions to the guest. People tuned in to see how she would treat the muckety-muck of the week. Would the guest falter under her glare or be charmed into revealing more than anyone would have thought possible? She approached each show with the same relish as her audience.

Even so, television was her stepchild. She got into it because power came from it. "These days Presidents call TV anchors, not columnists," she said to me. "If I want access to world leaders, I'd better have something pretty grand to offer in return." And she did. Nobody turned her down. Or turned her down twice.

By the time Leslie was eight, they were ensconced in their Georgetown house with a full-time housekeeper, a nanny, and Leslie in the most fashionable private school. When I came into their lives, Sarah was an established eminence, not only in Washington, but in the country; and Leslie seemed hardly aware of how they got there. In many ways, I thought, as the band readied itself for Leslie's entrance, today celebrated just that achievement.

The gate opened; the band and guests began "Happy Birthday"; and Leslie stood there stunned. She turned very red, and I was afraid she was going to cry or bolt; but, whichever, she caught herself and accepted the song as if it were a cold shower, something to be endured but good for you. And finally she smiled.

Wearing a blue angora sweater, a birthday present from Sarah, she looked better than I had seen her in a long time. With some care on her part — losing fifteen pounds and clearing her complexion — she could be lovely someday. Now her brown hair was combed and pulled back from her face, making it possible to see her pale blue eyes, her one really good feature. Usually she refused to wear blue and her hair hung in her face, obscuring those eyes from all but the most diligent observers.

As the song ended and the spontaneous applause began, the French doors connecting the pool to the house were flung open. Sarah, radiant in flowing white silk pajamas, arms extended, made her way to Leslie in a grand sweep around the pool. Her short brown curls gleaming, she hugged and kissed her daughter with the passion of a long-hoped-for homecoming.

The guests stood poised, ready to participate; and Sarah waved the band to begin playing while urging everyone to hug the birthday girl. On cue the group began to laugh and dance and wander toward Leslie.

Sarah began walking among the young people, kissing them on their cheeks, no pecks in the air for her. Her face was striking in its openness and pleasure — and its discipline and control. Fine and sharp, it forced distinctions. I envied its sureness, the aspect that always struck me most. She looked exempt from the doubts, misgivings, the minor states of hysteria that beset most of us, even on good days. Only her hair, that unruly trademark, and her quick brown eyes augured something more — a restlessness, an unleashing of passions merely hinted at in the composed face on the chic body — as if they had lives of their own that required more room, more play, more energy than one mortal frame could give them. An energy that could be a mixed blessing for those around it. On impulse, I decided to seek out Leslie.

She was talking to Gordon Simons, Sarah's on-again, off-again lover for many years and a vain, handsome man of about fifty. His vitality and triathlon body gave an illusion of youth and height. He ran one of Washington's main think tanks and consulted, somewhat mysteriously, with foreign governments on the side. At this time, he was having an affair with a twenty-eight-year-old social secretary at the British embassy.

Leslie was ambivalent about Gordon. He was caring with her, but she had seen too many quarrels between him and Sarah not to resent him. Sarah's unhappiness made Leslie feel even more responsible for her mother. Neither Leslie nor Sarah yet knew about his new interest in the British "special relationship."

Sarah had followed me over. "See how well it's working, Leslie? We could have been doing this for years if only you'd let me," she said.

Gordon grinned. "You were magnificent," he said to Sarah. She didn't respond, but turned her attention to me.

"I've just found out that the President is going ahead with the massive aid bill for Central America. Check with Walker about it."

I hated to think of all the notes I was going to have to send out for Sarah tomorrow. Almost without fail, high-level (and a lot of times, not so high-level) government officials would hear from her concerning their discussion, be it professional or personal. Except on occasions like this, she was hardly ever without her tape recorder to jog her memory and mine.

Sarah continued talking to me: "I also hear Walker has a good-looking son coming back to Washington. Maybe you should meet him." Whenever she sensed a restlessness in me, she'd start playing matchmaker.

But before I could respond, Leslie said, "I'm sure he's met hundreds of skinny blue-eyed blondes. What makes you think he'd bother with Courtney?"

"Don't be rude," Sarah snapped.

"It's OK," I said, though Leslie's tries at humor left a lot to be desired these days. I noticed Gordon had drifted off.

Sarah dropped the subject and put her arm around Leslie. "I've just had a nice visit with Suzanne. An outstanding personality. Such an outgoing girl. You should bring her around. So outgoing."

Suzanne Lake had a small, delicate nose, wavy blond hair to go with it, and the aplomb of a chief of protocol. I understood why Leslie never liked her.

"Mother, Suzanne could live with us, and it still wouldn't turn me into an outstanding, outgoing personality." The last bit was a mimic of Sarah's voice.

"Billy Long told me you were great auditioning for the part of Kate in *The Taming of the Shrew*," I said quickly, trying to salvage the festive mood.

"You didn't tell me that," Sarah said, sending me a grateful look. "What a lovely surprise! You'll be wonderful as Kate."

"I didn't get the part."

"You should have told me. No wonder you've been upset."

"I knew it would upset you."

"Certainly I'm upset. For you. You should have had that part. You would be wonderful. I feel like telling your headmaster — he's coming, you know — what I think about it."

"That's why I didn't tell you."

"Will you work on sets?" I asked.

"No, she will not. She's been a good sport with that bunch for the last time."

"I haven't made up my mind yet," Leslie answered.

"Who got it?" Sarah asked.

"Janice Ramsey."

"I don't even know her."

Leslie laughed in spite of herself.

Anthony Morris found us laughing. His most recent government job had been as the President's national security adviser: now he was back practicing law in his old firm. This statesman of considerable reputation and scion of a famous American family looked not so much younger than his sixty-three years as ageless with his close-cropped hair that ended with a cowlick on his crown. Five generations of good breeding had gone into his beneficent handshake; and his smile, like that of any American patriarch, welcomed you on your own terms. He could afford equality.

"One's dinner partner does have an obligation to be amusing, don't you think?" he had said to me recently at a dinner sponsored by the Foreign Service Institute. With surgical precision he had extracted an artichoke heart for me, his competent and graceful hands another signifier of his authority. On that occasion he found me amusing, or perhaps, found the companion on his other side unamusing, for he talked to her only minutes. Indeed, what really amused him was his own voice. I asked questions well. Even so, I was glad to see him again.

Then Sarah introduced us, and he said he was glad to meet me. Not placing people is a malady in this city, particularly for those who meet dozens of new ones a day. When I am his age and famous, I will have the same Washington problem, I consoled myself.

He had been talking to Senator Ditson, who joined us also; and Sarah teased Morris about the conversation. "Have you been giving poor Barney advice on Africa? Everyone else here is." Ditson was head of a subcommittee on Africa and was getting ready to put in place an aid program, especially for Somalia, to deal with that country's drought. So far, the story hadn't made the news, but judging by the interest at this party, that wouldn't be the case much longer. The interest had to do less with the plight of the people than the size of the package that Ditson was insisting upon, thereby putting himself in direct opposition to the President, a member of his own party. Morris, Ditson said, was the only one here who hadn't spoken to him about the situation, but that was because Morris probably knew more than he, Ditson, anyway.

"You represent Somalia?" Sarah asked Morris. His firm was known to have some African ties.

"Barney Ditson exaggerates my areas of expertise."

Ditson laughed. "No, I don't. It's just that Somalia can't afford you."

"Would it help if Somalia could afford him?" I asked. Ditson's cause was admirable. You didn't have to look at TV film footage to know that.

"I can use all the help I can get" — Ditson smiled — "including a sympathetic story from your boss."

Sarah turned to Morris. "Barney should be giving the upcoming dinner party instead of you and Sheila. Champagne and caviar. He's the one who needs our help," she teased.

"If you're not careful, I'll disinvite you both and ask Miss Patterson instead."

"But she is invited," Sarah answered and put her arm around me. "Sheila has taken Courtney under her wing."

And indeed Mrs. Morris had. I had helped her stage a celebrity tennis tournament, and she'd been kindly enough disposed toward me, not only to include me in one of her small dinners, but to choose as my dinner partner an up-and-coming young congressman, the new bachelor rage of Washington. If nothing else, she said, we'd be great playing doubles in tennis.

Right after I had settled in my job, Sarah had thought it a good idea that Leslie and I take tennis lessons together, thus providing Leslie with a playmate, and me with one of the more negotiable of Washington social skills. Though Sarah herself didn't bother to play, she vowed that I would have as many doors opened through tennis as I ever would as a journalist, and, so far, she was right. I had always played a pretty fair game. Sarah found me a good coach, and I worked hard. Sarah and Leslie faithfully came to watch me in my first matches. I always won. I was afraid not to.

Before Morris came up with a proper response, Madge walked over. Morris pulled Ditson to one side. And how could he help? I heard Morris ask the senator. Madge brushed cheeks with Leslie and told her she and Sarah were needed for hostessing duties. All kinds of people were looking for them. Sarah gave an Oriental bow to Madge and grabbed Leslie's hand. Madge and I watched them running across the lawn.

Madge sat down and lit a cigarette with the languid glamour of a thirties movie star. "She's driving them both crazy in the pursuit of Leslie's happiness."

"She needs a vacation. She worked too hard all summer," I said.

Madge shook her head. "You think a trip would keep her from finding out about Gordon?"

"Maybe."

We sat there watching the smoke blend into the golden haze and listened to the 4/4 beat of the second band. With her toe, Madge stubbed out her cigarette on the grass, then picked up the butt with a Kleenex. "For myself, I'd rather be a little lonely than put up with Gordon," she said.

In the three years that I had known her, that was the most

personal and revealing remark she had ever made in front of me. What must it be like, I wondered, for a woman, a beauty in her youth — a smart, vivacious, wealthy beauty at that — to find her possibilities diminished? To have her expectations met and then to find, not all at once, but ever so gradually, that they had not been met at all. And could she confide this to a Sarah Adams?

Rejoining the party, we found many more of Sarah's friends had come. For many this was the first fall gathering. Everyone was now back in town working and glad of the occasion to see each other. Along with the Supreme Court justice from across the street, and Ruth Howard, the head of the Smithsonian, with her husband Sam, a nuclear physicist — both friends of long standing — there were journalists, a couple of senators, and some of Leslie's teachers. In short, any of Sarah's friends who also knew Leslie.

They would come, kiss Leslie on the cheek, wish her happy birthday, chat with each other, say how nice to see young people have fun, possibly take a turn dancing, then leave.

The lights around the pool cast a yellow shimmer on the water. A keg of beer was being discreetly regulated by a friendly but firm college boy. Most of the young people were working hard to the throbbing beat of the music from Phobia. They came together and split apart — sometimes in couples, sometimes in groups of three or six. I caught a whiff of pot and hoped that Sarah wouldn't notice. I decided to relax a little. The music was infectious. Beyond the gate a siren wailed, as always in Georgetown.

"You look pleased with yourself," Bob Owens, the former attorney general, said to me.

"I'm pleased not to be seventeen," I said, and we both laughed. I liked him very much. His eyes had the bright honesty of a good little boy's.

"Will you two let me in on the joke?" Sarah asked, offering her cheek to Bob, who brushed her lips instead. He and his wife, Madeline, had been friends of Sarah's for years. I suspected he and Sarah had been even closer. "You've done a great job here,"

Bob said to her. "It is going well, isn't it?" Sarah asked happily. "Leslie is dancing every dance. Jack Kelman has asked her three times. These guys are great sports. I only had to hint and they fell right in. She is having fun. Don't you think?"

Bob's wife walked over, and Sarah asked her if this seemed a good time to cut the cake. "Don't put that responsibility on me," Madeline answered. She seemed to mean it as a joke, but it was laden with hostility, the way it happened when Madeline had too much to drink.

Sarah smiled and excused herself, but Madeline stopped her. "Leslie looks pretty tonight," she said. "Everyone says so."

"Thank you." Again Sarah started to leave, sensing Madeline's mood.

"She's not a thing like you, is she, Sarah?"

"How do you mean?" Sarah asked, smiling.

"You know, not your looks, not your personality. Is she like her father?"

For all the noise around, the quiet among us was deep and long. Sarah continued to smile.

"Yes. She is like him. And my brother. My brother is attractive. Do you have any attractive people in your family, Madeline?"

Sarah left before Madeline could answer.

The timing of the cake was perfect, for the golden day had turned into a creamy yellow twilight, helped along by little white lights throughout the garden. The cake, massed by yellow daisies and topped by seventeen jumbo candles, was rolled out and presented to Leslie as the guests, the bands, and the small chamber chorus from her school sang a medley of old songs and pop songs and, once more, "Happy Birthday."

This time Leslie took it as her due and graciously thanked everyone, though not Sarah specifically. Then the chorus serenaded her with "Greensleeves," an old favorite of Sarah's. After that, a balloon man delivered balloons and a funny verse, and some of the boys presented a singing telegram in the shape of a strongman wearing a bikini. Leslie appeared to be enjoying the spectacle, a major feat for our bashful girl.

I remembered my own seventeenth birthday. My friends had sung "Happy Birthday" to me in the school lunchroom, and I had been delighted. At home I was given underwear and a Safeway pound cake without candles, and I had been resigned. The most elaborate of my friends' seventeenth birthdays had been a backyard cookout. I was beginning to understand why Sarah was always thrusting things, events, ideas onto Leslie. There was something to be said for reliving your past, this time the way you wanted it.

Sarah was certainly getting a chance to relive hers. With the party well underway, she was relaxing and enjoying herself. When the music started up again, she joined in with a group of dancers. Billy Long and Jack Kelman asked her to dance. Soon the boys were all asking, and the crowd began clapping her on. She was splendid. She followed every step her partners came up with, and thought of some they hadn't. She was good, her gestures small, quick, and right. She did their dances better than they could. When the song ended, they applauded. The next one was hard rock, and she shook her shoulders in time to it, shook her shoulders hard and went into a back bend. "Oooohs" went around the garden. From the adults, too. They were enjoying having one of their own keep up.

When Leslie slipped around to the other side of the garden, I followed. I found her slouched in a chair, arms folded over her chest. I felt awkward standing there, silly to have trailed after.

"Is my mother still making a fool of herself?"

"She's having a good time. She thinks you are, too."

"Sure. Why not? I love to see her turn every party into a set for performance." She sat up and began to play with a fallen leaf. "Courtney, I'm sorry if you thought I was rude. It just came out wrong. I can sound angry even when I don't mean to."

"No problem."

"And thank you. I know how hard you work on these Adams productions. It is a nice party. A little Barnum and Bailey. But nice."

"Your mother worked a lot harder than I did."

I sat staring at the trellised roses climbing up this side of the house, and wondered what kind of mother it took to make a person happy. I had wanted much more from mine; Leslie wanted much less, or less of what she got and more of something else. That was the catch, I supposed. We knew what the something else was only until we had it.

"She really is trying," I said.

She crumbled the leaf and didn't say anything for a long time. "My father has said I can come live with him." Then so quietly I could pretend to myself I didn't understand her: "I'm leaving."

With that, she put her hands in her pockets and walked back toward the music, the lights, and Sarah's laughter.

2

THE WEEK after Leslie's party was not a good one. Every morning I opened the office door, not knowing how I would find Sarah. One day soon she was bound to find out about Leslie, whom I'd tried to contact twice. Leslie wasn't returning my calls, and I knew better than to push too hard. If she felt like confiding in me, she would; otherwise, I'd get a polite smile and a weather report.

Every morning I came a little earlier, out of no eagerness to discover what awaited me, but to finish my work before midnight. Sarah had been delighted with the party; delight energized Sarah; and more energy for Sarah meant more work for me.

This Friday morning I arrived a little before seven o'clock to find Sarah's secretary, Gladys Banks, a plump woman of sixty with defiantly brown hair, at work. Already she was typing at her desk, a hodgepodge of papers and books and file folders crowned with a small pitcher of red carnations perched precariously on a stack of newspapers. Her chaos was the focal point of the reception area, an otherwise nondescript room with an ancient brown leather couch, a couple of director's chairs covered in beige suede, and a few prints selected haphazardly by Sarah and arranged accordingly.

"Get you some coffee?" I asked, tossing my purse and tote crammed with papers into my broomcloset of an office.

"Not so much creamer. You're putting too much in lately."

"I'm trying to give us energy." This was as close as I would come to saying we were working hard. In this office we were as macho as any politician's staff; hard work was a given. One not only didn't complain; one didn't acknowledge anything to complain about. I handed her a mug with "Gladys" painted in bright red fingernail polish, the same mug she was using the first day I came for an interview. "Are we having an office party?" she asked, eyeing my perfectly pressed black wool dress.

"I'm capable of ironing just for the hell of it."

"I'm sure. You've just never done it before. I don't know that dress either."

The dress was new. I was going out tonight, but I'd be damned if I was going to tell her. "Any early morning instructions?" I asked. She was already typing again.

"If you think you'll get out of here tonight, you're dreaming. She doesn't have anything on her calendar," she said.

I didn't say anything, but, unfortunately, she had a point. When Sarah was on a tear like this, she availed herself of any free time to work. And her work usually included both my helping and keeping her company.

Out of habit, I took my coffee into Sarah's office, where I usually began my day by checking in with Sarah, or, as was the case this morning, checking her desk for notes she might have left for me. On her desk was a series of snapshots of her and Leslie taken on a carousel, both of them clowning for the photographer. The desk was a banker's desk; the carpet and walls, a doctor's office beige; a large ficus tree in front of the double window, the only touch of color.

The first time Sarah and I met, her office had disappointed me. It was as undistinguished as the downtown building that housed it. Anyone with impressive friends could have occupied it. The walls were covered with photographs of Sarah skiing with Betty and Jerry, walking with Jimmy, interviewing Dick, and talking and dancing with an assortment of other well-known politicians and personalities.

Her famous charm did not transfer to the deadly serious office, but neither did it translate into some intimidating superwoman. In fact, neither she nor her office had any of the puffed-up self-importance that finds ways of attaching itself to much lesser mortals around town.

I looked at her appointment book. Monday, a breakfast with the chairman of the Federal Reserve Board, a result of a phone call he made to her about last week's TV program, spotlighting the secretary of the treasury but, in the process, lambasting the Federal Reserve's monetary policies. Not fair, the chairman had said and agreed to discuss it over breakfast. Tomorrow night, a black-tie dinner party given by the new publisher of a magazine in honor of the old editor about to be booted out, a very Washington maneuver to keep all fences mended. Thursday night she had us down to go hear a chamber music group, one of Sarah's passions, not one of mine. I wasn't all that fond of chamber music, but Sarah was convinced that if I heard enough and she talked enough, all that would change. So far it hadn't; convincing her was another matter. Summer before last she had decided I should take up sailing with her. She scheduled lessons and accepted every invitation that put us close to a boat. I was forever sick to my stomach. Only that August did she relent and admit defeat. While I enjoyed her attentions most of the time, they could get too much even for me. Usually considerate, she could smother in her enthusiasms.

But nothing showed on her book for tonight. My irritation with this manic high she was on rose. How could she equate the success of a party with the well-being of her and Leslie? I was still annoyed when Sarah breezed in.

"Bastard," she said, slamming the paper on the desk. Her eyes had all the intensity of an owl's ready to attack. I wondered if we were talking about Gordon. "U.S. trade representative, indeed! In my own home and he didn't tell me."

We were, I realized, talking about Anthony Morris, who, according to the morning paper, was to add trade representative to his list of titles. Much was made over the importance of the post in this era of international economic interdependence.

"Maybe he didn't know," I replied.

"Of course, he knew. He also knew the President had no

business appointing him. The arrogance of those two! The unbridled arrogance."

I thought back to Anthony Morris standing, at the dinner party where we had first met, patrician head cocked to one side, listening to Vice President Burns with a deference bordering on condescension, and then to the kind of sharp attention laced with wit and delight he bestowed on Sarah when she said something. "He never had a chance to talk to you long," I ventured, but she didn't bother to respond. Sarah, I knew, could hold a grudge for a long time. Just as a particularly good source, up to and including Presidents, could count on some degree of protection, someone who was not forthcoming enough for her could be sure of retribution — anything from no mention at all by her, to an attack at some point in the future. I imagined Morris to be in for a chiding down the road.

The road was shorter than I expected. Those restless fingers began drumming the desk, a sure sign she was onto something.

"They can't be allowed to get away with this."

I risked the question: "With what?"

"Courtney, my God, sometimes you're stupid! This man is in a law firm that represents foreign interests all over the world. And why do they have these clients? Because Anthony Morris has contacts all over this government. And after all the stories that have been written on this problem and all the hearings proving the danger, the President has the audacity to reappoint one of the offenders."

"Morris has been going in and out of government for years," I argued. "Besides, no story has been written on him specifically. Compared to a lot of the others, he looks like a Boy Scout."

"So what? The point is, the President and Morris are playing by nobody's rules but their own. Trade representative! That firm is up to its ears in foreign trade.

"I want you to find out everything you can about the clients they represent. All it will take is one or two examples of their involvement with a regulation which works against some American interests — say textiles or computers. Something that will rile up an American lobby. That ought to be easy enough. Any of our lobbyist friends in those areas will know what's going on in the committees now. And you're bound to get a leak from a staffer or two. Just be careful of the stories you pick up, though, frankly, we get led down primrose paths more often by congressional staffers than lobbyists. Whichever, we're bound to come up with something before the confirmation hearings. If we can't shame them, we'll embarrass them."

A good idea, I agreed. But today I was determined not to be swallowed by this maw of an office, to be sloshed around in an ill-tempered stomach until evening. The head of Immigration, I told her, had agreed to cancel her appearance on both the morning show and a Sunday talk show in order to give Sarah first crack at the new U.S.–Mexico border policy this week. The competition to get first dibs on the celebrities of the week was fierce. Their representatives would negotiate with the shows' producers as to how much air time their pet would get; in some cases, how many plugs announcing said star's arrival; and, in the most valued prizes, how many days of continuous talks could be arranged. Sarah's program didn't lend itself quite to those extremes, but she fought to have exclusivity rights along with the other weekly talk shows. She never bargained; she usually won; but she never took the process for granted either.

Neither did she this morning. The news appeased her. Morris's indiscretion was forgotten. She began rifling through her day's stack of papers, but stopped and looked at my dress.

"It's very becoming. I'd like it better with a scarf." She looked at my hair. "Leslie and I are getting haircuts this afternoon. Want to come?" She laughed. "Not that yours doesn't look wonderful, but Matthew could blow-dry it for you. He gives it more fluff than you do."

Sometimes I knew exactly how Leslie felt. "I'll pass on this one," I answered. The last thing I wanted was to spend time with the two of them in a beauty salon.

Sarah had definite ideas on hair. She had convinced me to wear mine longer. On coming to Washington, trying to copy a hairstyle in *Vogue,* I'd cut it all off. While I was stylish, I was not particularly attractive. On the other hand, Sarah felt Leslie's hair was neither stylish nor attractive. The first fight I witnessed between them had been over Leslie's hair.

It was the day that, as a last bit of whimsy before giving up on the Washington job market, I had asked for and gotten an interview with Sarah Adams, the closest thing to a heroine I had. By then I was under no illusions about my chances, for I'd discovered thousands of young people just like me with the same credentials and motives. The difference was they all seemed to have connections and I didn't, though, admittedly, their connections didn't appear to be doing them much good either.

But Sarah had been wonderful to me. She had an opening and she hired me. That she expected more from me than to be just another ambitious, energetic assistant — that part a given — became apparent when Leslie dropped by her office during the interview. Not yet believing Sarah had offered me the job and a little dazed by how fast it had happened, I was slow in focusing on Leslie and understanding just how crucial she was to everything that touched Sarah, including me. About fourteen then, she'd been in jeans and an army fatigue jacket. Sarah had given her a bear hug and a noisy kiss on the cheek.

"I'm meeting Page at the movie down the street." Leslie had hurried her words and returned her mother's kiss without enthusiasm. She was as awkward and plain as her mother was beautiful.

"Is that a good idea? A downtown movie by yourself? You never know what stray off the street might decide to sit by you."

"Page is going, too."

"Not now, darling. Her mother doesn't think it's a good idea, either." Sarah put her arm around Leslie, but Leslie pulled away.

"Did she call you?" Leslie asked.

"Page called for you, and I returned the call. Anyway, since you're here, Gladys has made you an appointment for a haircut. Your time won't be wasted."

"You called her mother?"

"Page first. It really wasn't smart of you girls. On a weekday too."

"You had no right," Leslie choked out. "You shouldn't. . . ."

25

"Enough, sweetheart," Sarah interrupted, cupping Leslie's head with her hand. "It's more important to get you fixed up for the dance tomorrow night." Sarah turned to me and smiled. "Won't the boys be smitten once they see the new Leslie?"

Leslie twisted away and put her books down on her mother's desk. "I don't like boys." She spoke in a barely audible whisper.

Sarah laughed and included me in it. I smiled, but already she had turned away.

Leslie was insistent. "You shouldn't of . . . Page will hate me . . . she . . ."

"Shouldn't *have*, Leslie. Don't mumble." She looked at Leslie with a hint of displeasure. "Now wash your face before your haircut."

"I don't want my hair cut," Leslie said to her clogs.

"Of course, you do," Sarah answered. "It's too long and stringy."

It was hard to understand the fuss over her hair — limp and lifeless whatever its length. They should have concentrated on her eyes, bluebonnet-colored, slicing through her sullen face and set off by long, thick lashes.

Gladys came to the open door with some papers in her hand, but neither Sarah nor Leslie paid any attention to her, nor did she try to interrupt them.

Sarah was palming the back of Leslie's head. "We've been through all this. When your hair gets long, it gets stringier and straighter."

"I like straight hair."

"It isn't becoming to you. Your face looks that much longer."

"I'll be a total mutant. Nobody has short hair." Leslie's eyes filled with tears.

" 'Nobody' means Page Tuttie, and she looks cheap."

"Karen Sanders has long hair and you think she's perfect."

"Karen Sanders has a petite face. And I doubt that she washes her mane twice a day." Sarah let go of Leslie. "You're obsessed with your hair, darling, and it's unnatural. If it's shorter, maybe you can think about something else."

Leslie began blinking her eyes rapidly. "I like to think about my hair."

26

Gladys was pretending to ignore the exchange as she continued making notes and looking down at the papers. I was still standing there, reluctant to call attention to myself by moving, not able to decide how to appear least awkward in an awkward situation.

"You know," Sarah was saying, putting her arm through Leslie's, "I think on some level you're ready to cut your hair. That's the real reason you came down here today. Somehow you knew if you came, I'd see to it that we trimmed it up."

Sarah looked very satisfied with her analysis, which, I admit, didn't make any more sense to me than it apparently did to Leslie, who looked at a complete loss for a response. "I totally like it" was all she came up with. Sarah shook her head. "Leslie, between your hair washings and your 'totals' you may drive me mad."

"I *want* my hair." A few tears slipped from Leslie's eyes. I didn't trust them. She wasn't as vulnerable as she appeared. Though she didn't look especially old for her age, I sensed a wariness that belied innocence. Her pose struck me as another tactic in their quarrel. Understandable — Sarah as a mother would be a formidable opponent — but not all that genuine. I looked to see if Sarah knew that, too, but I couldn't tell. She didn't seem to. Maybe I was being too much the cynic.

"Believe me," Sarah was saying, "I want you to have what you want." She gently took her daughter's shoulders in her hands and, forcing eye contact, said, "But I don't want people to call you 'horseface.' "

This time there was no pretending. Leslie's face crumbled, then, just as quickly, tightened. Without a word she turned toward the door. We looked at her in embarrassed silence. At least, I was embarrassed. And alarmed: witnessing such an intimate scene could hardly work in my favor. And annoyed: why had they picked this time to have a squabble? I had an unreasonable desire to bop Leslie for her stubbornness.

Sarah followed Leslie into the hallway. Gladys shook her head. I wasn't sure whether I should sit back down or leave.

"Should I leave?" I asked Gladys.

"Why?"

"You know," I answered, following her back to her desk.

Gladys didn't exactly smile, but she no longer seemed put off by me. "Oh, that." She motioned toward the hall. "It's just Sarah and Leslie."

In a few minutes Sarah and Leslie returned to Sarah's office and closed the door on Gladys and me. Just Sarah and Leslie. What did that mean? It was disconcerting — not quite professional — having children running around a business office, disrupting everything.

I wanted to ask Gladys more about Leslie, about her place in the office patterns, but before I could think of inoffensive phrasing — something better than Does she bother us often — Sarah came out with her arm through Leslie's. "Gladys," she asked, "what will happen to us if you take Leslie to a movie now?"

Gladys glanced at her watch. "This" — meaning me — "is your last appointment, but I'm only halfway through typing your column."

"I'll type it myself."

Gladys hesitated a minute. "I need to call my sister and let her know I'll be late."

"Then call her," Sarah answered impatiently. "And reschedule the hair appointment for the morning."

I followed Sarah back into her office, where, once more, there was a regal queen above the fray. In detail she explained to me what was involved in her operation. She did most of the writing and reporting herself with the help of a research assistant (now my job), Gladys, and two college interns.

She also had offices at the television station, where the network provided her with an executive producer, two producers, and four researchers, as well as the technical staff necessary to get the program on the air. The two producers, she explained, saw to it that the shows were physically put together. They made sure the guests, if any, were invited and present at the appointed time, that all the tapes and slides and stills were in place with proper editing done on them, that researchers' work was done and organized. The executive producer also acted as a liaison between Sarah and the rest of the staff and was responsible for the overall planning of the programs. That included keeping both the guests and the program itself varied, spiced, and paced. Sarah tried to limit her time at the studio to a weekly planning meeting at which guests for future programs were selected and a rundown on the coming program was conducted, including a look at film clips that might be used. On the afternoon of the program she came several hours early for last-minute preparations; otherwise the staff came to her downtown office if other meetings were needed.

She discussed salary. She discussed work hours and vacation and sick leave. I had been mistaken in thinking that she ever intended to leave things as vague as I was willing to.

Then, quietly, she brought the conversation round to Leslie. Her only child, she said, and she (Sarah) hovered too much sometimes. But Leslie came first. Above everything. Careers were ephemeral; Leslie would endure. As she talked, she casually clasped a letter opener in her hands. They were graceful and slender, like one of those spiny seashells — fragile-looking, but tough enough to protect whatever was entrusted to them. I envied the sullen-faced girl those hands.

And I felt a little ashamed of my misgivings about Sarah. Of course, she was only trying to be a good mother. If she had been a little excessive, it was because she erred on the side of love. That was more than my mother had ever done. What it proved was that Sarah Adams was fallible like the rest of us. Not a mythic heroine, but a warm, caring woman and a loving mother. What else could anyone ask of, or even want in, another human being? Suddenly I felt strong and sure and ready to help her face the world.

The door opened and Leslie came in. "We missed the beginning. I didn't want to stay."

"Never mind," Sarah answered. "I want you to get to know Courtney."

Gladys, who came in slightly out of sorts behind Leslie, seemed pleased enough that I'd gotten the job. She insisted on typing the rest of Sarah's column before she left. Sarah steered Leslie and me out the door. She suggested I join them for "Ida's beans" and then take Leslie to an early evening feature. Leslie gave me a quick look — either sizing me up or cutting me down, I wasn't sure which — before nodding her head in agreement. Sarah turned to me. "All right?"

"I'd love to," I answered.

Sarah looked satisfied; Leslie, a little less so. I was delighted. This town was filled with smart people. I would be something more, I told myself that day. I would make myself indispensable to her, become so much a part of her life that she would include me in her worlds in ways I could only dream about.

Being included, I had found over the months that followed, was more than a little complicated and encompassed not only the large agenda — opening the right doors, establishing my journalistic credentials — but smaller agendas as well, such as she was doing right now: running her brush through my hair, "for fluff."

After she groomed me to her satisfaction, we got to work on her column. We went over my research, and she began writing but asked me to stick around to confirm some points as she went along. It was about an obscure House bill that would make it easier to deduct condominium conversion expenses. She was determined that it be obscure no more. "H.Res 212" became "the bill dear to the heart of your upscale realtor," the banking lobby was described as the House majority leader's "favorite lobby," an anti–low-income-housing provision as the "darling of the Republican leadership," and so on. She made a strong point to me that she was explaining it all for Congress as well as the public. That in spite of their staffs, most members of the House and Senate got many of their legislative "red flags" from the newspapers, magazines, and television.

Not to waste time, I brought in a box of papers to be filed. Since I was the one who used the materials most for research, I did all the filing myself, not wanting Gladys messing with my highly eccentric system.

I liked to file. I liked to see the stacks of papers disappear into proper file folders with their tabs all neatly typed. I was beginning a section on "The Third World and Its Economic Potential" when Gordon sauntered in.

Sarah froze. I shut the file drawer and rose from my knees to leave. Sarah stopped me.

"Gordon, we're busy now. Could you go?" Each word was a cube of ice. So she knew. She had known all week. Her manic energy was born of fury, not happiness; and I'd been too dumb to know the difference.

"After we talk. Courtney, you may be excused," he said.

"Stay, Courtney."

I felt like a cross between a dog and a not too bright child.

"Gordon is going," Sarah said.

"After we've talked." He sat on Sarah's sofa and draped his arm across its back.

Sarah took her shoulder bag out of the drawer. "I will not be back until he's gone."

"I'm not leaving," he shouted as she shut the door on us.

He lit a cigarette and slouched into a chair.

"I think she meant it," I said. "About not coming back."

Great sport could be had figuring out which one would triumph on any given occasion, but I was in no mood to have Gordon Simons spend the morning watching me file.

"Shall we bet?"

"All right."

"Fifteen minutes, fifteen dollars?"

"All right."

He got up to look out her window. I continued sorting. He turned to watch.

"Why isn't Gladys doing that?" he asked.

"Because when Gladys organizes, I can't find anything."

He made me self-conscious. It was going to be a long fifteen minutes.

"You'd make a great White House chief of staff," he commented. "You have all the qualities of the best of them."

"Thank you."

"I'm serious. Sometimes I ride you a little hard with the

31

faithful-lackey syndrome — you've given up your own life for Sarah's; but you're a perfect aide-de-camp. In the political world, of course, your role is standard fare."

"I know." I thought of all the deputy administrators and aides I knew on the Hill. Essentially our jobs were the same — to make the top dogs look good, which included going to extraordinary lengths to keep them happy and unharassed. Believing in them, or their causes, was a plus but not a requisite. They had the power and we fed off it; and whatever power we accrued — and some gained a great deal — we derived from them. We were parasites and considered damned lucky by the world we chose. So lucky we sometimes forgot what our luck was based on.

He put out his cigarette and lit another. "Have you many lovers?" he asked.

"Oh, sure. About ten. I work them in around appointments and deadlines. Keeps me off the street."

He laughed and continued to stare at me. "You women amaze me. You're more ambitious than most men ever dream of being."

I didn't answer but that didn't discourage him.

"I don't object. It's only a new form of the old impulse — a need to throw yourself into something — for women, family was big on the list, but everybody does it — country, God, sex."

I turned around. "Transcend through work?"

"Part of the Puritan ethic." He looked at his watch. "We settle for whatever salvation is at hand."

I went on filing and he went on talking. The frontier spirit, he opined, accounted for the emotionalism in this country, whether religious or patriotic or something else. It (this spirit) bred individualism and loneliness from the beginning. And the family, it wasn't just the women who had given up the family; each generation had loosened the tie — look at how we treated our old people.

I was tempted to ask him how he explained more fanatic cultures, the ones without the frontier spirit, but I didn't want to give him the satisfaction of appearing interested. I resented my role as captive audience. Abruptly he stopped talking, looked at his watch once more, went over to the window, and sat back down to wait.

32

"To kiss ass for professional reasons is one thing," he said after a lull; "to do it in a personal context is something else altogether."

I slammed shut the file drawer. "Gordon, what the hell are you talking about?"

"You know what I'm talking about. Your ambition boggles the mind, and I can admire that. Where you are screwing yourself royally is on a personal level. More and more you give in to Sarah. You're not nearly as tough now as when you first came here."

"I don't need you to tell me what I'm like. Or how to get along with Sarah." Then I couldn't resist. "I won't be here forever, you know."

"I know you say that and probably tell yourself that, but I think you are in great danger of sinking into Sarah's all-consuming needs. You are no longer making the distinction with yourself on what you are doing to get ahead and what you do because you've become too dependent on pleasing Sarah. More and more I see you doing things, not to get what you want, but only doing them because she wants them."

"If you say another word, I'll leave," I said. I was shaking. I didn't know how Sarah stood him. "And look at you. You play the naughty boy, but it's always her bed you come back to."

"It has occurred to me that is not so good for either of us. But you are right: I have no business trying to run your life. You have one too many doing that already, and now I will sit here quietly — I promise — until she walks in that door and once more forgives me."

I worked in silence until he interrupted again. "You want to know my secret weapon?"

"No."

"She thinks I don't need her. That's my secret weapon."

"Do you?"

"I've never allowed myself that question."

Fifteen minutes were up, but he didn't move. He closed his eyes and continued waiting. I couldn't remember the last time I'd seen someone idle. I'd come to consider it a lost art form and had to admire his ability to stay there thinking, daydreaming, or whatever it was he was doing behind those heavy lids. I left him there to go to lunch.

My lunch companion was José Eduardo de Marco Méndez, a noted Central American rebel leader, here to lobby Congress for increased aid to the guerrilla fighters in Garza.

"It is good to relax a while with such an attractive woman," he said, although we both knew he would work hard this noon to lay out his views. He had been putting in long days talking to members of Congress as each one was getting individual attention — "They are all their own foreign ministers," he explained. He personally was taking care of the Foreign Affairs committee.

Today José de Marco was not harping on the evils of the present Marxist regime as he did in his press statements but was concentrating on the benefits his party would bring to American business, which was now banned from his country, and to American banks, which had lost millions when the present government defaulted on loans. Everyone from the National Rifle Association to the American Bankers Association was behind the aid, he reminded me and continued to talk knowledgeably about the different forces in American politics.

José de Marco, I reminded myself, graduated from Notre Dame. Half the Cental American guerrilla leaders, whether on the right or left or center, graduated from Notre Dame or the University of Texas or some other North American college.

The waiter uncorked a bottle of Château Giscours for us, and my companion pulled the wine through his teeth with obvious pleasure.

"Whichever special interest is buying our wine certainly provides a generous expense account," I said.

He looked taken aback, then quickly laughed and said, "Wooing you Americans is not inexpensive. Nothing can be done too directly." I clucked sympathy and he continued in a confidential tone, "In the old days it was easier. You could hand a check over to a respected leader of your persuasion — whether the left or the right — and guarantee yourself glowing reviews. Nowadays you cannot count on such a procedure for results."

34

"I'm sure that's true," I said.

"My wife's father saw Castro give money to a Nobel Laureate." He said this with pride. "If we could be so lucky . . . but today your country is not enamored of intellectuals, no matter their leanings."

I looked appropriately in agreement with his sentiments. He had taken my attentiveness as concurrence, and I was was not yet ready to disabuse him of the notion. For one thing, I wanted to know which Nobelist, but de Marco was not undisciplined and went back to engaging me in matters closer to his concerns — political action groups sympathetic to the rebels' cause.

Once I realized I was getting no more confidences, I made my plunge. Could de Marco offer any explanation for the well-documented atrocities committed by the rebels? He looked as if he considered my question bad form, but what was the point of sitting here if the butchery was not brought up?

"There are good rebels and bad rebels," he protested quickly. "We are the good ones."

"But the money would go to all of you," I said.

"Not if properly channeled. And, please, do not lump us together. We are not the throat-slitters." He was referring to a picture in one of the news magazines showing a guerrilla, indeed, slitting a peasant's throat.

I assured him I certainly hoped that was the case and left as soon as possible.

By two-thirty, I was getting edgy. Gordon wouldn't leave. Sarah's column wasn't written. I went into my office to work on it. I knew the material as well as she did, and I knew her style better than my own. However, I needed to confirm it with Sarah, who hadn't called in and wasn't answering her home phone. The deadline was five o'clock.

At four o'clock, Gladys suggested I go over to the hair salon where Sarah and Leslie were getting haircuts. With reluctance, I agreed. When I took Sarah's briefcase out of her office, Gordon was napping on the sofa. He didn't wake up.

I was embarrassed to be tracking her down. Inadvertent as it was, she might resent my intrusion in her fight with Gordon.

Well, I wasn't the one misbehaving. It wasn't my fault that she was tangled up with an ass who also happened to be an exhibitionist. If she didn't want voyeurs, she should choose her men more carefully. I would get in and out of this shop as fast as possible.

When I got to the hairdresser's, Sarah hadn't arrived, but Leslie was already getting a trim — more than a trim. She was getting the limp stuff cut by the foot — something her mother had always wanted; but I didn't think this was exactly what Sarah had in mind. With the help of a blow-dryer and gel, Leslie was achieving Washington's version of punk.

Matthew, their hairdresser, looked nervous, as well he should. I sat down in the chair next to Leslie, who asked me what I thought of it. I shrugged my shoulders. Matthew rolled his eyes at me. None of us noticed Sarah until she was on us.

"My God!" she said over the blow-dryers, over the shop's chatter; over the shop itself. "What have you done to my daughter? Leslie, what have they done to you?" She turned to Matthew. "Make it below the chin, you fool." She ordered him to restore it.

"It's not his fault," Leslie said. She was bright red. Even she hadn't expected this response.

"You look fat," Sarah said, spitting out the last word. Then I watched her making great efforts to get herself under control. When she spoke again, her voice was calm; she sounded amused.

"Things were bad enough to begin with. You've gotten so lumpy I can't tell your front from your back."

By now the entire place was silent. Matthew looked near tears. So did Leslie. She stood up. "I hate you." She said it calmly. She took off the barber's apron. In one rapid movement she picked up Matthew's scissors and threw them toward Sarah's head, just missed by a couple of inches. In two strides Leslie was out the front door.

"Mrs. Adams, I'm sorry," Matthew was saying, but Sarah didn't hear. She ran out after Leslie, who had disappeared. I felt a tear on my cheek. How strange, I thought, to be crying and not know it.

When I caught up with Sarah, she grabbed my arm. "God, Courtney, what have I done? How could I be such a bitch?"

"I'll try to talk with her," I said, without much conviction. She had been exactly what she said she was. Then I remembered the column. Did she want to take a look at the copy before Gladys mailed it?

What was wrong with me, she wanted to know. Her baby was wandering the streets and I was interested in a column. I took a deep breath. It was, I reminded her, due. Could I have Gladys send it on without her approval?

Her look held all the fury of the past week, but quietly she asked me to take her home. Then she shrugged and told me to have Gladys put the column in the mail. On the way to her house, she kept saying we would find Leslie and all go out tonight. Not this time, I thought. This time Leslie won't go, and this time I have my own plans. I'd had a bellyful of Adamses for one day.

At the house, I took three calls from Gordon before Leslie's came saying she was spending the night at Page Tuttle's. By that time I had already called my date to say I'd be late. He was probably surprised to hear how much I was looking forward to the evening, which I was determined to have.

After Leslie's call, Sarah sat forlorn, like a little girl, all defenses gone. "Wait until you're a mother, Courtney. You'll understand this better. It's all so much more complicated than you ever expect. There's all this love . . . but a kind of hate builds up, too . . . we're so vulnerable to each other." She pulled her knees into her body and hugged them. "People shouldn't need to count for so much. It's a mistake," she said.

Was she talking about people you love or people in general? Sarah had a need to please. She wanted Leslie to please, too. In the same way she pleased. Was that why she had worked so hard to be a success — to count for so much? Or why I worked so hard to count so much with her? What kind of salvation was it, anyway? I was too tired to make much sense out of it. Now Leslie would tell her about leaving.

To this extent I faced myself. I did and did not want Leslie to leave, any more than I did or did not want to leave myself.

As long as we both stayed, no matter what the frustrations, we were cozy, a family. If either of us left, my family would disintegrate and a part of me with it. But we were disintegrating — my ambition and Leslie's fury equally to blame — and I didn't know what to do about any of it.

"I have an idea," I said, looking at Sarah, her arms still squeezed around her knees. "Let's go to Le Pavillon. The food there is always good."

3

By the time I pulled in front of my building, only a little after ten-thirty, Maxie was the only streetwalker left plying the beat. The glow from my dinner with Sarah had faded, and I was furious with myself for canceling my dinner date. Cheryl Dalton, my neighbor and the person responsible for the date, would be furious, too; and I dreaded explaining to her in the morning.

Maxie came around to open the car door and greeted me with a "you know better than to come in this late by yourself." Maxie's uniform never varied: a white lace blouse with a white lace bra underneath, size D cups by the looks of it; a brown leather skirt slit all the way up the side; and gold wedged sandals. Sometimes, if Maxie was displeased with a potential customer's response, the slit would be twirled dead front, revealing Maxie's true sex.

If I couldn't sleep, I would sit in my window and watch Maxie work his trade. He would hop in a car; the customer would continue driving. In ten minutes or less, Maxie would be let out, the customer never the wiser about Maxie's gender. From April through October, Maxie was also on duty in the early morning rush hours. He had several regulars who took a few minutes out on their way to work. The winter months would be as lucrative, he maintained, but he hated getting up in the dark and cold. Winter evenings weren't his favorite, either, but he usually stayed at his post, his light brown delicate face all but hidden by his long frizzy hair and rabbit coat.

"You should go home and get some rest," I said as I opened

the first of a series of doors that had to be unlocked with different keys.

"Mr. Duc is waiting inside for you," he said.

"Why?" I asked, never mind how Mr. Duc had negotiated himself through the barricades. I was too tired to deal with Mr. Duc tonight. Maxie shrugged and walked down the street. "Sooey Pig!'" he shouted over his shoulder — the University of Arkansas football yell. I had no idea where Maxie learned it, but I got a small pleasure at this reminder of my cultural roots.

Before coming to Washington, I had passed my life in northwest Arkansas, most of it in a small town close to the Missouri and Oklahoma borders. By the time I was three, my two older sisters had already left home. Only Jane and I would share our parents' weary silences, until Jane eloped to Oklahoma City with a cocaptain of our high school football team.

That broke my mother's heart. Not because Jane was gone, but because we had drawn attention to ourselves. My parents, especially my mother, went to great lengths to see to it that we were not out of the ordinary. So I chose to stand out. I won spelling bees and math races and an essay contest on "Razorbacks for Democracy," eventually getting a scholarship to the University at Fayetteville. There I developed a passion for politics, wrestled with and then abandoned God, and didn't look for a husband.

This was only mildly disappointing to my parents. After all, I had been a disappointment from birth: I was to have been a son, named after my bachelor uncle Courtney, who had made a modest amount of money in the lumber business. Though I was said to resemble him, with my scrawny build and white-blond hair, he was not for one minute taken in by a *girl* named Courtney. His money went to an animal shelter in Fort Smith.

Now I no longer needed his money or my parents' approval. I dreamed myself a life and was making it work. Well, almost.

Mr. Duc was sleeping in the fetal position in front of my door, and taking up no more room than the door width. He was even smaller than Maxie.

"Mr. Duc, you're supposed to be at the shelter," I said, touching his shoulder lightly. He looked at me and smiled; my irritation disappeared.

Mr. Duc had sat on my front steps a month before we spoke, not that unusual, since most of the steps in the neighborhood were taken over by transients, some of them peddling drugs during the day. At first, he had sat there playing with a ball of string or moving a half deck of cards around. Some days he did nothing. He appeared not to know any of the street's regulars or be much interested in either them or the street's residents.

Then he started showing up with a book. Next, he began copying from it onto paper with a pencil stub he'd probably found in the trash. One evening, on impulse, I'd given him a pencil out of my purse. He nodded but we didn't say anything. Two days later I brought a half-used composition book from work. "Maybe this will help," I said, knowing as I said it I was now involved. He thanked me in precisely spoken English. The next day he handed me a letter written in a formal, flowery turn-of-the-century prose, the body of which appeared to be from a son to his mother, extolling her virtues. The letter began, "Dear Mis" and ended, "Your good friend, Mr. Duc."

Mr. Duc, it turned out, copied letters from famous people and usually sent them to people he read about in the paper, trying to choose a letter to match the recipient. That he had no addresses or stamps bothered him not at all.

Now that my largesse kept him in pencils and paper, I had received two more letters, one entreating me to join the Civil War, the other urging me to take care of myself with many suggestions for home remedies.

"The shelter is no good tonight. A stabbing . . . the blood . . ." He made a gesture of blood flowing from his shoulder and shuddered. Mr. Duc had been in the South Vietnamese army — a general, he said, though I doubted that — and he abhorred violence. Even the street arguments made him uneasy. A general and an engineer, he sometimes said. He planned to go back home as soon as he earned some money. I couldn't make him understand that there was no home to go back to or that a job was needed to earn money.

Only last week, after two months of my filling out forms and

41

making countless trips to the District welfare office, had I gotten him into a shelter for homeless men at night and off park benches and sidewalk grates.

Cheryl Dalton stuck her head out her door. "I thought that must be you," she said. "So how did it go?"

I told her, and waited for the scolding and lecture about not living my own life, which she delivered. The three of us were still standing in the hall. Oh, hell, I thought. "Some coffee?" I asked and opened the door.

Cheryl looked at Mr. Duc. "Why aren't you at the shelter?" she asked.

Mr. Duc looked at me. "There's been a stabbing. Mr. Duc got upset," I answered for him.

"He can't stay here. Mr. Duc, Courtney has gone to a great deal of trouble for you and I expect you to be more appreciative. You can't stay here."

Mr. Duc started to leave.

"Have some coffee first." I went to the kitchen to put water in the kettle and got out the cups. Cheryl followed me in.

"What happened?" she wanted to know.

"Don't be rude to Mr. Duc." I opened the Instant Taster's Choice. "Do you want real or decaf?"

"I mean, what did you tell Dave? He's my friend, you know. Give me half decaf, half real. I need to know what to tell him when he calls tomorrow to find out why you stood him up."

"I told you. I got busy. Sarah has a lot going on." I put a two-pound bag of sugar on the tray with the cups. "Mr. Duc has a lot of pride," I whispered.

"I wish you'd learn to make brewed coffee," Cheryl said, ripping off three paper towels. "Someday I'm going to teach you." She shook the towels in my face. "Do you realize it's been six months since you've had any sex life? That's unhealthy."

"Listen, I don't even have time to fuck myself, let alone a man!" I said in the fiercest hushed voice I could manage and went into the living room.

"I don't have any milk," I said to Mr. Duc. "Would you like some toast?"

He shook his head no.

"Of course, he wants toast," Cheryl said. "He doesn't like that shelter food."

Cheryl, as usual, would be right. She was right about the sex, too. I was clearly not cut out for celibacy but was left with neither time nor energy to do much about it. I went back to the kitchen to rummage up food and to answer the telephone.

"Sally Henson," the slurred voice said. "Thought I should tell you I'm leaving — since we're old friends and all. . . ."

Old friends? She and I had known each other slightly at the University of Arkansas. Then, not long after I moved here, I ran into her and discovered she, too, had come for fame and fortune. Equipped with a good mind, a gorgeous face, and a job on the *Post*, she had every reason to assume she would achieve it. She graciously gave me a few pointers on whom to meet, where to go, making it clear she was too busy to do much more than proffer advice over a drink from time to time. Since neither of us had found the other sufficiently interesting to share a beer in school, this arrangement was fine with me.

Over the course of the next two years we ran into each other occasionally at parties or press conferences and somewhere in there switched roles: I knew more people; I could drop more names.

Now she was calling to tell me she was going home. The town was eating her alive. The paper was a jungle, the social scene worse. "I use to feel pretty good about myself; now if one more person ignores me or looks over my shoulder when I'm trying to make conversation, I think I'll shrivel or shriek, and I'm too young for either. I'm getting out and you might consider the same."

"I'm OK for now," I replied.

"You're damn lucky is what you are." She was close to mumbling. I had to listen carefully. "It's not fair at all. You haven't worked nearly as hard as I have. Half the time, you don't even know where the bases of power are."

I asked about her new plans. She had a job as a producer at one of the local TV stations and a promise for a crack on the air in a few months. She thought she could get me a job writing copy — no on-air stuff, though; my voice wasn't good enough. "Arkansas will treat you good," she laughed and hung up.

That's all I needed: to bite the dust and let Sally Henson save me. Then I could spend the next fifty years back home in her debt. Terrific. To avoid that, I could give up a lot of dates with Cheryl's friends. The kind of access I'd enjoyed so early and so fast was a direct result of latching on to someone with real power; and that latching had a price. That latching was also the name of the game around here. Just one big pyramid of latchers-on. I supposed I could even include Mr. Duc. After all, he had me.

When I came back out, Cheryl and Mr. Duc were smiling. "Mr. Duc understands he can't stay here, but he's no longer afraid, so it's fine."

This time she was wrong. Smile or no smile, Mr. Duc was obviously frightened or he wouldn't be here. He'd have gone to his street places.

"We'll see." I looked at Mr. Duc to reassure him we could work something out once Cheryl left. If she ever left.

"I'd rather have a senator for you, anyway," she was saying, as she absentmindedly stirred her coffee.

For the two of us, Cheryl had made a list of the suitably marriageable men in Washington. She'd included four senators, two congressmen (congressmen only got on if they were wealthy or showed senatorial promise), one cabinet member, three superlawyers, and one lobbyist, qualifying only because he was rich and sexy. Journalists didn't even get honorable mention, either being too poor or two swell-headed. When I complained that some on the list were old enough to be our grandfathers, she told me to take a lover. When I protested that I wanted my husband to be my lover, she dismissed me as Arkansas naive.

"Cheryl, I have to go to bed," I said, but she wasn't listening.

"Maybe we should expand our range," she said.

"I'm all for that."

"Listen to me. Nobody does 'corporate' in this town. Women forget about it because the others sound so much more glamorous, but there are hosts of men to be tapped out there in business, with more money than most politicians and probably a lot less ego. A veritable gold mine of eligibles."

"If this gold mine exists, you'd think someone else would have gotten word of it by now."

"This town has as many unattached men as women. I read it in a study. The problem comes because nobody perceives it that way; so the men stay spoiled and the women stay needy."

"Greedy," I said and yawned.

"Don't be dismissive. You could easily end up joining the Washington legions of transitional women."

"What does that mean?"

"You know perfectly well. The town is made up of them — the ones who get the guy in transition, just after the split and before he's found himself — either with another true love or a bevy of them. You've watched half the women we know go through it and you haven't seen one of them end up with the man, have you?"

"Oh, Cheryl."

"You know I'm right. He's lonely; ego's low. You pet him, make him feel good. Then after a while he'll decide having women pet him and make him feel good can be had from any number of attractive creatures. And — poof! — he's gone; always, of course, remembering you with special fondness for being the one to get him through the hard time."

"I give up! If we can change the subject, I swear not to become a transitional. OK? Besides, we're boring Mr. Duc."

"No, we're not, are we, Mr. Duc?"

Mr. Duc smiled and said "no" about ten times.

"Now this is what I have in mind for us," she went on.

She wanted us to have a party featuring Sarah as the center-piece. With Sarah as the star attraction, we could get anybody to come, Cheryl said. As it was, Cheryl did pretty well. She'd call up Senator So-and-so, saying Mrs. Important Jane Doe was coming and so wanted to meet him. He'd accept, and then she'd call Jane Doe — one of the oldest of social con games, but somehow she made it work for her. She seldom got caught, and the word spread that Cheryl Dalton had interesting parties, just a little offbeat, maybe, but even that was appealing to Washingtonians who spent most of their time going to standardized, homogenized functions. Cheryl's parties made them feel a little younger, a little naughtier. So far, I'd never invited Sarah. She'd made a real effort to include me in her social occasions, and it hardly seemed fair to exploit her for my own.

"Look," I said. "I promise to socialize more, and I promise to find some trophies for you, enough to people three parties. OK? Now I have to go to bed."

"If you'll get my name in the paper, I'll fix you up again with Dave. Betsy Johnson got her name in the 'Personalities' column last week, and she got spoken to by media stars and politicians who'd found her invisible before."

"The power of the *Post*," I yawned.

"Some of them didn't remember where they'd read it, but they recognized it right off."

"Maybe they're all graduates of the Evelyn Wood speed-reading course."

"We could have a really tony party, stage something funny, and get us both in," she said.

"Wonderful! Only I don't work on a paper, and Sarah isn't given to writing columns about the likes of you and me. Not unless you can come up with a solution, say, for the care of the homeless," I said, looking at Mr. Duc.

"That wouldn't get any play either, unless I could figure out some way to make it sexy — maybe bomb the shelter or something."

"Well, you're the one in p.r., you get your own name in the paper." I stood up.

"All right, I'll go," she said. Mr. Duc stood up, too. Mr. Duc looked distressed. Cheryl saw me looking at him and led me into the kitchen. "You are crazy," she hissed, "but he is crazier. He cannot stay here."

"He's not crazy."

"So sane people call themselves General, and turn down jobs because they aren't stimulating, and talk about going back to a country whose leaders would kill or imprison them?"

"He's not crazy."

"What if he dreams you're the Viet Cong or something?"

I walked back into the living room. "Mr. Duc, you can sleep in the hallway if you promise to leave by dawn. The other tenants get picky about these things."

Mr. Duc thanked me over and over. He looked relieved. Cheryl looked relieved. I looked ashamed, or felt I looked ashamed.

In bed, I was glad to find my mind too tired to do much spinning. The dinner with Sarah had gone much better than I'd thought possible. We both had made a great effort at gaiety, never once alluding to Gordon or Leslie. I could tell she was grateful to me. A great storyteller, she'd told me stories about her first years in Washington. For my part, I told her about the time I wrote an editorial advocating doing away with the University of Arkansas football team, and almost got thrown out of school because of it. A couple of times I made her laugh.

And Sally Henson's call had been a good reminder of how well I was doing. So long as I didn't "do" it for too long. But then I didn't intend to.

Viet Cong indeed. That idiot Cheryl. I would find Mr. Duc a job he didn't think beneath his talents. Maybe, I would make him a United States senator.

4

HER SMILE didn't quite make it.

"You all right?" I asked, as she climbed into the car.

She nodded. We drove from her house in silence.

At the stoplight on Wisconsin Avenue, I watched two early evening strollers window-shop in upper Georgetown. "A nice night for the party," I said.

"Mmmmm." She closed her eyes. She looked ready to cry, an alarming possibility. I had never seen her cry. Then she said, "It's Leslie." She didn't elaborate, but she didn't have to. Another fight. Underneath her blusher, she was bleached out, her face slack and claiming its forty years.

"Anything I can do?" I asked, though we both knew the futility of that question. Whatever was happening these days was out of my control, and — more frightening — out of Sarah's control as well, I felt. Until some sort of personal order was restored, I couldn't possibly think about leaving. As long as her life was chaotic, mine was on hold. She had been too decent for me just to walk away.

"You know the speech I couldn't find last night?" she began almost hesitantly.

I said yes. I certainly did know. Sarah, in a panic, had called me at the office about six-thirty the evening before. She had misplaced her speech on "The Politics of Economics" she was to deliver at nine for an American Stock Exchange dinner.

Because the subject was so specialized, she'd spent a good deal

48

of time writing it and needed, more than usual, to rely on the prepared text. The night before the dinner she'd been working on it at home and was sure she'd left it there, but would I check the office.

I looked everywhere and, not for the first time, cursed Sarah's stubborn refusal to get a word processor. She had to be the last journalistic holdout in all of Washington, maybe the world; but she insisted she could only think using the electric typewriter she had had for fifteen years. "Nobody mails in columns anymore," Gladys and I would twit her and express amazement with her transition from manual to electric.

Neither the speech nor her notes showed up at either place. She ended up piecing the subject together as best she could, but this morning she'd said that, while the talk hadn't gone too badly, the audience definitely didn't get her standard fee of $15,000 worth. Even giving free speeches, she couldn't stand to be less than stunning.

"Late this afternoon," she was saying, "I went into Leslie's room looking for my black camisole to wear underneath this blouse tonight. She never puts back anything she borrows of mine, and she knows it bothers me."

She paused long enough for me to wonder if this was the end of the story, but she spoke again, every word costing her. Almost never could she bring herself to tell a story unfavorable to her and Leslie's dealings with each other. Even to me, who saw the problems at close hand.

"In one of her drawers I found the speech and notes — everything. When I confronted her, she said she must have picked them up by mistake. But no other books or papers were with them. I persisted and she began accusing me of snooping in her room. I could not get her to focus at all on what she'd done."

"She could have picked it up by mistake. Then hidden it when she realized what she'd done," I said and meant it.

Only two days earlier Leslie had confessed she hadn't yet told her mother that she was leaving because of worry over what the news would do to her. She didn't want to hurt Sarah, she told me, at that moment probably believing what she said, but her

49

mother would never let her live her own life. "Sometimes I wish my mother would disappear. Then I could do what I wanted without hurting anybody."

I had the feeling she was still determined to go though the guilt over leaving might make the move impossible. In light of Leslie's earlier concern, this act of deliberate malice — taking Sarah's speech — didn't make sense.

"She made a mistake," I reiterated."Don't you think?" Her eyes remained closed, and she didn't answer. Her exhaustion sat between us like a palpable presence. Sarah could put forth so much effort, could squeeze herself into such distorted shapes, in trying to arrange life according to her terms, that when life, or Leslie — teased, coaxed, forced — didn't yield the expected results, she felt betrayed. All her energy erupted into the very chaos she worked so hard to avoid, especially with Leslie. She was a different person with Leslie. Her wisdom disappeared.

"We could cancel tonight. I could say you were sick," I said, slowing down the car. She looked up interested and surprised, as if such an idea had never occurred to her. Parties were as much a part of Sarah's life as going to work in the morning. She did not take them casually, certainly not this one given by Sheila and Anthony Morris, whose nomination as U.S. trade representative Sarah was still determined to thwart.

The Morrises lived in Kalorama Square, one of Washington's urban fortresses. Atop a hill, protected by a block-long brick wall, the enclosed townhouses afforded the best view and the best security in the city. We walked into an entrance that resembled an upscale doctor's reception area, and a pleasant voice asked our destination over an intercom. I answered into a bowl of fresh yellow roses, and waited to be given directions by the disembodied voice. From here, we proceeded to the inner court-yard onto which the houses faced.

Another warm evening, a real Arkansas autumn evening. I liked to think of this day beginning here with me, passing through a softer Virginia, now down the interstate, on by the small mountain towns tucked away in Tennessee, through the subtle rollings of Knoxville and Nashville, until it headed straight through the humidity and moss, crossed the Mississippi around Memphis, and deposited itself in Arkansas, all the while bringing with it accents and attitudes and a gift for adaptability. And even here tonight, even in this enclave of privilege, I felt the spirit of the day. This thought cheered me considerably.

Arturo Rios, a waiter hired out to many private parties, answered the Morrises' door before we had a chance to ring. He led us into a great expanse of room, done in beige linen overstuffed chairs and couches, with a few French country antiques thrown in. People milled about in groups of twos and threes; any number above four seemed unacceptable. Already the room was filling up, its rhythms quickening.

Anthony Morris greeted us with an enthusiasm he couldn't possibly feel. By now, he had to know Sarah was making inquiries about him, and Sheila Morris, while it had not originally been part of her plans, would hope to use the evening to defuse her. But Sarah had other ideas. She would approach Morris while I sniffed out everybody else. "People open up to you," she said. "You make them connect below the surface." I appreciated the flattery but I wasn't sure how well either of us was going to connect; nor was I comfortable accepting the hospitality of someone we were pursuing, never mind that he was aware of the game.

The day after the announcement of Morris's appointment as U.S. trade representative, the game had begun in earnest. In the morning mail Sarah had received a note suggesting she look into his African connection. Lots of crank mail came to Sarah's office, and most was thrown out by Gladys. This one was a grudge letter; but, since the typing was neat and the grammar passable, Gladys handed it on to me. Before bothering Sarah with it, I checked it out and discovered that Morris had been registered as a lobbyist for the Lumbanese government for seven years. Lumb was his only African country, however.

"Anthony Morris part of a shady deal? Hard to believe, but

we'll check it out. If it's true, it sure helps make my case to the President," Sarah said. "Find out who represents the neighboring countries. His competitors might have information we can use."

"Or they'll invent it if they don't."

She laughed and began listing other interested parties — staffers on the African subcommittees, disenchanted lawyers who had left Morris's law firm, a couple of other lawyers and p.r. types who wanted the job themselves, and the former secretary of defense, who had been a bitter rival when the two served in the Administration together.

While she began making calls, I began my search through documents. Sure enough, his firm was involved in several large foreign transactions for hundreds of thousands of dollars. In one of the largest, Morris had worked to change a regulation for a large South American computer company to expand its sales in the U.S. According to a lobbyist for IBM, Morris himself had made a couple of phone calls to the right places.

He had also represented a Japanese electronics firm fighting a trade complaint brought by the administration. The deal brought $950,000 to the firm. A South American client had brought in $450,000. And the Chinese government had paid $250,000 for advice on trade matters.

However impressive these sums were, they weren't out of line with the going rate. As for Sarah's tying Morris to the trade deficit (by our buying more foreign goods while inhibiting U.S. sales in other countries), only the scantiest of cases could be made unless we could somehow scare up a source on the Japanese regulation.

In the case of Lumb, other than a hefty $850,000 for "advice," nothing looked out of line. True, the country was now receiving $25 million in financial aid and had been granted most-favored-nation trade status, but aid had been forthcoming in large amounts ever since this regime had taken over from a corrupt and incompetent dictatorship. The U.S. had given to them, too — the last year before the takeover produced a sum obviously meant to bolster them up. Sarah was sure one of us would turn up something, but I was beginning to have my doubts.

Morris certainly didn't look concerned. He made a joke about when the interrogation was going to take place. Sarah patted his arm. "Depends on how good dinner is tonight." She turned to me. "Come. I want you to meet Carl White."

After two minutes, I realized I could have done without meeting Carl White. He was a commentator on one of the network's nightly news shows and every bit as serious and earnest in real life as he was on the air. He was down from New York and was truly, truly delighted to see Washington and old friends, like Sarah, again. Sarah did, indeed, count him as a friend. She held no brief for his brains but declared him a decent person — admonishing me not to be dismissive of anyone exhibiting so rare a quality as decency. I couldn't quarrel with her assessment of either the man or the trait. And decent and dull I was willing to accept. But decent and glib?

He was accompanied by Angela Sells, who covered the Pentagon for the *New York Times*. With her short French haircut and St. Laurent dinner suit, she was most striking, though, if a couple of other occasions were any indication, not the most promising of companions. In the most casual situations, her conversations had a business-dinner tone to them. The idea of the two of them in bed together struck me as hilarious.

So hilarious that when Carl politely asked me how I knew the Morrises (by now, savvy Angela had pulled Sarah to one side), I had a hard time composing my face, much less my answer.

It turned out Mr. Commentator's connection with the Morrises was more personal than Sarah's: he had been their neighbor when he lived here. He was a great admirer of both the Morrises. We discussed the energy and determination of Mrs. Morris, and agreed that it would be hard to come up with a more formidable foe in all of Washington.

When the conversation got around to Anthony Morris's new appointment, he declared there was no more deserving appointee. "He has served his country well," he pronounced.

"Then you can foresee no problem at all in this passing Congress?"

"None whatsoever. He's as clean as they come."

"Does that mean that there's nothing there at all, or only that there's no more there than would be found for anybody?"

His expression quickened for a second, but his instinct to trust me won out. He put his hand on my shoulder and leaned close. "No one, my dear, has 'nothing at all,'" he said, in a conspiratorial whisper.

Observing this intimacy, Angela stepped back into our orbit, so he finished in his pleasant, if pontifical, voice, "But in this particular case, I wouldn't want to find out."

As if on cue, Sheila Morris came over. "Forgive my negligence," she said, hugging Sarah and Carl and Angela, and extending her hand to me. "We're waiting for the Ditsons. The vote's on the floor now, I think. Thank goodness I didn't include more senators. They're always a risk."

Sheila Morris calculated her risks carefully. She was from that long line of women who had used their husbands' positions to secure power in their own right. She was the leading force behind the family foundation, which had benefited community service projects throughout the country, including the city of Washington. If her husband were to die tomorrow, she had enough strategically placed loyalists to call in favors for the rest of her life. She had cultivated the younger players, having seen for herself how much the prestige of the old was dependent on the succeeding generation of power. And she would always be useful to know. According to Sarah, she had more bases touched than anyone she knew, with the possible exception of the President.

Larry Blake appeared, and Sheila Morris gave me a knowing look. He was the young congressman from West Virginia she wanted me to meet. Larry Blake was very smooth and very good-looking, too much so on both accounts for my taste, but a large number of other Washington women found him irresistible. Clearly, he had already established himself as a favorite of Mrs. Morris. After hugging her, he kissed my cheek as if we, too, were the best of friends.

However, our conversation remained impersonal even after Sheila Morris left us. As it turned out, we stood there admiring

Sarah, who was talking to Matthew Todd, secretary of the Navy. In spite of frequent interruptions from other guests, he was explaining why he disagreed with her piece on amphibious warfare, and she was listening politely.

With her color returned and her body alert, she looked ready to begin a race or a performance. The laugh lines around her eyes crinkled and her eyes themselves glanced everywhere, taking in the room, examining, acknowledging, commenting. Her famous calm enveloped her.

As Larry and I watched her, I understood once more why I had been content to stay in her shadow for so long. She was, I had to admit, worth one hell of a lot of bad moods. Like the best of the politicians (and there has to be some pol in the best of the journalists), even her "hellos" were special. She touched you. She asked about your mother or your child's first year in college or if you'd felt good about the story on you in the *Post*. Always something for you, and with a look that said she could hardly wait for more time with you. She was "Mister Rogers' Neighborhood" come alive for grown-ups.

As she walked away, I heard Todd tell the man standing next to him that she was now persuaded of his position — a fact not discernible from anything we'd witnessed.

We laughed at Todd's foolishness, and the sharing of this small intimacy turned me into Larry Blake's confidant. At any rate, he felt obliged to tell me he found Angela Sells beautiful, but not sexy, implying that this opinion was based on closer scrutiny than observing her across dinner tables.

"But leave it to Sheila to pull off a twofer," he said.

A twofer was two stars in one couple; in this case, two media stars: one in print, one in television. This meant not having to waste space with two extra spouses, and freed hostesses up to include an entirely new category, say Culture, Law, Sports, or, with luck, Entertainment.

Then he turned to his media topic of the week and asked me how I felt about videotape press releases. He was referring to the latest Washington mini-scandal, in which videotapes of former journalists interviewing foreign heads of state were being sent to TV stations by p.r. firms. The propaganda tapes were distributed as representing legitimate news. At any rate, the TV stations were running them that way, without any disclaimer.

Reprehensible, I said. From time to time segments of the press get lazy. Also just another dimension to the problem of foreign governments petitioning us directly.

So insightful of me, he said. Hardly, I answered, but he was moving on to what he really wanted to know.

"Do you have much contact with the Sunday talk shows?" he asked. "Sarah pops up on all of them."

"You've noticed."

"Sure. Say, how does she decide on what her column or her show is to be about? I'll bet you're a big help to her there. Does she take your suggestions?"

"Sometimes."

"But what's the decision-making process? How and why does she decide to interview someone? I'm interested in the process."

"In your line of work, I'm sure that's a plus." I looked around the room for someone to rescue me. The only eye I caught was Sheila Morris's, and she thought I was signaling how pleased I was with her "find" for me.

Now he was onto a banking bill he was sponsoring in the House but was worrying about its passage through the Senate. "I haven't a clue what Jones will do with it over there." Jones was head of the Banking Committee.

"He's going to oppose it," I said, not able to resist showing off and knowing full well he was finding out exactly what he wanted to know. Not the specific facts. That was easy enough, but how well I knew Senator Jones or someone around him. Oh, why not, I thought and settled in for the inquisition.

We were on to Pringle in the House and Sampler over at Treasury. But now I was enjoying myself, and if I didn't know, I lied. Let him think my access boundless. Just so I didn't have to spend the evening with him.

On our way into dinner, he explained how he used his stud book, the little book containing pictures of everyone in the Houses. He tried to memorize the faces, especially those who held positions which could be helpful to him. He was so brash and open

56

that I felt an urge to protect him. At least, to warn him. He was on the verge of being taken either for a fool or a brilliant politician. If the brilliant label stuck, he could spend the rest of his life walking into dining rooms like this one.

Our particular room was massed with crystal candlesticks and white mums in large crystal bowls, counterpointing the mauve walls, which could have been awful but weren't, at least not in the shimmering light. Sarah pointed to my place card and winked. Senator Ditson, the head of the African subcommittee, was on my right.

This meant I could make a few discreet remarks about Morris. Sarah had already called Barney Ditson to see if he had any information on our host for the confirmation hearings, but he'd said no. He asked Sarah if she had anything, but she evaded since Morris was an intimate of his and both had African ties. Ditson himself might somehow be connected to whatever was going on between Morris and Lumb. An unlikely proposition, however, for Ditson's reputation was impeccable. He had gained power through a consistent understanding of issues and hard work. To have intelligence, information, and a sense of fair play did not go unacknowledged by his colleagues.

Secretary Todd was on my left. He was large, had brown hair parted low to hide a balding spot on top of his head, and wore a pink paisley tie. Did I have children, he asked. I saw him glance again at my place card to see if I belonged to someone.

With resignation, I asked about his family. His wife was at their family place in Rhode Island. With their children grown, she stayed there more every year. He was only sorry he didn't have more time to spend with his family, but then who did? he said. But who did? his wife would repeat, while never forgiving him, and his children would echo, when forgiving. For this man, according to those who knew him, was not petty and was as intellectually honest as you could afford to be and still function in government. He was also ambitious and single-minded in his pursuit to change things, to influence things — whatever things there were.

I stole a look at Sarah, who was laughing with Wilson Kane,

the President's chief of staff. Her whole body pitched into what appeared to be a momentous discussion, but she was probably talking about his family, too.

I turned back to Todd. With Family out of the way, I could try Geographics, though I really didn't care where he was from or where he lived now, or I could move right along to Issues. Whichever I chose, it was obvious that *I* would have to interview *him*.

"Have you known the Morrises long?" I asked.

"We're both navy men," he replied, as if this explained something, which it didn't, since Morris was ten years older.

"Was he your commanding officer?"

"Of course not." He frowned. "Good man, though. Would have been honored to have him."

"The people in this room seem to think he's a saint." I said.

"Good man, " he repeated to himself, as he stuffed a too-large piece of roll in his mouth. He chewed contentedly for a minute, then, in a burst of expansiveness, he continued, "As smart as good."

"Don't tell me his family loves him, too."

"What?"

"I mean, he's good, he's smart, he's universally respected. Isn't there even a small blip on the man who has everything — say, ungrateful kids?"

"Of course not. Even his in-laws love him. My wife says he's the only one of the 'outsiders,' as she calls everyone who marries into her family, whom every member of her family likes."

"Your wife is related to him?"

"A cousin of Sheila's. Now Sheila's something else again."

So, he hadn't wanted to admit his wife was the reason he knew the great Anthony Morris. But before I could find out about Sheila's "something else," he had switched back to Anthony.

"A real public servant in the broadest sense. You know, he has this liberal image, but he's been a real friend to business, too. Grove Systems tried to make him board chairman, they thought so much of him. We're all indebted to him," he said, motioning around the table.

"I hear even foreign governments are beholden," I said, with an inspired thrust, if I do say so myself.

He actually chuckled. "You've got good information," he said. I think he was ready to go on, but Sarah took over the table.

She directed us through the crab and avocado, and most of the main course — not by talking, but by asking questions. Sarah, the ultimate listener. Sarah, the impartial judge. Always that little mystery with her, a sense of holding back. It worked.

When the conversation retreated to dinner partners, I grabbed Barney Ditson before Angela Sells could get hold of him again. Everything else aside, politicians usually made good table companions; that went with the job description. With no trouble, I steered us into talking about the graciousness of our host and hostess, their charms, abilities, historical ties.

Then I commented on what a wonderful source Morris must be with his knowledge of Africa. Ditson agreed.

"He must be invaluable where Lumb is concerned, especially with its Marxist government."

Ditson understood me. "He has single-handedly kept Lumb from becoming a radical Soviet satellite. He uses his knowledge well."

I felt properly chastised but also a little smug. Now I was ready for the party to be over. I wanted to tell Sarah my hunch — that Morris's connection was more complicated than we thought and that, whatever he did, he had Ditson's stamp of approval, not an easy thing to come by.

Watching Anthony Morris as he told an anecdote, a gift to us both private and funny, about another administration, I felt a momentary pang of conscience. He just *seemed* good, and I didn't much care or want to know whether or not he truly was good. It was sufficient to appear that way. But the room began to relax as Sarah once more entertained us.

Blake was hanging on her every word. For that matter, so was the chief of staff, Wilson Kane, attractive in a three-piece-suit sort of way. Since he controlled access to the President and the President was known to have complete trust in him, it could be argued he was the second most powerful man in the country.

He was a young-looking fifty-two, but his demeanor aged him. Maybe being surrogate President caused that weighty look. But for now he was laughing.

We were all laughing and basking in our laughter. We listened intently to one another. The sparkle of the bowls and candles and words made us worthy. For a little longer, secure. Refracted light and refracted feelings only enhanced. We were special, we told each other with our laughs and our eyes and our attention.

We were all aglow. No one was slighted. And if Sarah's mind was racing too fast, veering around corners, careening slightly off-track, she was also having a great time, not unlike an evangelist with her followers. She would throw out the good word. There would be the testimonials, the amens. She would praise us for our goodness and begin again. My amens were as loud as the others'.

Then, as arugula salad was served, Wilson Kane asked Sarah about China, and she answered with all the intensity of a prize student herself. We discovered she had a favorite, and Wilson Kane was it. Without changing the tone of her voice or a facial expression, she turned a recitation of facts into a seductress's call. Pat Kane, his wife, shifted her shoulders. Nothing else changed. Sarah's recklessness floated around us.

By the time Grand Marnier mousse replaced the salad, and champagne the red wine, Wilson Kane, looking younger and aware of his own sensuality, was in an expansive mood. Together, he and Sarah brought us back into the circle. To show our gratitude, we twirled more wildly and forgot that we had ever felt anything but included. Only Pat Kane might remember otherwise. Or so it seemed to me.

For a moment, Sarah looked ready to propose a toast, but must have thought better of it, and settled for a thank-you to our hosts instead. Soon after that, we disbanded, because the next day was a workday.

Carl White came over to assure me I was working for the best journalist in the country. He wished he'd had such training when he was young. I was sorry I'd been so quick to judge him — to type him — earlier in the evening. Larry Blake made a point of coming over to say good-bye, and suggested we get together soon.

Angela Sells made a point of ignoring me altogether as she walked past on her way out. I stopped her and smiled sweetly. I'm sure it was sweetly. "I saw the story about your conversation with the secretary of state yesterday. Very informative."

"Thanks," she said and started to move on.

"Your version was much better written than the one in the PBTS." The Press Briefing Transcript Service transcribed all the press conferences held by government officials. Any reporter who wanted was welcome to the briefings, but a few tried to make it appear as if the words were just for them, or, at the most, a small group. Now it was my turn to walk briefly by her. I didn't wait to see if she had the decency to blush.

In the car, Sarah threw herself against the seat, her energy visibly draining away. I told her what I had found out about Morris; and she told me that Morris, according to his wife, had only been to Africa once. I wanted to ask if she'd felt guilty about spying on our hosts, but already she had left me and the evening.

"I think Wilson Kane and Larry Blake have crushes on you," I said, trying for one last time to bring her back.

Slowly she turned her gaze from the window to me, but I don't think she saw me.

"Do you think you could talk to Leslie?" she asked. "The way you used to."

5

ALMOST IMMEDIATELY Hank Brown spilled coffee in my lap. I winced. He took out his handkerchief and wiped and apologized. His secretary brought paper towels. Then we all wiped. I kept assuring him I was fine, my dress could be cleaned, but the incident upset me. I refused more coffee and couldn't think of anything other than his ex-girlfriend for small talk.

Not that Hank and I had ever been close. We didn't even rate high on the acquaintance scale. On occasion he'd seen a friend of mine, and on a few of those occasions they had seen me. Although separated from his wife, he'd never really fit in as a bachelor. He discovered that changing women brought him no more satisfaction than changing hobbies or jobs, always government jobs. He reconciled with his wife and stayed on here in Interior.

In fact, Hank was part of that Washington breed of men, mostly in their forties, stymied at midlevel in their careers and discouraged from exercising initiative, who wait out their pensions. For the most part, they start out with the best of resolutions: work hard for a few years, then either get out or run the place. They planned to distinguish themselves. They were bright, capable, and hostile, sometimes noticeably so. They pervaded the bureaucracies.

"No one speaks to anyone here," I said.

"True. We are all molecules refusing to connect with one another," he began as if lecturing to a classroom. "This refusal is against the natural order of things; therefore we stay in an uncomfortable and unfriendly state of isolation. We are all practicing up for Purgatory in the afterlife." Then he changed tone. "But you didn't come here to do a philosophical treatise on the Interior Department."

I smiled. I'd forgotten about his offbeat sense of humor. "I need some information on Lumb."

"It's been eighteen years, and I was a junior Foreign Service officer at that."

"I remember once your saying you'd kept your ties to the place even after the revolution," I pressed.

"Yeah, the same men I played tennis and discussed Nietzsche and Marx with now run the country as revolutionaries."

"But moderate?"

"As revolutionaries go."

"Do you have any idea why our government upped the aid ante right after the Marxist takeover?"

"The ways of the State Department are even more mysterious than those of Interior. That's why I got out."

Which was not exactly true, I knew. He left to work for one of the more glamorous senators, who had promptly gotten bashed a few months later in an election upset. Hank Brown's one gamble and he lost.

"Who would know?"

"Ted London, maybe. He was on the African desk at State at the time. Or Ditson over in the Senate. State works pretty closely with him. They think twice before crossing him."

I thought back to Sarah's recent attempts to crack him. "Ditson isn't talking now," I admitted.

"Try Dobotu. He's a salesman at Neiman's. When the coup took place, he was stationed at the embassy here. He was sympathetic to the new government's cause but opted for permanent exile when it looked as though the more extreme element was going to take hold.

"In fact, we probably started pumping money for the very unmysterious reason of keeping the real radicals at bay. And there goes your story?"

"Not just yet." But I stood up to leave and asked my last question. "Has Anthony Morris's name ever come up in your discussions with these old friends?"

He actually laughed. "So he's what this is about. And the answer to your question is yes. He's sort of their patron saint. When any of them come to town, he's always on their agenda. They're very proud to have a man of such great reputation as their flack or hack or whatever men of that caliber and ilk call themselves."

The bitterness in that last remark was too raw and we were both embarrassed. I left quickly before I could feel sorry for him and embarrass us both again.

The afternoon yielded little. Mr. Dobotu was less than forth-coming with me. Whatever he knew, he was keeping to himself, but I was determined to make as many trips as necessary to cultivate his trust.

Old records didn't help much either. Lumb was on the General System of Preference list, unusual for a Marxist country but not impossible. Nor did I have better luck going through microfilm of the *Times* and *Post* stories on Lumb, a tedious job at best. To begin with, there weren't all that many stories.

A little discouraged, I trudged off to a reception at the British embassy in honor of one of their visiting dignitaries. This event I could have done without. The night before had been a late one, thanks to Leslie, and it was catching up with me. I had just dozed off when she called, around one in the morning.

"Damn her, damn her, damn her," she'd come on the phone. At first I didn't know who was calling or who "her" was. The thin voice hardly resembled Leslie's. I would have hung up, but she started talking about "telling" her and how she'd just laughed, hadn't taken her seriously. Half-asleep as I was and incoherent as Leslie was, I finally got the gist.

"She laughed." Leslie must have said it to me a half-dozen times. Sarah refused to consider Leslie's leaving a possibility. Leslie would show her. One day she would leave. Just walk out without telling her. Teach her not to laugh. Hated that woman. "If she hadn't driven my father away in the first place — just like she drove Gordon — this wouldn't be happening," she'd said. "It's all her fault."

Finally, I calmed her down, assured her I understood her frustration, persuaded her she could consider her alternatives more clearly after she'd had some sleep, reminded her how unrealistic it was to expect Sarah to accept the separation so quickly. With promises to continue our talking, we hung up. Though I intended to try to help her, I doubted that we'd have many more discussions. Leslie seldom opened up to me any-more — as she'd said, she saw me as Sarah's ally. I was afraid this call was a fluke with little chance of being repeated.

I also doubted that she could leave Sarah, or even wanted to all that much. For all her talk of independence, she was bound to Sarah — hating her, loving her, worrying about her, needing her; and all of it more than most children her age. She still kept scrapbooks on Sarah, still saw Sarah's problems as her own.

To separate or to punish? Leslie probably didn't know herself. Or was punishing her only way of separating? And if she could punish enough, make Sarah pay with enough pain — would that suffice for separation? If rebellion could give Leslie a sense of independence, maybe a complete break wouldn't be necessary. Unless Leslie thought only parting would extract enough pain. At any rate, many more nights like last night and she'd end up punishing me, too.

"You've come," Ian Webster said. He was the embassy's press attaché and the reason for my coming.

"How can I refuse you?" I asked, and we both knew it to be true. Ian had helped us out on more than one story and always gained us access to any of their people Sarah was interested in.

He took me with him to meet the guest of honor, whom I sounded out to see if his economic line had changed from the accounts I'd read. Unfortunately for my friend, there was noth-ing to warrant an interview with Sarah. When I didn't pursue matters, Ian looked disappointed but didn't press me.

My mission accomplished as far as both Ian and I were concerned, I calculated how much longer I had to stay. Long enough to speak to the Under Secretary of Defense, I decided when I spotted him across the room.

Yes, he was glad to see me. Always too long. My tennis game still great? Sprained his wrist, hadn't played in weeks and, by the way, had I heard old Lester was on his way out? (Old Lester was head of the joint chiefs of staff.)

I wondered to how many others he'd passed along the rumors. His boss was singularly unfond of old Lester. But it was always possible he was right, so I would have to check it out.

Frank Carmichael walked up and kissed me on the mouth. Thirty and already balding, Frank had met me just after we'd both arrived in Washington; and we'd been sort of friends since. We had formed a bond because we were both lonely, both southern, and both ambitious. The catch came because Frank decided to realize his ambitions by marrying wealthy women of "good family." Law wasn't getting him where he wanted quite fast enough. He was in the process of leaving his first wife for another of equal rank. Over these few years I noticed his background had become southern aristocratic rather than southern gentry, and he would have loved it if my background had kept up with his. He could have referred to us as old, old friends, implying childhood attachments, the kind his wives were surrounded by. Had I tonied myself up, we could have been cousins.

"How did you get in these fancy surroundings?" he asked, not quite joking.

"Hard work counts, Frank," I answered, not quite joking either.

We walked to the buffet table. Melanie Myers was in front of me. Years ago she had been a social reporter for one of the now-defunct Washington papers. Now she eked out a living as a stringer for small-town newspapers and somehow had managed to keep her name on the roster of invitees for a few embassies. She was one of what Sarah dubbed "the embassy bag ladies" — women, once prominent, now poor, who could be caught stuffing their bags with rolls and cheese, smiles and talk, anything to get them by until the next gathering.

Melanie had also managed to retain the haughtiness of the best social doyenne. While she had come around to acknowledging me, her reserve was formidable. She did not speak to Frank at all. We discussed the Indian summer and the relative merits of the canapés on our plates. I was not one of the few with whom she gossiped.

I would help her out anyhow. "Senator Wood hasn't touched his plate," I said and pointed towards a full plate of hors d'oeuvres. The buffet was closing down, but the food on that plate she could easily filch.

Frank came with an espresso to reclaim me.

"Some jerk spilled coffee in my lap today, and he wasn't even sorry," I said to him. But as I was saying it, I realized I was exaggerating. He had looked sorry; he had acted sorry. Only my mother hadn't — when she'd done the same thing to me a few years ago back home. At a missionary meeting at our house. The discussion had been about Africa. Lumb included? Unsettled, I told Frank good-bye.

Then I remembered what else happened in Lumb, and one of the staff found me a telephone in a quiet room. Not yet nine o'clock. I crossed my fingers Neiman's stayed open this late on Thursday nights. On the fourth ring, the operator answered. Two mintues later Mr. Dobotu was on the phone. He was less than thrilled to hear my voice.

"Miss Patterson, we really have nothing else to discuss," he said with great politeness.

"A terrible accident happened that year — the year of the coup."

He paused to remember or to stall.

"Yes."

"But what?" I asked when nothing else was forthcoming.

"A train. Many people died. More suffered injuries. How did you come to know of an accident?"

"I read it in *My Weekly Reader*. Thank you, Mr. Dobotu. You've been invaluable." Not exactly what he wanted to hear.

Ian Webster walked me to the door. "You should come here all the time. You look a lot . . . livelier than when you came in."

"Tell you what," I said, "if you can get your guy to make

67

just one statement to Sarah about the trade imbalance or the lack of cooperation in controlling the currency, I'll get you a column."

He kissed my hand and clicked his heels. "At your service."

"At yours," I started to say and checked myself, not prepared for him to take me up on it.

Sarah would already be gone for the evening, and the libraries had closed. Never mind. First thing tomorrow I'd put some more pieces together — enough to make a TV program. I was sure of that.

Back at the office, I wrote up my notes and looked over information I already had. The puzzle had a few more pieces in place. The Navy Secretary had told me of Morris's connection with Grove Systems, who, among other ventures, manufactured trains. Now I had to find out what happened after the wreck. I could hardly wait to tell Sarah. She might even cheer up. I leaned back in my chair and put my palms over my eyes to rest them — to calm me.

"How did you come to know of an accident?" Mr. Dobotu had asked. How did I indeed? The coffee, I could have said. The coffee, my mother, the *Weekly Reader*, the creep, and all of them together.

Back in Arkansas, the creep — my one-and-only live-in lover — had been a graduate student, putting himself through school on my teacher's salary. When he told me he was taking a teaching position elsewhere, and didn't invite me to go along, I had said nothing — no cursing, no crying, just nothing — and had gone out to teach the remedial reading class I had volunteered for. That's when I read the *Weekly Reader* story to the class. I had clung to every word of it, as if focusing on the words would keep away the pain. Words had always kept away the pain. They could do it one more time. And they had until class was over.

After class, I had gone for coffee, then to an all-night hamburger stand. Finally, I had lain by the side of the snoring creep for the rest of the night, making sure never to touch him. The important thing was not to touch him, never mind that meant keeping an all-night vigil. Never mind that I closed my eyes only while he dressed and fixed his own coffee and toast, making as much noise as possible in the hope that I would get up and do it for him. After he left, I called my school to report an emergency back home. I left for my parents' only because I could think of nowhere else to go that didn't cost money.

I was under no illusions, but the visit was a disaster anyway. Whether I was more aggrieved with the loss of my future, or the reminder of my past, was hard to say. My parents had not grown more talkative over the years — the vibrations of their silences filled every corner, pushing me, the intruder, out, just as they had always dismissed anything "different." I made them apprehensive. I felt I should reassure them that I wouldn't streak through town, or pull out a gun and shoot them, or stand up in church and yell "bullshit!"; but the longer I stayed, the more I contemplated all those possibilities.

One afternoon, my mother had her missionary group over to discuss, as usual, the conversion of the heathen, this time the heathen of Africa. One of the women had heard about the terrible train wreck which had taken place in Lumb the week before. Over a hundred had been killed and four times that many injured. Couldn't a letter of sympathy be sent to the government? she asked. More information was needed, my mother said. Pleased to have something to contribute to the conversation, I helped the woman out as best as I could. I began reciting all the facts I could remember from the *Weekly Reader* story. In the middle of my recitation, my mother managed to miss my cup and poured hot coffee in my lap.

With the pain of the sting came a terror I controlled by taking myself to the kitchen, and dabbing my legs and skirt over and over. I made a pack of soda and water and applied it, more to keep from crying than to ease any pain. I heard my mother assure everyone I was fine, but in a few minutes, she came into the kitchen.

"You did this to me once before," I said, my hands trembling.

"Everyone's waiting for the rest of your story."

"When I was a little girl." I kept applying the soda pack.

"Maybe you should change skirts."

"Don't pretend you don't remember scalding me. I still remember that pain. In the same place."

"Don't be silly," she said, taking out a cup towel and blotting my skirt. "It wasn't coffee and it wasn't me."

A nice young doctor, she went on, had done it. She didn't know how I remembered any of it, I was less than three at the time. A lot of trouble, too, I was. I had the croup, and the doctor made a tent over my bed with a steamer in it to help me breathe. His device worked until the vaporizer tipped over while he was examining me.

"You got a good dose of that hot steam on your legs. Not enough to hospitalize you, but enough for you to set up a howl. I thought you'd never stop screaming," she said, taking out the milk to refill the cream pitcher. "I felt so sorry for that young man. I thought he might cry, too. I was so embarrassed." She started back into the living room. "If you're not going to change, you should come back in. You're holding everybody up."

But that was all another world. That world didn't exist for me anymore. Now I had this desk and these notes and friends who had never once been to a missionary circle meeting. I tried to call Sarah again. Maybe she was home. She would bring back my excitement. When nobody answered, I took a tube of hand cream — expensive hand cream — out of my desk drawer and rubbed it on my legs, where the coffee spilled. Then I went back over my notes one more time.

6

ANTHONY MORRIS knew what he was in for, but he'd had no recourse. For any other talk show, a guest of his caliber had a choice and often exercised it. Some would only come with stipulations — certain subjects were to be avoided or a particular subject was to be the only topic; other guests had to be of the same rank or stature, or there were to be no other guests at all. Sometimes ideological enemies refused to appear together. But once Sarah asked, that was it. One way or another — using her columns, her parties, her power lunches — she persevered until you came. If you were a good politician, you understood and respected this tenacity in her, for many of her skills — having the right contacts, touching all the bases, knowing when to call in chits, and not ever taking No as the final answer — were the same skills you and members of your staff cultivated. Better to accept her the first time around, be a good sport. Sarah did not abide bad sportsmanship.

Tonight the control room was crowded. Besides the usual crew — the director, assistant director, technical director, audio person, producer, and executive producer — a researcher, the makeup woman, and a couple of other staff people not involved with tonight's program had shown up. Word was out that Morris was in for a bashing. At least the possibility was there. The rumors had started at the Wednesday meeting.

On Wednesday mornings Sarah, her show's producers, researchers, and I met to discuss the final details of that week's show and the guest and issue to be spotlighted the next week. Included in the decision on the guest would be the kind of film, tape, and stills available, the other guests, if any, who might be involved in a discussion, and the focus — whether it would be on the guest or the issue represented by the guest. Out of the four or five names submitted by the staff, Sarah would make the final selection. Usually a consensus ensued. This time Sarah hadn't bothered.

Anthony Morris was it. The only film she expressed any interest in was that showing him in foreign countries when he was national security adviser, especially any of him in Lumb or another African country. (There was none.) The researcher, who usually assumed the role of reporter, was this time given to research alone, Sarah making it clear she and I were handling the story. She didn't even tell the executive producer — the person in charge of translating Sarah's desires into a finished product — exactly what the story was all about. I was the only one who knew.

She also decided the interview would be conducted in the studio instead of Morris's office or home, the usual place for a one-on-one live interview of this importance to take place. "We'll put him on my turf," she insisted when the executive producer pointed out that the story would be more visually interesting in his setting. The producer was a woman in her fifties who had been with CNN, CBS, and ABC and was considered one of the best in the business. She had come just three months before from the Brinkley program to Sarah's. She tended to treat the rest of Sarah's staff, and possibly Sarah herself, with scorn. Clearly Sarah both annoyed and intrigued her with this latest mystery.

Only an hour before the show began had Sarah clued her in to what she was going to do. Her response was somewhat short of ecstatic. I suspected she liked Morris as much as everyone else did. Sarah had a lot of work ahead of her this evening. The producer's reaction would not be atypical.

So far, Morris was conducting himself well; easy enough, however, for Sarah was only warming up. She had shown film clips of him with past Presidents, of him signing bills as secretary of the treasury, of him at arms negotiation talks. He was a living civics lesson, and she said as much. She did not try very hard to catch him up on a couple of early policy decisions that were less than commendable. She let his explanations slide by gracefully.

Morris wasn't fooled. As unflappable as he appeared, he had to know something more was coming. Not that Sarah had a reputation for always "getting" her guest — she didn't — but he knew well enough of Sarah's poking, and unless he had a lot more skeletons, which I doubted, he knew what she would find.

And because of the confirmation hearings coming up, she'd been able to discover more than enough to make the show interesting. Once the Hill found out she was looking around, phone calls started coming in: to verify their information, to trade information, to spread wrong information, to pass on legitimate damaging information, to pass on legitimate favorable information about Morris. We had followed up on all of it and sifted through to Sarah's satisfaction until tonight's show evolved.

She was bringing up trade regulations. How he had represented the South Koreans on a textile bill that benefited them to the detriment of our own shoe companies.

He was unperturbed. He had only helped the South Koreans make their case known. He had not used his influence to obtain a favorable vote.

"Making their case known is not influence of a kind?"

"I saw to it their information was properly disseminated."

Sarah tried again. "You may not personally involve yourself with individual legislators, but having someone from your firm walk these people through the halls of Congress with your blessing is not without consequence. Would you agree?"

"These people could gain access on their own with enough time and information. Our firm facilitates the process. Also, Sarah, may I point out to you that we always give the other side. Legislators are entitled to know the negatives in any situation. We see that they do."

She pressed on. How could a man actively involved in working against American interests — the textile bill, for example —

73

properly represent them in his new job? By any standard, wasn't that a conflict of interest?

He became indignant. He never worked against American interests. Not the interests of the nation. He would remind her that in any piece of domestic trade legislation some interest that was American was going to be affected adversely. His record, the record now before them, did not warrant this kind of innuendo.

"This is not the only country in your debt, Mr. Morris. Your help has been extended to others." Sarah began matter-of-factly. "In the last few years you have been a lobbyist for Lumb, giving them the benefit of your insights into American government. For instance, they have a larger share of the hemp quota than would normally be allocated to a country that size. They also have come under the General Systems Preference — a status all Third World countries desire from us and one that the AFL-CIO is against giving in the case of Lumb. Theirs is a human rights argument — that GSP status should be reserved for countries that have free trade unions." She paused, as if waiting for a response. Finally, he nodded. She continued: "Do you have any problems making this kind of expertise available to a foreign power?"

"First, in regard to the GSP, let me say that I believe we should stay neutral on trade. Second, while I provide material to help my clients, I'm not giving away government secrets." His voice denoted a pat on the head for such a simplistic question. Then came the hands. He sliced his right hand away and down as if to put a period to that thought. Sarah countered with her right hand palm-out like the safety patrol on the corner.

"Would you acknowledge this could be a problem for the United States government," she asked, "since there is no assurance that some of the information might not hamper relations with the countries involved?"

"The assurance is my word, my record, and my discretion," he replied in a tone that left no room for doubt or further questions. Some attributed to him brilliance, but Sarah thought it was a combination of wide reading, much more so than most of his peers, and sound instincts, properly acted on.

Sarah wasn't pleased. "In your case, of course. But I was speaking generally." She went on to point out the large numbers of former cabinet officers with great access to government peddling ideological wares of foreign powers. "As your numbers increase, hasn't this become a real danger to our country?"

"I don't think so."

Sarah was making her points to the President, who almost certainly would be watching. He usually did. Still, she was spending too much time on this part. The rest of the press had been covering it more than adequately. The arguments on both sides were getting stale.

"But you will acknowledge the potential for problems is certainly there?"

"Move in close to Morris," the director yelled. "Hold it on him. No, no. Camera Three! Camera Three!" Though Morris appeared as composed as ever, a still life of exact proportions, we all smelled the fear, felt it would somehow make itself known through the camera.

"I am not given to theoretical answers," he said and smiled, which took the edge off.

The camera picked up Sarah's touché smile back. "Isn't this form of employment for former cabinet officers becoming so commonplace, that someone in that capacity could automatically assume such a position, a highly lucrative position, would become available?"

"I suppose so."

"And if that is the case," she went on as if any answer he gave was of no consequence, "would it not become a temptation to make yourself available for dispensing favors to other governments, knowing later benefits will accrue?" She might be right, but she was beating a dead horse. Even Sarah couldn't arouse the public on this issue. She should have backed off by now.

Morris apparently thought so, too, his irritation beginning to show in the clipped tones of his answers. "May I point out to you that governments change?" he asked. "There is no guarantee the party you helped would be around a few years later, if, in fact, one were so tempted; and I have to add, I don't think most are."

"When you were national security adviser, did you do the Lumbanese a favor?"

"Close in on Morris," the director said, and whistled. My stomach tightened. Now she had to make her case. The harassment had to pay off.

"I have never, as a public or private person, done anything at any time I thought was not in the best interest of my country, and I think my record speaks for itself."

If this had been a live audience, applause would have followed. The hurt and indignation on the man's face were moving. I wished Sarah would get on with it.

"Mr. Morris, did the Lumbanese receive a loan while you were national security adviser?"

"I don't remember. A lot of countries receive loans."

"Lumb received a loan for fifty million dollars."

"I don't remember."

I thought I heard a tremor in his voice, but he hadn't gotten where he was by giving himself away. The worst was, I felt compassion for him, and if I felt that way, the rest of the audience must be sympathetic. Sarah never lost her audience. She should make her case.

"Are you saying you didn't arrange the loan?"

"Quit, Sarah, baby, quit," the researcher on the piece was cooing.

The producer and I looked at each other. "Maybe we should suggest she move on," the producer finally said. This was no small suggestion. Several months earlier, Sarah had become distracted by the number of voices coming at her through the earpiece, giving her suggestions, and she had banned everyone but the director from talking to her while the program was on the air. Before that, she had prided herself on her ability to remain calm no matter how much shouting was coming at her; but since that outburst, she had stuck with her decision.

"She won't like it," the researcher said before I could say anything.

"Real professionals do not refuse to take suggestions on a live program," the producer said.

Morris once more was repeating his earlier answer, this time more calmly.

"Sarah, move on, please." The producer spoke into her mouthpiece and thus into Sarah's ear.

"A few days before the loan was arranged, I believe there was a train wreck in Lumb. Do you recall that?"

"I do."

"In the wreck over one hundred people died. Scores more were injured. It was a terrible accident."

"Yes, it was."

"The train was American-made by Grove Systems. I believe at one point you sat on the company's board of directors. Your law firm represents the company now."

"What has that to do with anything?"

"By several engineers' best guess — and that's all it is, because the accident was never properly investigated — the brakes didn't hold and the cars weren't sufficiently strong to withstand even a modest impact.

"Engineers at Grove Systems told me the brakes hadn't passed inspection. They had to be redesigned for American trains. And the steel used in the cars wasn't up to American standards."

Actually, the engineer had told me — I went to Des Moines to drum up a disgruntled middle-management type who might know something about the wreck. As it turned out, my type was all over the place. My information came from three different sources. What had happened was common knowledge. The fishing expedition had taken me less than forty-eight hours.

With that information I was able to go back to Mr. Dobotu at Neiman's, who confirmed my story. Still we had no absolute proof.

"I had no contact with anyone at Grove Systems at that time."

"But you had plenty of contact with Lumb. You arranged the loan. They arranged the cover-up. Neat and tidy for the company and for Lumb. But who compensated the victims, Mr. Morris? The ones with no legs? The two women with broken necks? The families left without a father or mother?"

"Oh, Sarah, you are good!" yelled the director.

"I assume the government took care of its countrymen." No expression crossed Morris's face, but the sureness was gone from his voice. He went on to explain that the loan was arranged to purchase goodwill between the United States and the new leftist government. That was the purpose.

Sarah hounded him. Both his condescension and his stone-walling had brought her close to losing her temper. The purpose was to protect Grove Systems from lawsuits, she insisted. She let herself be drawn into the argument just at the time she needed to make her triumphant exit. She had won. What had gotten into her? Sarah understood timing better than anyone I'd ever seen — both on and off TV. She knew when to press, when to let up, when to tease, when to taunt, when to bear down. No matter how tired or distracted she was, her professional instinct didn't fail her. Maybe she needed a few days away. Madge Hudson-Marsh would understand and help arrange it. I didn't intrude into her personal affairs unless asked, but I hadn't seen Sarah quite this way — first the beauty salon, now here.

"Sarah, shut it down," the producer said to her.

"Tell us briefly, Mr. Morris, what you hope to accomplish in your new post."

Both Sarah and Morris ended on a grace note, but the show was bound to create controversy. Tonight's show was expected by a great many in Washington, if nowhere else, to be a tribute to Morris and the quality of public service he rendered, the kind that doesn't appear all that often on any scene. The audience would have expected a searching for concepts, a gathering and ordering of a man's life, for Sarah could do that, could in the course of thirty minutes turn a life into a work of art; and every-one felt the better for it. Only tonight she didn't choose.

"She was dynamite," the researcher said.

"That remains to be seen," the producer mumbled.

Sarah came out of the studio furious. "I'm not through with Anthony Morris yet," she said. She called the producer into a conference room, and in a matter of minutes the woman was back out. "She fired me," the woman said to all of us standing around. "Just for talking in her ear." She looked in shock.

Everyone looked at me, but I had no more explanation than they. I turned away to look out the window. Usually I watch the whitecaps in the distance and stay with them as they come in, higher, more powerful, until they crest; but I don't feel the throb. Sometimes I'm caught in them, feeling the pull, knowing the wetness will invade my body even through tightly closed eyes, half-fearful, half-excited by the thrust and the abandon of their force, then waiting, waiting for the breaks — the definition of its end. Sometimes I detach and only observe, feeling nothing at all. Experiencing or observing, I wait.

7

THE WEEKEND away was not a success, according to Madge. Sarah had fumed the whole time about the Morris story — the lack of one, really. Only the *Washington Post* had picked up on it. The paper's notice was not good, however. An editorial had roundly praised Morris and, while not mentioning Sarah directly, had gently taken her to task for getting concerned about "men of Morris' stature acting as lobbyists, or anything else of a legitimate business nature."

Unfortunately, most of Washington appeared to agree with the editorial. An aide to a senator on Morris's side called to suggest it might be hard to work with her in the future. Under the circumstances, past favors no longer counted. As an added indignity, establishment Washington, of which Sarah was very much a part, had closed ranks around Morris. He was one of their own, of their best. If she could do this to him, she could do it to any of them. With this story she was bordering on the extreme and needed to be put back in line. Extremism was anathema in this world. While invitations to Sarah didn't drop off, warm responses did. So far as I knew, no one, with the exception of the aide, said anything directly to her about it — no one wanted to take her on — but also no one murmured even faint praise.

A couple of TV critics had been emboldened, however, to question her judgment. One even went so far as to insist that while this program was bad, her others were worse — and for the opposite reason! "Balanced critiques are dull," he wrote. "It's like reporting on the people who didn't have a car accident."

To joke that Washington's collective memory was very short and all would be forgotten tomorrow only outraged her. To remind her it was often weeks, months sometimes, before lone voices were picked up by the rest of the press (citing as precedents Watergate, the Bert Lance scandal, and even the Mike Deaver one) did no good. To suggest that once the media overcame their innate sense of rivalry, the entire press corps would swoop down on the story got no further. Nothing like this had happened to her before. While she was not always followed, she most certainly was never crossed. Of course, all it did was make her more determined than ever to prove her point. She had told me that last bit over the phone, and I had winced. I was ready to forget what the point was.

Leslie came with me to the airport to meet her mother. Whatever the problems between them, Leslie rallied when Sarah was attacked. To attack Sarah was to attack Leslie. The boundaries between them blurred.

"They have no right to say bad things about my mother," Leslie said on the ride to the airport. "She would never do anything she thought wrong. We just don't do things like that."

Sarah was delighted to see Leslie with me. For whatever reason, she chose not to mention the Morris episode, a good sign, I hoped, although with Sarah I could never be sure. When Leslie said she'd fixed dinner for us, Sarah and I were both thrilled. If possible, I was more grateful than Sarah. If Leslie had been partly the cause of Sarah's getting off-track, then maybe she could be the instrument to get her back on. For this minute, on this day, I loved Leslie.

In the car, they chatted like best of friends, the way they used to. Then Leslie had still talked to Sarah; and Sarah did the same with Leslie, confiding her disappointments in work, in love, in friends. For all the mother-daughter arguments — and some were bitter — they had been close, maybe too close.

When I first knew her, I'd been shocked that Sarah confided so freely in a fourteen-year-old girl. Sarah's supposed rejections and disappointments were a large burden for a young girl. A burden Leslie had come to resent; and, for all this afternoon's bonhomie, I wondered if they would ever be friends again.

Still, seeing Leslie this buoyant was a good sign. She had announced she wanted to cater a dinner party for Sarah, who became ecstatic. I relaxed a little myself. This must mean Leslie had given up her plan to leave. As they discussed their plans, my mind wandered. But not for long. Sarah was suggesting a trial run be done with Leslie's friends in attendance.

"Forget it!" Leslie snapped.

"Why?" Sarah persisted. "Some special old friends — Page and Suzanne, maybe Jack Kelman, whomever else . . ."

Leslie let out a shriek. "Are we talking about the same person?" she asked in exaggerated tones. "The dangerous Stud Kelman who is on the make for homely little girls like me?" Leslie rasped in mock horror.

"Leslie, stop. I was trying to help."

"What a crock of shit!"

Sarah looked stunned. "That's disgusting. Let's not entertain Courtney with our dueling scene just yet."

"I'm curious about Jack Kelman," Leslie went on. "Why is it OK to be an easy mark now? Or am I so corrupted it doesn't matter anymore? You think Rich Sanford fucked me up." Then she laughed. "Or just fucked me."

"Don't talk like that!" Sarah yelled.

"Don't shout at me!"

Sarah opened her mouth, swallowed, began again in a calmer voice. "I'm not shouting."

"That's right. I forget. You never shout. I just hear loudly."

"Leslie."

"I mean it. I used to think something was wrong with my ears."

"Courtney is going to think we're monsters."

"Courtney knows we are," Leslie continued. The effort to repair, to contain the anger had been too costly. It would spill out on its own. "It's fascinating to think Jack Kelman is going to leap into my arms at the mere crook of my little finger, which is, in fact, the same little finger I had two years ago." Leslie scrutinized her finger.

"Please, stop, Leslie."

"Please, stop, Leslie," her daughter mimicked. "Please be good, Leslie. Please be wonderful, Leslie. Please be somebody else, Leslie."

Sarah had tears in her eyes.

"OK, Les," I said in a barely audible whisper.

Leslie continued to look at her little finger, but said nothing. We drove along in silence. An autumn shimmer lay across the countryside, covered in golds and reds and browns.

I remembered other, better fall weekends spent in this Virginia countryside. A house lent Sarah by friends on sabbatical; the dune buggy Sarah delighted in driving up and down their rolling hills; Leslie and me grabbing for each other as she gunned it on curves, raced it against deer; evenings in front of the fire with her friends driving down for the night or coming over from their places nearby.

On one of those times I first realized just how thoroughly Leslie had walled herself off, and, in doing so, had lost all claim to innocence. I caught her smoking pot in the pasture and, for the first and only time, delivered her a lecture — a friend-to-friend one, but, nevertheless, a lecture.

My horse kept moving around with about the same amount of contempt for me that Leslie was showing. She was polite. She listened obediently to all my reasonable, well-constructed arguments, but I saw the same glaze on her face that came when Sarah scolded. She calculated her responses, but, more than that, though nothing I could put my finger on, she conveyed a deep cynicism which forbade any genuine response or feeling, not just with adults but with herself — as if any real emotion was too painful to bear. She had sealed her lifespring. Or so it seemed to me.

This new angry humor and venom, then, could be sparks of real life flashing to the surface and, in the long run, serve her well. For years, she had kept her small rebellions mild and mostly to herself. Over the past year, that passivity gave way to a barely controlled militancy, her nerve endings all in her tongue. No wonder Sarah was bewildered. For me, there was something so audacious and transforming that I was fascinated — repelled and drawn, frightened and admiring.

When Sarah shouted for me to stop, conversation had ceased altogether. Braking too quickly, I skidded onto the road's shoulder. Only the seat belt kept Sarah's head from hitting the windshield.

"Shit!" Leslie muttered, echoing my sentiments.

"That dog back there, he's hurt," Sarah snapped.

"Shit!" Leslie repeated loudly, but Sarah was already out of the car. Leslie followed, cautioning her to be careful.

"You'd better help, too," Leslie said to me.

I hated dogs. I was scared of them. Leslie knew it.

Getting out of the car, I saw that it was a large black-gray dog with a German shepherd ancestor. His left ear was bloody, and he limped. In my recurring nightmare, dog jaws fastened onto my crotch, and I would wake in terror. Sometimes the dog would hold my neck, paralyzing me. Again, I would wake, the stillness and silence engulfing me.

Sarah crooned to the animal, which was whining. Leslie backed away. I climbed into the car.

"Let's go," I called. "We'll call the Humane Society."

Sarah ignored me.

"He could attack," I said.

"You won't, will you, good doggie?" Sarah continued crooning.

I watched from the front seat. For a minute it looked as if Sarah could get closer, but he began barking at her. The sun was losing some of its warmth and the wind was coming up in wafts. I got back out of the car, hoping to persuade Sarah we should go. "Isn't this futile?" I asked, walking close to her, though keeping her body between me and the dog.

With much coaxing, she got hold of his collar. "Good doggie," she said, stroking his fur and leaning closer to get a better look at his leg. "It's probably not broken," she said to Leslie, "but we can't leave him on this highway. He'll get hit again."

As soon as Leslie approached, the dog growled. I backed the car to where he sat. Sarah looked at the two of us, rejecting each in turn as we stood, abject that we had somehow failed her. Then her eyes came back to me. "Let's give it a try," she said.

"What do I do?" In a stupid way, I was almost pleased. She had chosen me over Leslie. I am crazy, I thought as I listened to her instructing me how to push its rump. I am crazy to care and crazy to do it. My mouth was dry; my stomach, iron. But somehow I managed to help her lug the animal to the backseat.

"Leslie, drive us to the vet. Courtney and I will try to calm him down a little more."

Then I understood: the element of risk precluded Leslie. Compared to that possibility, my fear didn't count for a damn.

The dog's rump was against my thigh, and I felt claustro-phobic in the back. If this dog moves at all, I thought, I'll throw up.

He didn't. He allowed Sarah to look at his ear, which, ac-cording to her, was only nicked. "He's a lucky dog," she said, pleased, willing to accept us all back into her good graces now that the dog had been declared lucky.

"If you say so, Dr. Doolittle," Leslie said, speeding along. I didn't like my car driven this fast.

Sarah turned to me. "Leslie thinks I have ESP with animals."

"You did with Spanky," Leslie said. Spanky was a cocker they had before I knew them. He and Sarah had been inseparable, so the story went. I was in no mood to hear it again. "It was eerie," Leslie encouraged Sarah. But why? Leslie knew the story better than I did.

"I cried for days when that dog died," Sarah said, and patted the one in her lap.

"But you never let us get another one."

"Go a little faster, Leslie," Sarah said.

"I have never understood why I couldn't have another dog."

"Maryland tags here. This poor thing came across the river. It's disgusting how some people don't take care of their pets. If you're going to have an animal, you have to control it, take care of it."

"But we took care of Spanky. We both did."

"I can't stand loss," Sarah said quietly. "You must know that."

When no one was at the vet's, Sarah decided to take the dog to her house for the night. Leslie didn't look much happier with the news than I did.

While Sarah fussed over the animal, I went into the bathroom to wash my hands for five minutes, and then to sit on the toilet seat for half an hour calming down. Don't take your neurotic fixations out on the dog, Sarah had said to me in the kitchen, only half kidding. But the dog was a fixation. And so what? I could think of better ways to use my Good Samaritan gestures besides wasting them on some damn dog, I thought, looking at the brown carpet between my feet. Bathroom carpet was idiotic; conspicuous consumption and nobody even knew it anymore. I would tell Sarah so, too, about the dog, if she made any more comments. My navy shoes were more scuffed than I realized, maybe past polishing. "I should take better care of my things," I said out loud, as I got up and took a look in the mirror.

They were out by the pool having iced tea, pleased with their arrangements for the dog in the kitchen. The evening, cool black silk in its loveliness, had brought a blurring of tensions. Words, soft as down, floated around unhurried and undirected. Whatever strains we carried, we managed to keep to ourselves.

From the out-of-doors, we moved seamlessly to Sarah's cozy breakfast nook, with its glass-topped table garnished by crystal containers of small flames and fishbowls of flopping daisies. For a while, we were all content to be part of the set Leslie had conjured so carefully. She had fixed a cold lobster and pasta salad, which Sarah greeted with the wonderment of a small child. I looked carefully at Leslie, who seemed pretty pleased herself. Maybe I had become too cynical and too pessimistic. Maybe this could work out after all.

But our structure started shifting before we'd even finished the salad; and, as usual, once begun, it crumbled rapidly. Sarah became effusive over Leslie's last soccer game of the week before, describing her plays, explaining the difficulty of her position; and Leslie looked more and more uncomfortable. She accused Sarah of hyperbole — in this instance, an apt description. But Sarah was careless of the warning signals, and she continued bragging about Leslie's athletic abilities, as if I hadn't seen them, or the lack of them, a hundred times myself.

Leslie looked at Sarah. "You think I've got to be a star or it doesn't count."

"That's not true; but if you listened to me, you would be a star." Leslie and I looked at each other and laughed. Sarah frowned. "You need to be more aggressive," she said.

Leslie put her fork down and got up from the table.

"Don't be silly. Finish your dinner."

"I'm not hungry," Leslie said and left.

She reappeared in the doorway and announced she was going to Page Tuttle's. Sarah resisted. "You've got Courtney," Leslie said. "I'm not leaving you alone." Sarah followed her to the front door.

I could hear the shrillness of their voices, but not the words. The kitchen clock hummed, and the dog snored, and I finished my salad.

"You'd better not see him," I heard Sarah warn. "I'm going to see Page!" Leslie shouted.

The door slammed. Sarah came back composed, but subdued. She washed some ripe pears and made coffee for us. Her mother, she said, had died when Sarah was fourteen. Sarah saw her vomit blood, then leave for the hospital. That was the last time she had seen her alive. For years, she told me, fountains of blood were a part of her nightmares. Her recitation was flat, inviting no response. We moved into the living room.

As Sarah poured the coffee, she began her question. "Did you know," she asked, not looking at me, "that nineteenth-century physicians believed a child's genes were solely the product of male sperm? The mother provided only blood and a nice warm place to grow?" She handed me a demitasse.

"Meaning?" I asked, stifling a yawn.

Sarah cocked her head to the side. "I thought I heard the dog." She listened another few seconds, then tucked her bare feet under her on the couch. "Leslie feels the same way these days. She sees herself as her father's child. I provide place — in utero." She laughed.

Stunned is the best word to describe my reaction. I had never heard Sarah mention her former husband before. She was Zeus, and Leslie had sprung from her head. She had not even hinted of Leslie's threat to leave.

We took our dishes back to the kitchen and checked on the dog, who appeared listless but not in pain. Sarah stroked his head, cooed to him, tried to give him water. The dog whined back its acceptance of her succor. She looked up at me. "Don't be timid. The dog won't hurt you."

I laughed and made a remark about hardly seeing myself as timid, but I was annoyed. Timid I was not. That wasn't fair of Sarah. But I would not have walked out like Leslie did, I realized with a force that left me depressed. Leslie, the weak, the incompetent, could do what I no longer would, or could. Vulnerable in an area I prized most about myself. A little too independent, a little too combative, I'd always been told; but I'd spent a long time cultivating those qualities, drew strength from them, and they were the very things that had attracted Sarah to me. She had, in fact, openly applauded them. So long as she was excluded from my bravura. So long as I minded her. No wonder I was so ambivalent about Leslie's excesses with Sarah. They were my vicarious rebellions.

Without asking, Sarah poured us each a brandy. "It really is hard to raise her alone," she said.

"And with whom would you share her?" I asked. It came out prissy and sharp, but I didn't care. I was sick of discussing Leslie.

She drew in her breath audibly, then smiled and picked up a cloth to wipe the stove. "Ida is great on the flourishes but lacks attention to detail," she said, referring to her housekeeper, as she cleaned the counters that were already clean. Together we rinsed the dishes and cleared the coffee tray.

But that taut controlled energy couldn't be so easily dissipated.

She scrubbed the breakfast table with Windex; she attacked scratch marks on the floor with steel wool; she extracted dust from the corners of drawers. When I suggested she leave the rest — whatever the rest was — for Ida, she ignored me. When I suggested we use the time to work on her Cincinnati speech, she dismissed the idea. She looked tired, haggard, even a little frantic. I regretted I'd cut her off.

"You know," I said, pouring myself — against my better judgment — a bit more brandy, "at least, you fight. My mother never cared enough to bother."

She looked pleased. I went on. "Maybe you two could plan a trip for Thanksgiving."

She put down the baby oil she was using on the chrome and hugged me. That had done it. She put up the oils and cleaners and scouring pads and began planning a trip to Bermuda, to Morocco, to the Pennsylvania Amish country. Yes, the Amish trip would be best, she decided. Leslie hadn't seen nearly enough of her own country. Sarah loved making plans like this, loved the maps and plane schedules, though in this case they would drive, she thought, loved figuring out all the logistics. She wouldn't bother with a house sitter; her new alarm system would be quite adequate unless, of course, I wanted to use this place for a change of scene. I declined and, again, felt another little sting; she assumed I had no other plans and wasn't going with them. Chiding myself for turning into some sensitive, precious creature, I vowed to bring more people into my life on a regular basis. I would get rid of the emotional vacuum I had created for myself.

I was about to ask Sarah if she detected any signs of the spinster in me, but she had moved into the burglary that had occurred here a month before. "Violated," she was saying, "exactly the way that magazine article says victims feel." She had been saying much the same thing every two days since it happened. This was the only subject I had ever heard Sarah repeat herself on, usually in the same words, as if saying it over and over would perform an exorcism, which I hoped eventually it would.

Someone had pried open their back door on Ida's afternoon

off and taken some silver and an expensive stereo belonging to Leslie. Not too much of a loss, but an unnerving experience, especially for Sarah. Leslie, usually the first person to be spooked, had handled the whole thing remarkably well. Sarah was commenting on that, too. "We've reversed roles," she laughed. Then she suggested we go to work on the speech. "If I haven't worn you out," she added.

I shook my head no. I knew she wouldn't rest until Leslie got home, and she preferred company. Not just preferred, but needed company. At first, I'd been flattered to be included by her in so many late-night vigils of one kind or another until I realized that just about anybody would do when it got late enough. She liked warm bodies around. If they were interesting and fun, so much the better, but when the crunch came she would settle for anyone without bad breath. For duller companions, she would simply provide entertainment herself. She was as fond of audiences as she was of companionship. It made life easier that way.

In her study we sat at Sarah's desk, an antique reading table that stretched the width of one wall. Sarah rescued the small, narrow room from being cramped by covering the walls, the windows, the short sofa, and an easy chair in a brown and white French country print. What wasn't covered in print was covered in bookshelves. To get to the desk meant navigating between the sofa and chair, but, once inside, a comfortable, womblike feeling emerged. I could spend whole days working in this room.

We began making notes for the speech. She'd decided to take after the defense budget, one of her favorite targets, and show how little oversight Congress really brought to bear on the problem. We had done a formidable amount of research on it, so it was mostly a matter of sifting, deciding on which facts to focus, making points without overwhelming her audience, a World Affairs Council in Cincinnati.

After only a few minutes, though, her mind was wandering back to Leslie and she kept looking at her watch. Finally, she gave up entirely and began pacing up and down, her arms folded across her chest. I stayed at her desk and continued to make notes.

"Courtney, stop that and talk to me," she said after an unusually long stretch of silence.

I yawned and raised my hands over my head. "Sure thing."

"Is she deliberately disobeying me — seeing that drugged-up punker Rich Sanford?" she asked, somehow turning her question into an accusation toward me.

I shrugged my shoulders, and we went back to work.

We continued working on the speech until after two, and Leslie still wasn't home. For the last hour, Sarah had been tensing everytime she heard a car go by, waiting for the sound of an engine shutting down. Actually, I was the one working on the speech, for Sarah roamed the house — checking the dog, staring out the window, watering her plants.

Three times she told me that she was not getting angry with Leslie whatever time she got in, not going to let their quarrels spoil the attempted truce. Her intention sounded good in theory; in practice, the outcome was doubtful. Sarah's temper hit straight on, then evaporated immediately. When she tried a different tack — holding back or attacking obliquely — the result was usually more disastrous for her and her target than if she'd followed her first urge to have it out. Because have it out she would, one way or another, until that emotional pasture had been grazed clean. Only then could she move on. Not that she flared up often. She didn't, and almost never in her professional life.

Tonight her eyes had a strange look about them — flashing but with a cold, calm center. Was she aware of just how angry she was with Leslie? I hoped so. Control counted on awareness.

When we did hear the slam of a car door, followed by Leslie's slow footsteps, Sarah sat down at her desk. When Leslie came in to say goodnight, Sarah remained bent over her work. If Leslie was nervous, she wasn't showing it. She looked self-assured, belligerently so. An airy goodnight and she started to leave the room.

"Don't be smart with me!" Sarah said, jumping up out of her chair. The veins on her forehead stood out and her face muscles were as rigid as a mask. Her voice startled me, but Leslie looked amused.

I didn't want to see this, but Sarah was now blocking my way out of the narrow room. I slumped back in my chair.

"I've tried so hard," Sarah began. "Done everything I know how. Never remarried. Never . . ." Her voice broke. She looked at Leslie, tears streaming down her face. "I might as well be dead."

Leslie's face remained impassive, though I thought I saw her nostrils pinch together. "You've used that line before," she said. She left the room.

Leslie might just as well have struck Sarah, who eased herself into a chair, hands shaking. I started out, too.

"Where do you think you're going?"

"To talk to Leslie. You two have done so many numbers on each other you can't play anything straight anymore. Both of you should be ashamed of yourselves."

Leslie was in her room undressing. Reluctantly she let me in. I went straight to the point:

"Leslie, it's sometimes hard for you around here, but this has got to stop. You're tearing each other up. What if the three of us sit down and talk calmly about what's going on? Use me as a buffer. Or, if not me, Madge or somebody." She continued getting ready for bed and wouldn't look at me. I went on, anyway.

"You know she loves you and doesn't want to lose you. I know you love her. I think if you tried to talk it out calmly . . ."

"Talk it out calmly? What world do you live in? She doesn't hear anything she doesn't want to. She doesn't love anybody unless it's convenient. I hate her!"

"That's not true."

"Not true? I'll show you what's true." She took my hand and pulled me down the stairs to Sarah, who had moved to the living room couch.

"This is what's true," Leslie said to me as she stood in front of her mother, who looked up expectantly. With deliberate slowness, Leslie put a finger down her throat, bent towards Sarah and vomited into her lap.

Sarah screamed. Leslie gagged herself again just before Sarah ran out.

"Leslie, my God," I said weakly.

"I'll clean up the mess myself," she said. "But don't go home. My mother may need you."

Not knowing whether or not Sarah would be down, I went back to the study, but I couldn't get rid of the stench. When she did come, she had showered and changed into jeans. "I don't feel like bed," she said.

"Leslie needs help," I told her.

"She's fine now. She came in to apologize. She's been drinking, I'm sure."

"She needs help," I repeated.

But she didn't answer, and we sat in quietness. No cars passed. The clock didn't hum; the dog didn't whimper. She sat staring at a spot on the carpet just beyond her feet. I looked at the bookcase and counted the number of letters on each of the titles, trying to make them into a pattern. I looked at Sarah and away again quickly. I had never been more disgusted with either of them. I went back to the bookcase.

I would have preferred working on the speech to this unproductive hand-holding, but that wasn't too appropriate. Finally the dog made a noise and I volunteered to check him. She nodded her head yes.

I had hoped he would rouse her, but she was perfectly willing for me to go. Not my plan at all. He looked uncomfortable. The bathroom, I thought, and went back to tell her. Slowly, in a stupor, she stood up. She looked tired and older than I had ever seen her.

"I can let him out myself," I said quickly, regretting it as I was saying it. "You go to bed. I'll lock up." She nodded her head but didn't move.

In the kitchen, the dog whined, and I opened the back door to let him out. Standing on the porch, I watched him frisk in the moonlight, and wondered how I would ever get him back to his bed without touching him. It was such a fine evening, though, the weather still so warm that Sarah had not yet enclosed the pool. I wished I'd taken a swim; the water, dotted with burnished leaves, looked pretty and inviting. The fresh air must have invigorated the dog also, for within minutes, hurt leg and all, he leaped over Sarah's fence and headed down the street. I ran through the front door to tell Sarah.

"You fool!" she shouted at me. "Sloppy, stupid fool."

I was too surprised to be either angry or upset. "Should we try to catch him?" I asked quietly.

We ran after him, not even having a name to call out. Chasing a no-name something, I thought, in the middle of the night. Thanks to his injury, he stayed only a block ahead of us. "Damn fools," Sarah kept saying, "damn inept fools."

Her anger with me, our chase through pleasant streets stirring with fallen leaves, the peacefulness of the night, was like a dream. I felt adrift from all of it.

Whatever possessed me to chase something I feared so much? And just what was it I did fear? Fear that I wouldn't count — with the world or with anybody? It was a hoax, anyway, that counting. It didn't save us after all.

I felt myself gaining speed. I might, just might catch up. But what if I did? Who would save me? I didn't give a damn about this dog. I didn't know why I was running, outdistancing Sarah. To prove what? I felt sick. I was only vaguely aware a car was coming towards us.

When the car struck, we saw an outline of a dog against the streetlight and heard a muffled thud. Then silence. The car didn't slow down. Sarah leaned against the closest tree.

"Go see what happened,"she said weakly, breathing hard.

The dog began to twitch. He wasn't dead. I would somehow have to get that dog out of the street and into a car. In my nightmares, when the dog's jaws locked on me, I was unable to scream or to move. My palms were perspiring and the cold, sick fear of my dreams spread its tentacles down my legs. I was not Sarah. I could not do this. This time, in his fear, he would attack. I turned to Sarah, but she didn't move.

Now it was my turn to be angry. She should understand. My need. My terror. I would never ask of her what she so casually asked of me. I would never ask anybody. This was her problem, not mine. She could damn well get her precious Leslie if she couldn't do it herself.

The moon silhouetted her by the tree. Stooped, head hanging down, she was without defenses, without hope, it seemed. Sarah, who had shown me how to make the patterns of dailiness count. This Sarah.

Without any more thought, I stooped down to examine the dog. He looked at me and whimpered briefly. I sat down in the middle of the street. I talked to him as I had heard Sarah do. I cradled his head in my arms. Did dogs mind being alone when they died?

Sarah walked over. "He's dying," I said.

"No, he isn't," she said fiercely. "You don't know anything about dogs. Let's take him home."

Dark brown blood trickled from his mouth as she tried to take him from me. She looked at me in horror and abruptly backed away. She shuddered. This wasn't supposed to happen. This, she couldn't control.

She began walking toward her house.

"Sarah!" I yelled. "Come back here!"

Startled, she twisted her head toward me, but kept walking.

8

SARAH WAS on her best behavior. She apologized for the dog incident about fifty times. She sent flowers. She explained. Not so easy to raise Leslie alone. And then that blood from the dog's mouth. She knew I'd understand. Understanding be damned, I wanted to shout. Sarah and Leslie made up. Sarah and I made up. Still, all the flowers and apologies hadn't quite got rid of a lingering bad taste in my mouth.

Now she was asking me to play doubles with Richard Lorton, publisher of a chain of newspapers that ran her column. He was in town for the weekend and wanted me for a tennis partner.

"He's a prick," I said.

"But you can stand him for an hour and a half. Besides, you'll be playing tennis most of the time."

"He plays tennis like he talks."

"An hour and a half. Please, Courtney."

As soon as we were in the car, he'd started talking about what was really on his mind — and it wasn't tennis.

"She's way out of line on Morris, even if she's right. People say she's gone too far. I want you to tell her to back off. I understand she listens to you." He made his points by jabbing the air with both hands as he drove along. "She may end up dropping off the limb and pulling the tree down with her. Extremes don't work around here. You should tell her. I tried but she thinks I don't know what I'm talking about — because I don't live here. Even when I quote people to her," he finished a little lamely.

I wished I were more in the mood to enjoy the deliciousness of having one of the most powerful men in the country petition me to petition one of his employees on his behalf. These last few days I'd had plenty of lectures and snide remarks on Sarah's crusade. I always defended it and her, but everytime the subject came up, I felt a little queasy. I tended to agree with her critics. She had made her case, and a good one, but no one else cared. Saints, they don't grow in Washington summed up the general attitude. The Lumb train wreck victims had been out of the news for too many years to capture the media's, and therefore the public's, imagination again.

"I'm sure Sarah doesn't need advice from either you or me. She's done pretty well for herself following her own hunches," I answered him.

"That I can't dispute," he acknowledged, and this was the reason, we both knew, he would let Sarah be on this matter.

Sarah could tell him herself that she wasn't about to let Morris go just yet. As we talked, she was working her sources for a column. I had only yesterday found from Ted London in the State Department that the Lumbanese were trying to get arms from us when he was stationed there during and after the coup. I went back to Hank Brown, who had suggested London to me in the first place, and he remembered the Lumbs talking about Stingray missiles in recent years but didn't know if they got them. Financing was always a problem for the Lumbanese. There was a possibility, however, that Morris had managed to get them a "soft loan," one with long-term financing and no interest, instead of the usual commercial terms.

Sarah had been delighted with the information and was sure she could pull something out of her contacts at Defense if State wasn't talking. Since Stingrays could shoot down low-flying aircraft, they were particularly lethal. But the main thing was to keep the story alive, she had told me. And maybe she'd told Lorton, too. Maybe that's why he was so upset.

For all his newspapers and television stations, he was no class act. Among other vices, he was a braggart. He even boasted about his open-mindedness. Why, one night at dinner, his companion (another media mogul) complained about a story unfavorable to the man's company. Our Mr. Media Mogul made the paper write a retraction, explaining why the first story was unfair. I happened to know the reporter and happened to know the first story was accurate and told him so. Oh, it wasn't the facts in dispute, he admitted, only the presentation of them.

"I'll bet you're in great demand as a dinner guest," I said, but the dig was lost on him. He began to tell me just how in demand he was.

Although he had a wife and she must have gone to some of these fetes, her name never came up. He was the one to balloon with the Forbeses or sail with the Kennedys (back when it counted) or ski with . . . (and here he listed five celebrities and described the houses of each). Somewhere during a recitation of what he'd said to a senator at a Washington dinner the night before, I vowed not to play tennis with him ever again no matter that Sarah's column ran in his papers or that he might someday put me in charge of his empire. Admittedly my resolve wasn't too significant, since, so far, no woman in his organization had gotten above midlevel management.

In the car I decided the tennis couldn't be as bad as the talking. Now that we were playing, I'd changed my mind. He was so busy checking out the other courts, he kept slamming his ball into the net. He was especially taken with the two men playing next to us — a former head of the CIA and a former Soviet spy. We were going to lose the game.

"Just look at that," he'd said to me twice now.

"Yeah, well, they've played together since they were twelve. Anyway, he hasn't been a spy for years."

"You people in this town shouldn't take pairings like that for granted," he chastised me, and was probably right, but I wasn't going to admit it to him.

"Good shot," Tom Wyrick, our opponent and the President's press secretary, said to me when he was unable to return my ball. Because of Lorton's importance to the President, Tom could no more refuse this game than I could. Tom's partner was Amy Freund, deputy assistant to the President. She'd been pressed

98

into service when Tom's wife bowed out because of family commitments. Both Tom and Amy had given up their much-needed Saturday afternoon off to play tennis with this jerk.

Tom and Amy were gracious winners until I managed another ball just out of Amy's reach. Suddenly we were ahead by two points. The game became serious. If we won this one, we won the set. Even Lorton, when he saw what I was doing, started paying attention and held his own.

On the next court the two old spies were in an argument over whether or not the ball was on the line. At some other time the quarrel would have amused us, but we were now caught up in our own battle and with all the intensity we brought to our work. For the most part, we weren't good at differentiating goals. What we did well, however, was to keep our veneer most amiable — as much as possible, anyway. We counted on form to civilize us.

The ball came to me, no spin on it. I took my time. A lob and I caught both opponents off guard. Victory was mine.

Tom and Amy congratulated us and pointedly praised my game. Lorton was forced to applaud me, too. As pleased as I was, I hated giving him an opportunity to brag tonight about his afternoon victory. In another fifteen minutes he would emerge the hero.

Certainly, I told Lorton as we headed for the locker rooms, I would love to play the next time he was in town. I accepted a ride home with Tom.

Coming out of a toilet stall, I ran into Leslie, here to play racquetball with George Rollins's daughter. George was the quiet-spoken head (a story in the *Post* had called him that) of the IRS. His home, according to Leslie, resembled a military boot camp.

Twice this week I had tried to make contact with Leslie, but she'd avoided me. This afternoon, however, standing in the middle of a busy locker room, she was ready to talk. After sending her friend outside, she began telling me her latest plan.

She was leaving. She already had her ticket to Colorado Springs, where her father lived. He was her best friend. Didn't I think she looked better? She'd lost a little weight. If she'd been prettier, he'd have stayed with them. Now she could show him what a good daughter was like.

The dinner party she was catering for Sarah was to be a farewell of sorts. Afterwards she would tell Sarah, and this time her mother wouldn't laugh. But everything would be all right. Because of the party. Her mother would see just how mature and responsible Leslie was. Sarah was going to be so pleased and satisfied that the leave-taking would be forgiven.

Having convinced herself Sarah could be placated, Leslie was close to euphoria; and reasoning with her, useless. Her thinking was strange enough for me to suspect drugs, but I knew her "good daughter" role wouldn't allow anything more than grass. I would wait until the mood passed, as it was bound to. At least, she was talking to me again. Eventually I could get through to her.

On our way home Tom stopped at the Safeway. His wife needed a couple of items and did I mind? On the contrary, I could pick up things, too. He joked about gossip run rife since we'd be seen together by half of Washington in this Georgetown supermarket. Tom made lots of jokes. He seldom let the press rile him, and he was much respected by the majority of its members. As far as I was concerned, his only drawback was his physical appearance, uncannily like my once-upon-a-time and only live-in lover's.

While he headed toward the ice cream, I made for the apples. A teenage boy, walking rapidly, accidentally nudged Tom with his cart.

"You son of a bitch! Why the fuck don't you look where you're going!" Tom shouted. So much for veneer, I thought.

"Sorry, mister." The boy looked shaken.

"Sorry's not enough. You need to pay attention."

"Look, I said I'm sorry."

Tom continued to lecture him. I paid for my apples and went to the car to wait. The pressures do it, I rationalized while watching a Rolls-Royce pull up in front of the store. But are we all time bombs? That loss of proportion — Richard Lorton, Tom, Leslie. Leslie's behavior today was bizarre — her pressures just as real as Tom's, for instance.

100

Though by now I understood the perils of living on the edge, Tom surprised me. Perhaps because his mannerisms and surface calm reminded me so much of my old flame, the creep, who — whatever else could be said of him, and a lot could — certainly did not have a temper. Maybe, living here, he would have developed one.

I had adored that bastard. He moved in with me in September and stayed through the spring term. We had a cozy nine months together. When I got home from teaching, I'd tidy the apartment and start dinner. When he ambled in from the library, we'd have a beer together and I would tell him about the latest shenanigans of my history students, and quote him some of my more penetrating observations on American culture, as viewed in an eleventh-grade classroom. If he didn't exactly solicit my recitals, he didn't discourage them either; and that was all I needed to ramble on until after dinner, when I would clean the dishes, grade papers, and make lesson plans. He would take his books to the bedroom, close the door, and study until past midnight. I tried to stay awake until then. Even if he was too tired to make love, which he often was, he didn't mind cuddling for a while.

If it was something less than a grand passion and he was something less than a great communicator, I didn't care. No one before had ever asked how my day was. He didn't reject me and he didn't judge me. In a way, his quietness made it easier for me to project on him any fantasy I wished: he could be or feel whatever my mood desired. It was a happy and secure time. I felt myself unfolding, giving, trusting.

Then spring came. The Ph.D. took a job in Nebraska without including me, and I huffed home for those miserable two weeks. I stood it that long only because I was in shock.

Neighbors and old acquaintances were more welcoming than my parents. Now that my headstrong ways were no longer a threat to their children, already escaped or safely married and trapped with babies, these townsfolk were glad enough to see me. Some whispered how they admired my spunk the time I organized an Arkansas Mothers' March for Peace. (There were eight of us; none, mothers.)

One great busybody laughed about my lecture to the Women's Garden Club on Zero Population Growth instead of the beautification of Zumlat High School. Nobody mentioned my participation in the town's one black boycott of white businesses. Maybe nobody remembered. My sister Jane had discovered me carrying a sign in front of the local dime store and dragged me home. My parents never mentioned any of this, nor had they appeared to notice. Indifference always gave them the final victory.

Two weeks were enough. I thought I understood a little better what kept pushing me. I thought I would try once more with old truelove. I thought my absence would have made him see the folly of his ways.

I arrived at the apartment a day before he was expecting me. From the looks of things, he was never going to expect me. At its best, our apartment was none too tidy; now, it was a disaster. Plates and cups and dirty glasses were scattered through the living room and kitchen area, not even an attempt made to pile them in the sink. In our bedroom, his clothes were everywhere — the floor, the bed, the chair, the desk, the windowsill. But the bathroom really did it. Out of some misplaced need for cleanliness, I guess, he had drawn the tub full of water and deposited his dirty socks. Pair after pair floated near the surface, a green slime adding a touch of color to the darkened stinking water.

Then I saw the rat. Its eyes and mouth open, its tail as long as its body, floating on the surface of the fetid socks. Had those socks killed the rat? I was afraid if I screamed I would lose control, and if I lost control I would never get out of there.

I picked up my suitcase, still standing by the front door, and dumped out enough clothes to make room for my books and tapes. I slammed the door behind me and ran down the two flights of stairs, grateful to be out before those socks killed me, too.

I ran to the street corner where the rage hit. The suitcase no longer felt heavy nor my feet clumsy. Without really thinking about what I was doing, I turned around, climbed the stairs again, and reopened the door. In the kitchen, I picked up the longest-handled pot I could find. In the bathroom, I scooped out socks and emptied them onto the bed. Back and forth I went, piling the socks. Finally I topped them with the wet-haired, gaping-mouthed rat. I pulled up the covers. I threw my abandoned clothes in the back of the closet. Let him find out in his own good time. When I closed the door, I had lost the need to cry.

As Tom walked back to the car, I marveled at just how strong the resemblance was and how little sexual attraction he had for me. Maybe the creep had ruined me for a certain type forever. He had also served a purpose, for after him I stopped counting on white knights to rescue me. Any more than Leslie's searching for a fantasy father would help her. If I could just make her understand how lucky she was to have one parent who paid attention, albeit excessive attention, I might have a chance with her. Make her understand that parental approval that's never been there will never be there. Another fantasy to let go.

Affable as always, Tom got in the car and didn't mention the incident inside the store. Instead we talked about his wife's family, who were here visiting, and the lineup of guests for the Sunday morning talk shows.

"Up yours," I muttered when my doorbell buzzed the next morning. I hadn't bothered with a robe. I knew who it was: only Krys would show up at eight-thirty on a Sunday morning to clean house. She stood there in her painter's pants and baggy man's shirt tucked in, a black braid hanging to her waist, her broad freshly scrubbed face and black eyes appearing open, but hiding everything. She had to be twenty-seven, but could easily pass for a teenager.

"I thought Cheryl told you last week not to come on Sundays anymore," I said, letting her in.

"Did she?" She looked surprised, which I was sure she was not.

"Sundays are really not a good time for us." Cheryl was convinced she came on Sunday morning as a form of harassment. I guessed it was for the Vie de France croissants Cheryl and I shared over a late Sunday morning cup of coffee as we watched "Face the Nation" and "Meet the Press." .

She continued standing in the door, staring out of that immobile face. "So long as you're here, you can do a wash for me." She nodded and stepped inside.

Cheryl's original idea had been to hire someone once a week to clean our small apartments, press our clothes, and cook up a couple of simple but nutritious dinners we'd otherwise not get. As young professionals, we owed it to ourselves, she'd argued.

I had called the George Washington University placement office to ask for a college student — cleaning was one of several ways I had put myself through graduate school. They posted a notice, answered a few days later by Krys. She was the only applicant. She came three times before we discovered she wasn't a student at G.W. at all.

Krys was, in fact, a campus bag lady. Only she used a backpack instead of a shopping bag. Staying in the stacks until everyone had locked up, she spent her nights on a couch in the G.W. library. She spent her mornings there also, reading books and improving her English. Afternoons, she swam in their indoor pool or walked around campus. Unlike Mr. Duc, she was satisfied with her situation and spurned all my offers of alternatives.

As a teenager, she had left Poland to visit an aunt in France and never returned. A young French couple brought her to New York to be a companion for the man's elderly mother. While the couple traveled, Krys and the mother watched television continuously. A year of this, and Krys became fluent in English. How she got to Washington was vague. What she planned to do here was even vaguer.

I sorted through my clothes for washing, no longer trusting the job to her after my panties and blouses had come out pink a couple of times. Nor had the ironing worked out; she pressed the wrinkles into the clothes. The cooking I couldn't bear to let her try. At least once a week we discussed letting her go, but I kept hoping we could help her. Along with a good ear for languages, she was smart. With the proper training, she could do well for herself. To give up on her was to watch her talent wasted.

By the time I had put back laundry to do myself, Krys was

left with only towels and sheets and flannel gowns, but those would get her out of my place and into the basement washroom. I would dress and get out of here. Sarah had asked me to drop some papers by her house this morning; by now she would have jogged, read the *Times,* and finished her first cup of coffee. I would deposit her papers, pick up the croissants, and eat them in whichever apartment Krys wasn't in. Krys could make do on Special K. And if she showed up again on a Sunday, I would fire her, I swore to myself.

In the living room, she was Windexing my mahogany desk top. Without shrieking, I explained for the fifth time what Windex was for. "Someday," I added, "you'll want to know this when you have your own apartment."

"I won't have to clean my own place," she answered.

"Then you'll want to know about these things to tell whoever works for you."

"Anyone who works for me will know what to do." She took the laundry from me and left.

The morning papers were gone from the front walk, but the house looked closed. I let myself in through the side gate. If Sarah wasn't up, I would leave the papers with a note wedged in the screen door and come back later. The pool hadn't yet been enclosed for the winter, and the late begonias lent a leisurely summer feeling to the quiet, cool morning.

My mood blossomed. Leslie, sleeping over at the Rollinses', couldn't have delivered any crushing news, and probably wouldn't now until after the party, by which time I would have talked her out of it. Even Sarah's fury with Gordon had dissipated. Granted, she was still furious with Anthony Morris and the press for not backing her, but she was bound to calm down soon. She just had to. As for myself, admittedly, I was nowhere nearer independence of any kind. Still, if I could keep her life steady, I had a chance to get back to my own with more success. On the steps to the kitchen, smells of coffee and bacon met me. I nudged the door. "Sarah," I called, stepping in.

On the kitchen stool sat a man, newspaper opened wide, with

only black hair showing above, white legs crossed, dimpled knees and bare feet showing below. I began backing out.

"Courtney," Sarah yelled from another room, "I'll be right there." The paper didn't move.

"I'll come back later."

Sarah came in, wearing a crinkled black cotton dress with nothing under it. "Don't be silly. Have some coffee. Wilson, you remember Courtney, of course."

There was nothing for it. The paper came down. Chief of staff to the President, confidant to the mighty, Sarah's star pupil, Wilson Kane, was sitting at Sarah's white marbled counter, a gleaming wooden floor beneath, clad undecorously in what appeared to be faded blue boxer shorts. He was trying hard to cover them with his paper. He tried to cover his chest, too, but gave up for fear of looking more ridiculous. For my part, I was concentrating on his forehead. When Sarah spoke again, I was still looking at his forehead.

"Well, Courtney, do you or don't you?"

"Don't I?" I turned to Sarah.

"Want some coffee. Pay attention. You'd think you'd never seen a man before."

In that case, I wanted to say, Wilson Kane looks like he's never seen a woman either. I declined the coffee, but Sarah was already handing me a cup.

Baby blue. Wilson Kane wore baby blue shorts with tiny white whales on them. Had his wife purchased them? — taking them home as a surprise — "Look at the cute whales, darling." Or had his mother, perhaps thinking of her baby boy, bought them in a fit of nostalgia? Or had Wilson Kane himself found them, taken a fancy to the whales, and decided to live it up a little? More than a little by the looks of things.

"Do you have the papers?" Sarah asked me.

"Mr. Kane has the papers."

"Not the newspaper. The ones you brought for me."

My face flushed. Sarah laughed. Even Kane smiled, but not for long. Sarah leaned across the counter and took the paper from him. "Wilson, you can read later." He folded his arms across his chest, but his stomach was suitably flat for this kind of exposure.

"Not much of interest here, is there?" Sarah said, thumbing through the reports. She wanted to do a piece on the administration's veto of a bill affecting our allies. So far, we had only come up with the surface excuses.

"Wilson, would you want to help us out, by any chance?"

I wondered what had happened to Sarah's rule about not sleeping with sources. "Stay away from sources and married men," she'd cautioned me when I'd first come to town. But then maybe she never meant to apply the rules to herself. She probably didn't see herself vulnerable on either score, and she was, at least, half-right: who would dare accuse her of getting a story because she slept with a source? You might as well have been accusing Walter Cronkite.

"No comment," he said.

"Courtney says the President's just being a good guest. The Europeans were nice to him on his visit there last week and he's returning the favor."

Kane looked at me. "I think he's trying to establish better relations with our allies, the way you in the press are always advocating." On "advocating," a limp, round, flesh-colored protrusion gaped through his whales. He shifted position and it disappeared. Neither he nor Sarah seemed aware of it.

"Do we think our esteemed White House chief of staff is biased against the press?" Sarah asked. For all the syrup in her voice, she could just as well have been asking him to bed. Maybe he would prove enough of a distraction to get some balance back into her life. Maybe his white whales could help her forget the Anthony Morris controversy.

Mr. Kane looked uncomfortable, but began an earnest monologue on the irresponsibility of some segments of our beloved profession. As he talked, the protrusion again reared its head. So to speak.

With great effort, I brought my gaze back to his forehead. Sarah looked at me in amusement. She asked Kane for examples of his grievances. He recrossed his legs, once more banishing the flesh, and gave a recitation. I marveled at the obliviousness of a man listening to his own voice. Only when Sarah expressed a little too much shock at his report did he realize she was putting him on.

With that, he got up to get himself more coffee, either overcoming his self-consciousness around me, or too irritated with Sarah to care. As he stood, Sarah placed her hand on the back of his neck. "I wonder what the government and media folks would have to say about all this?" she asked, her whole face smiling at him. Behind the whales, his protrusion went from Parade Rest to Attention.

This he noticed. He quickly turned his back and began readjusting.

"Why don't you bring the pot back with you? Courtney would like a refill." Sarah's grin was contagious. We quickly looked away from each other. "By the way," she said to me, "Leslie has decided on next week for the dinner." Turning to Kane, "Isn't that sweet? She wants to cater a party for me. Would you and Pat like to come if Pat's back in town?"

Kane only smiled and rejoined us, with the pot functioning as a fig leaf. Before offering me coffee, he sat down and crossed his legs. With great aplomb, he picked his newspaper back up and asked us to defend the press bias against this administration. Sarah looked to me for comment, but I shook my head no. With all the discipline and soberness I could muster, I waved my fingers good-bye and shot out the door. I had to hand it to him, though: the man had class.

In the car, I laughed until the tears came. In the bakery, I started laughing. The woman behind the counter looked alarmed. I ordered a half-dozen more croissants than usual. "These are for Krys," I said, and began laughing again, only to realize how rare a commodity laughter had become in my world.

9

As the phone rang, I unlocked the office door and knocked over Gladys's chrysanthemums, reaching across her desk to answer.

"Where the hell is everybody? Why aren't you getting ready for the big bash tonight?" It was Gordon Simons, whom Sarah was now referring to as her estranged friend. That meant she hadn't given up on him. Or him on her. He was coming to dinner. "She's taken the goddamn phones off the hook over there. I can't get through on hers or Leslie's."

"Leslie may have done it. She wanted Sarah to take a nap."

"Sarah hasn't had a nap since she was two months old."

"It's something to do with Leslie's friendly catering service; probably a way to keep Sarah out of the kitchen and make grand amends at the same time."

"Leslie, the solicitous. A new one," he said. "Maybe she should give me a few lessons in the care and assuaging of her mother."

I didn't answer.

"I could be late — an hour or so." He hesitated. "But I'd better tell her myself. I don't want to screw things up between us."

"I'm on my way over with her book galleys now. I'll ask her to call you." I looked at my watch and wished he would get on with it.

"I'll give you this number."

"Fine."

"Courtney?"

"Yes?"

"You tell her. Tell her I'll do everything I can to be on time. It's an out-of-town client who leaves first thing in the morning — really."

"Gordon, deliver your own mail," I said, hanging up.

If Sarah wanted to entertain us, Gordon would certainly be useful. Both were equally adept in the dramatics of quarreling with flourish and making up the same way; and tonight they would be in prime form — playing off the other, wooing each other, vying, all the while, for center stage. Great sport could be had figuring out which one would triumph on any given occasion. This evening, I thought, wiping up the flower water, Sarah and Gordon might be exhausting, but they wouldn't be dull.

The galleys were on top of her desk, where she said they would be. She had called my apartment asking for them, suggesting I come early to look over them with her. I suspected they were a pretext to call about an article of hers she'd just seen in print. Whenever possible, she liked the instant expression of displeasure. This time she had used the adverb "truly" twice in the course of three paragraphs. Sloppy editing irritated her. I apologized for not catching it, but she chose to blame the magazine, their "excuse for copy editors." I didn't mention that most copy editors weren't about to take her on, especially over an adverb.

On the way out, I tossed my hair and smoothed my new navy silk dinner dress in front of the bathroom mirror. I was fine, I decided, and, for the first time, started looking forward to the dinner. Sarah had chosen comfortable friends to sample Leslie's culinary skills. Comfortable and captivating — Madge Hudson-Marsh, who, since Leslie's party and the shared secret of the Brit, had been more open with me. Ruth Howard, as solicitous of Sarah as she was of the prized Smithsonian, and Ruth's husband, Sam, who commuted from M.I.T. to be with his wife; Madeline Owens, charming when on her good behavior, as she had been recently, and her husband, Bob, included, I felt sure, to lend moral support to Sarah in her bout with Gordon, in the role of both loyal friend and former lover. The Wilson Kanes had declined Sarah's invitation. Whenever I thought about leaving Sarah, going out to do something on my own, I'd remember the lovers and friends and parties and travel, and know my life would never have the kind of drama that Sarah provided on a daily basis.

The streets were already filling with cars for other dinners in the homes and restaurants of Georgetown, and I had to park four blocks from Sarah's house. I walked briskly, looking forward to putting the finishing touches on the party. I'd need to redo the florists' arrangements to make them less formal, and put out ashtrays and place candles all around. The evening might even be cool enough for a fire, a satisfying beginning. I smiled. Leslie was right about one thing: I got as much pleasure out of Sarah's home as if it were my own.

It wasn't large, but it was inviting. The living room and dining room and one upstairs bedroom had been built in 1780, the library in 1820, the kitchen and one other bedroom added about 1910. Sarah loved repeating the dates to people.

"These rooms are my ancestors," she'd once said to me. "My father's family got off the boat and promptly forgot where they came from, and my mother died before I was old enough to ask about her family."

It amused her that her friends sometimes assumed a John Adams connection, and she did nothing to dispel the assumption. If pressed, she would simply say that her husband was from the Midwest branch of the family. Since the whole business with her former husband was a little mysterious, people would drop it.

I waved to a friend from the Canadian embassy and got a satisfying feeling that Washington was becoming a small town for me, that, at last, I could walk the streets and run into people I knew. But even if Sarah's drama could be mine, I thought, stepping aside for a little girl barreling down the sidewalk on a tricycle, even if I could have all the intrigues and affairs and mysteries, I wasn't emotionally capable of handling it. My parents and the creep had made me shy of caring too much, wanting too much emotionally. As a result I enjoyed vicarious living, maybe more than the other kind. And if that made me timid . . . I paused on the sidewalk, remembering Sarah's reproach of me on the night the dog died . . . well, I would deal with all that later. I increased my pace.

*   *   *

A half block from Sarah's, Gordon fell into step. He carried an armful of flowers, a signal that he planned to swaddle Sarah in attention until she relented. Sometimes this ploy worked, though usually not. Usually he would have to wait until Sarah arbitrarily declared a halt to their battle, at which point his escapade would be put behind them. Or appear that way. Now he was anxious to please.

"See, I did better than on time. I'm here early," he said. "I've probably created some ill will with an important client, but this is worth it. We're both being childish, and I, for one, am putting a stop to it."

"Is this a dress rehearsal?" I asked.

He laughed. Then the play left his face. "Has she mentioned me?" I shook my head no. "Not even in a bad way?" he pursued. Again no.

"Well, what about the flowers? Do you think she'll like the flowers?"

Already trying to figure out how to make those florist-dyed daisies and carnations look presentable to Sarah, I assured him she would love them. Before I could get to it, he rang Sarah's bell with his elbow. When no one answered, I knocked loudly. Then I tried the door.

The brass knob was cool. A fire this evening was definitely not out of the question. I wondered how Sarah would take Gordon's early arrival. He would throw off her timing; but, of course, that's why he'd done it. The door was stuck but, unexpectedly, not locked. It gave.

We stepped inside. The small entrance hall, with its pots of mums and ferns, looked festive. A sweet, vaguely familiar odor came from the direction of the kitchen. Sarah had already turned the light low in the living room, and the firewood was in place and waiting for the match. The Richard Estes lithograph above the mantel and the rows of books on each side added just the right note to Sarah's stage set.

I took the flowers from him. I would put them in the kitchen, then go upstairs to check on Sarah. It was unlike her to leave the door open; I hoped she and Leslie weren't at it again.

As I pushed open the swinging door with my hip, I viewed the shambles. Canned goods and pans were everywhere. A carton of milk was turned over and trickling down a cabinet. A platter of cherry tomatoes and carrot sticks lay toppled by the butcher block.

Then I noticed the bright red stain on the kitchen floor. I felt the pressure of Gordon's hand on my arm. Wordlessly we opened the door onto the back garden.

Sarah was kneeling by the pool, her back to us. Rivulets of blood and water ran down her robe, forming a pink puddle around her and Leslie. They were both soaked through. Leslie's legs sprawled on the ground, her head cradled in her mother's arms, her face half-hidden by Sarah's breasts. Her eyes were open and very red. Water trickled from her slack mouth. Blood had ruined the embroidered violets on her old blue work shirt. Her jeans had a small hole up on her thigh — an old hole, I remembered. She was still wearing yellow kitchen gloves.

Gently, Sarah rocked her back and forth.

Gordon tried to take Leslie, but Sarah clung fiercely. It no longer mattered. He put his jacket around Sarah, and I held it tight to stop the bleeding. He went to call an ambulance.

Momentarily she stopped rocking and looked up at me blankly. Gordon came back.

She began rocking again. Over and over she smoothed the thin, wet hair back from Leslie's forehead. A bee hovered over a tub of late-blooming geraniums decorating the pool. The pattern of leaves floating on the water formed a golden mosaic, as new leaves drifted lazily onto the others. Where the leaves had separated, there was a reddish tinge to the water. The sun, gray-pink in its decline, caught the gold in Sarah's hair.

Gordon patted her shoulder, but she was completely absorbed in rocking Leslie.

Somewhere down the street I heard a child laugh. Everything else was still. The scream in my head didn't disturb the day. My body rocked with Sarah's as I continued to clutch her arm, even after the bleeding had stopped.

10

In a concerted effort, Gordon, an ambulance attendant, and a police sergeant pried Leslie from Sarah's arms. Someone said, "She's dead"; and, for an instant, I thought he was lying. Leslie could not be dead. She consumed too much space to be dead. "Liar!" I wanted to shout.

Another young attendant tried to examine Sarah, but she rebuffed him, concerned herself only with the blanket-encased body she followed into the ambulance. Although Gordon followed after, the sergeant stopped him for questions, causing Gordon's usual phlegmatic demeanor to disappear. Face contorted, he looked ready to take on all of us until he was promised he could go to her soon. As the ambulance drove away, he calmed down.

Whirling lights and siren noises had attracted a crowd. Neighbors looked from their windows, and curiosity-seekers, from the nearby business and restaurant district, clustered about. Police were everywhere. Two fire trucks appeared. I was glad when the sergeant, his cap too small by a size, led us back inside, away from the gawkers.

"This yours?" The sergeant held up Gordon's blood-soaked suit jacket that he had put around Sarah. Gordon nodded and reached for it, but the sergeant told him it had to be checked out. Still Gordon held out his hand for it, addressing the officer as he might a recalcitrant child: "I want my jacket."

"Later," the sergeant replied, and handed the jacket to a plain-clothes detective, who joined us. The detective wore sneakers, jeans, and close-cropped hair. He was dark black, rather tall, solidly built, with a sureness about his carriage.

"I want it now," Gordon continued to insist, beginning himself to sound like the child.

"It's OK, Gordon," I said. "You can't wear it, anyway." I would swear his nostrils flared. No one had ever looked at me with such intense hatred in my life.

"We need your help, Mr. Simons." The detective's voice was quiet but authoritative. His focus was sharp and strong, almost tangible. I was glad he was here. He introduced himself as James Brill. Patiently, he waited for Gordon to regain control of himself; then we recounted what little we knew.

"And the front door, was it usually locked?"

"Yes," I said.

"But she was expecting us," Gordon added.

I looked at the detective. "She's been compulsive about the door ever since the burglary."

Brill was interested, asked for details. I recited the missing items — some silver, and Leslie's expensive stereo. I told him how the back door had been pried open, how Sarah had put in an alarm system, which she'd been conscientious about using.

Brill asked my relationship to her.

"Her assistant," I answered, wondering how to begin to explain what that one word meant.

"And you knew her daughter well?"

"Yes."

"Can you think of any reason for this? Anyone with a grudge?"

"No. Sarah has upset people professionally, but they're hardly the kind to . . ."

"Everyone loves Leslie," Gordon interrupted. "And Sarah," he added.

"Of course, they do. But Sarah's writing affects a lot of people. That's all."

"Don't be so goddamn condescending." Gordon edged himself between Detective Brill and me, and turned his back on me. "While I don't presume to know as many facts as Ms. Patterson, I do have an understanding of their lives."

Brill did not ask him his relationship to them; instead he took us on a tour of the house to look for something missing, something out of place. The entrance hall, the living room, and Sarah's study looked exactly as they should — spotless, festive, intact. The dining room was dramatically lovely, the table splendid with its crystal and candles and mirrors. All that was missing were the rubirum lilies I had come early to arrange.

We were asked about her valuable objects, including papers. I explained that most documents were in a wall safe at the office, but led them into the bedroom, where the spread was turned back, the pillows propped, an indentation of her head on them. So she had rested in the afternoon. I pulled out a small drawer inside the armoire. It held her gold chains, her pearl earrings, an elaborately jeweled pin that I'd never seen before. I saw nothing missing. Gordon insisted upon looking himself but had to agree with me. We finished the upstairs and started back down. Toward the kitchen.

"Who would have keys to her house?" Brill was careful to include both of us in his questions. He was probably a great parent if his handling of us was indicative of anything.

I answered. "Me. Ida Turpin, her housekeeper. And, of course, Leslie."

Brill looked at Gordon, who looked down. But we were entering the kitchen, and our childish game ended. I gagged. Gordon stepped in and stepped out hurriedly.

I was determined to check out every possible detail, to impress on my memory every spot of blood, every overturned object. The clue had somehow to be in this place, hidden in the midst of the wilting lilies lying next to their broken vase or in the bright collage of vegetables scattered about — Sarah's contribution to the health- and calorie-consciousness of our nation's capital. Yet in all the disarray, I found nothing but bright, caked blood that didn't belong. When I shook my head, we left the kitchen without speaking.

I breathed better in the hall, where Gordon stood waiting for us. Remembering the guests, I suggested notifying them, but Brill preferred to meet them and set up individual interviews for later.

"They won't appreciate getting messed up in this kind of thing," I told him.

Gordon turned toward me. "I guess you think Sarah does."

"You're hysterical," I said calmly.

"You are the smuggest bitch I've ever met."

Detective James Brill quietly watched our road show.

"Do you have children?" I asked him with an unreasonable urgency to distance myself from this house and Gordon and Brill's pertinent questions.

"Two boys," he replied, slightly taken aback.

"How old are they?"

"Courtney, for God's sake!" Gordon yelled. But it didn't matter what I said. None of this was real anyway. Soon this would be over and our lives would be back to normal. Sarah and Leslie would start fighting again, but this time I could stop it. All we needed was one more chance. This time I could make everything all right for all of us. Even for Gordon.

"We're going to be OK, Gordon," I tried to assure him. Without bothering to reply, Gordon walked to a waiting police car and headed for Sarah.

"Do you want to sit down?" Brill asked me. I shook my head no, for not for one minute could I let up. I could afford no more slips, and I would have none.

Bob and Madeline Owens were the first to arrive. Following them was Justice Lemon, a neighbor, not a party guest. Madeline greeted me with a brush of cheek. "What's going on here? Did Sarah snare the President? You look lovely in that dress. Doesn't she look lovely, Bob?"

Bob Owens looked around the room at the police and took my hand. "Hush," he said to his wife. His hair was graying and thinning out, but his vigor was that of a twenty-year-old. His vigor and his eyes would always keep him young.

"Can I be of help?" Justice Lemon asked. "I just got home," he added apologetically.

James Brill, a little flustered, began explaining what happened. It wouldn't be easy for him to have a Supreme Court justice and a former attorney general breathing down his neck for the rest of this case. After he talked briefly to everyone, Justice Lemon insisted that we come to his house for a drink. I thought I should stay and wait for the other guests, but Brill insisted I go with the others. On the way out, Brill gave me permission to come back later, to wait for Sarah's return.

Leaving the house was a relief. Only a few curious strays were left in front. The trees arched over us, and wood fires scented the early night air. The evening was as crisp as I had once hoped it would be. We walked through the burgundy and gold leaves glistening under the streetlight, our feet making a whooshing sound. I wished myself part of this tranquil scene and was angry that I wasn't — might never be again.

The justice's home was comforting, its reassuring air belying the possibility of the past hour. The drawing room with its over-stuffed sofas and armchairs covered in quilted chintz had a permanence about it, without in any way appearing dated. Cheerful pots of red begonias perched randomly on table tops. The tone was light and casual. No Louis, no gilt, no layers of window covering. The only bow to important furnishing was four American Hepplewhite chairs scattered about the room.

If it weren't for Sarah, I thought, I would never see the inside of homes like these. But if it weren't for Leslie, I might never have seen this room in particular. The nausea started to come back, and I reached my hand toward the sofa for support.

Madge Hudson-Marsh suddenly was by my side and guiding me down on the sofa. She sat by me and patted my hand. I wanted nothing so much as to cry in her arms, but neither my sense of privacy nor her reserve allowed that.

We watched Justice Lemon, giving us all time to get our bearings, fix drinks and reorganize chairs. "I should help," I said.

"Stay still," Madge ordered.

Sam Howard came over and handed Madge and me a drink. I was glad to see him and Ruth. The others began joining us, and I steeled myself for conversaton. Nobody else sat down. I tried compressing my mind and body into a sliver that would go unnoticed, but Madeline Owens didn't allow it. "You look like the wrath of God," she said to me. At least, we'd dispensed with my lovely dress. Ruth put her hand over mine, and suggested Madeline find me a wrap since I was shivering, though I was hardly aware of it. I assured them that a few more sips of scotch would solve the problem. I wanted no favors from Madeline Owens. Not even small ones.

Madeline turned to Sam. "I don't know what's going to happen to Sarah," she said.

"Bless her heart," the justice murmured. Their voices had the hushed quality heard wherever people are waiting — in churches, hospitals, airports, or train stations. The rhythms were different, but the inflections could come out of any home in Arkansas. I was comforted by their lull and by the soft, warm light in the room and even by the table of family photographs in antique silver frames. When my shivering stopped, Ruth turned and smiled.

"Better?" she asked, and I nodded yes. "It's good that Gordon is with her," she continued.

"I guess," I answered, then couldn't help adding, "He's a belligerent bastard. I've never seen him so . . . so . . . proprietary."

"You've never seen him so guilty. He's been acting like an ass and he knows it."

"Has anyone called her brother?" Madge asked me.

But I had forgotten about her brother Andrew. A hotshot with one of the multinational corporations, he lived in Belgium and never made it to Washington, though sometimes Sarah and Leslie would meet him in California, company headquarters. With a pang, I remembered Sarah's high hopes for the upcoming Thanksgiving holiday with him.

It turned out only Madge had met him, and that had been on a ski trip in Switzerland. She would call. She had her doubts as to how much real support he was going to be to Sarah. He'd made so little effort in the past.

"Even Sarah said he was spoiled," Sam said.

"He's Sarah's little brother, isn't he?" Madeline clipped off each word. From past experience I knew it best to let remarks like that from Madeline drop, but tonight I wasn't so inclined.

"What's that supposed to mean?"

"That if he's spoiled, we know who did it. It's one of the surest, swiftest ways to dependency I know of. Look at poor Leslie."

Madge's face flushed. I wanted to punch Madeline Owens in the mouth, and Bob Owens looked as if he might, but instead, wandered away to replenish his drink.

"Don't everyone act so righteous," Madeline continued in a voice that sounded more amused than defensive. "I hate this as much as anyone. I bleed for Sarah. But that doesn't make her a saint. And, with the exception of Courtney, we're all of us too old to be sentimentalists. Right?"

No one responded. The justice suggested everyone sit down and be comfortable. No one looked at Madeline. The most maddening thing about the woman was the way she could take a disturbing trait — Sarah's desire to do everything for Leslie — and turn it into an obscenity. Without wanting to, I remembered the fights Sarah and Leslie had over homework. Then one evening I had delivered to Sarah a lecture on leaving Leslie's homework to Leslie, who was plenty capable of doing it herself. But Sarah had listened, had even announced that night to Leslie that she was leaving her on her own, and had succeeded in doing so more often than not after that. Sitting on the justice's couch, I wished I'd intervened more often.

Someone asked the justice how an investigation like this proceeded, and we listened attentively to his answer. We wanted to follow the correct procedure, the right form, wanted order restored. All of us had spent our lives garnering power in one way or another, and not for nothing had we all been more successful than not in gaining some control over our lives. We had all bought into the illusion of control, and to be reminded that it wasn't worth a damn, that all this fetch-and-carrying was just so much manure, left us shaken and angry.

Or was I speaking for the others? Were they enough older or wiser that they'd already figured out pretty flowers and pretty rooms and pretty conversations — the trappings of illusion — could be wiped out by some nut they were unlucky enough to cross? It could happen to any of us, and it had taken me twenty-eight years and a murder to make me stop long enough to acknowledge it. What do I do now, I wanted to shout at them. But nobody looked in any shape to answer.

We had formed a chorus; we testified, singly and as a group. We banded to cast out the evil spirits, to give witness to Sarah's love. Sarah's doting. Sarah's protectiveness. Sarah, the giver. Sarah, the nurturer. But did that make Leslie nurtured?

"Once," said Madge, "on a muggy Saturday morning, Leslie called Sarah from camp. She was fine, but she'd gone off without her allergy medicine, and could Sarah send it to her. Sarah had been in a great mood — we were on our way to the Weinsteins' country place — but she panicked after the call. She told me she thought Leslie was sick but trying to protect her. Nothing would do but for her to drive to the camp, six hours away in North Carolina. I finally wrangled the conversation out of her, but couldn't convince her she was imagining trouble. So, we set off for North Carolina — she was too distraught to go alone.

"I was so irritated — giving up such a lovely day. I also felt so sorry for her. I'd never understood before quite how vulnerable she was. And so guilty — as if forgetting to pack Leslie's medicine would bring down some awful punishment on her, Sarah." Madge stopped, apparently lost in the enormity of Sarah's feelings.

Sam nudged: "What happened?"

"We arrived to find Leslie playing volleyball. She was very embarrassed that we were there." Madge laughed. "Had we stayed very long, I think it's possible that we would have made her sick."

"Once," said Justice Lemon, "Sarah forgot a swim meet of Leslie's — she must have been around eight. For the rest of the summer, Sarah brought her over every afternoon — this was before she put in a pool — and watched her swim for an hour, whether Leslie wanted it or not."

We laughed. "She was turning into such a beautiful young woman," Sam said, his voice failing to keep the bland, neutral tone the rest were working for.

But Madge quickly began telling us of the time Sarah left the President's dinner table because she had called home to find

Leslie's fever had hit one hundred and three. By the time she'd gotten home, Leslie's fever was under control and she was sleeping peacefully.

"Leslie got a get-well card from the President," Madge continued, "and half of Washington must have called the next day. Sarah made me swear to report that Leslie was on her deathbed, if anyone asked. Even she realized she'd been a bit excessive this time around."

Then Ruth recalled the time that Sarah had gotten a call during a snowstorm, saying that Leslie had slipped on the ice and was in the emergency room of Sibley Hospital, getting stitches on her eyebrow. Traffic was immobilized, so Sarah walked five miles to be with her. I knew the story well, for Sarah was fond of telling it in front of Leslie, who always looked trapped.

What I had not heard, until Ruth told us, was that Sarah had grieved for months over the scar, so small as to be invisible. I watched as Bob Owens stood and began fiddling with a small blue and white Chinese vase on the mantel. He made me nervous, and he looked ready to go, which meant we would all leave with him. I didn't want to leave. What little comfort I could get was in this room. At Sarah's, I would need all my control to get ready for her, and, right now, I didn't see how I could do it. Just thinking of Sarah made me feel guilty. Were the circumstances reversed, Sarah would already be planning, organizing the next day's events, charming the police into conducting the investigation on her terms. Just thinking about it made me weary.

Now everyone was standing. Madeline came over. "Don't try to be Superwoman," she said. "Go to bed."

I nodded.

"I know what I'm talking about," she went on, as if I were arguing with her. "Age counts for something, and you're still wet behind the ears, you know."

I smiled, or tried to.

"Anyway, you must get bored with us old fogies."

I didn't say anything.

"I mean, your own friends must be much trendier than this stodgy Washington scene."

I thought of Cheryl and Maxie and Mr. Duc. This time, I smiled. "Not really." I still wasn't sure of her point, and I was too tired to care.

"Then find yourself more friends, dear. More like you — young and not so important . . . self-important. You don't want to get embalmed in our political tomb." Madeline smiled and walked away to take her husband's arm. How long had she been waiting, I wondered, to tell me I am not one of them? Until Sarah no longer protected me? I shuddered. For this strange evening, Madeline was the descant. I quickly walked over to the Howards and Madge.

She took my arm. "Be patient with Gordon," she said. "He cared very much for Leslie."

"Gordon?"

"I believe he loved her as much as he allowed himself to love anybody. She was as close to a daughter as he would ever have, and he knew it. He worried about her, though I'm sure he never let Sarah know it."

Before I could pursue this startling idea, the justice came over to suggest I bring Sarah back to his house. I declined his offer, knowing Sarah could not allow him close tonight. Madge offered to wait with me, but by now her hands were shaking badly. She seemed in no condition to keep a vigil, but I wasn't sure just what I should say to her. She had as much right there as I did. I assured her I would be all right alone and left it up to her to decide how much help she would be to Sarah. With obvious relief she took my answer as the last word — declaring she would be over first thing in the morning. Sarah would be knocked out anyway. Doctors always did that. More important that she herself be fresh tomorrow. I promised to call if I needed any of them in any way.

Before we parted, we spoke once more of Leslie's death, of Ruth's beautiful stole — such fine wool, it would go through her ring, she showed us — and of how uncommonly lovely the last few days had been.

11

"HAVE THE PAPERS called yet?" she asked, as soon as she walked in the door. Her left forearm was bandaged, the blood gone from her face and arms. Only her dazed face and the short caftan, still soaked with blood, hinted at the earlier catastrophe; and her voice — flat, matter-of-fact, without resonance.

"Not yet," I answered, helping her remove a sweater someone must have loaned her. Gordon helped, too. She had been stabbed, he said hurriedly, under his breath.

"I've got a lot to do. People to contact. Does my brother know? Have you made a list? The obituary. Does my brother know?" She was mobilized in the exact way she was for any deadline — taut, with a cool, impassive veneer, shutting out everything extraneous to the matter at hand. Only now, I felt no intelligence working under it. Now she was all form.

Gordon touched her arm. "Let's sit a minute. You need to catch your breath. I'll get a brandy."

"Is that a good idea?" I asked. "If she's been given a sedative . . ."

"It's been a rough few hours," he said.

"Madge has a call in to your brother. His answering service is trying to reach him." But she no longer seemed interested in that. In one quick movement she unzipped her dress and jerked it over her head. "Get my robe, Courtney. And I don't want a drink. I don't want anything."

I ran upstairs for the robe, while Gordon helped her off with her slip and shoes. We wrapped her carefully, but she hardly noticed.

Then she roused herself again. "Courtney, get Father Dalton on the phone for me. This is to be a very private family service in the chapel. Episcopalians do these things right, don't they? Dalton will say the right things. To the papers, I mean. This is all to be kept as low-key as possible. In good taste. I will not have this turned into a circus," she said, as if I were thinking of doing just that. Then, "Don't you need to be taking notes?"

I got a pencil and pad, the same one I'd already been making notes on. I tried to tell her. I tried to ask about her arm. But whatever force was keeping her going was working from the inside out. She was receiving nothing. Shut down except for this stored-up energy.

"Gordon, get in touch with Leslie's father. His name is Philip Adams. He lives in Colorado Springs. But insist that he not come. If the press finds him, he should express his regrets — coherently, if possible. He is not to come. Make that clear." She got up. "We can finish in the morning." Again, she turned to me. "Have things been reorganized?"

"Not yet. Not until the police have another look around in the morning. Justice Lemon wants you to stay at his house tonight."

"That's absurd."

"But . . ."

"It's no use," Gordon interrupted. "I've already been through this with her."

She touched the white cyclamen on the coffee table. "My brother brought me one of these when Leslie was born. Andrew was the same age as Leslie now, but he was trying so hard to be grown-up for me." She smiled at us. "It was the only flower we got." Her mask crumbled as she put her hand to her mouth, but she stood still until the lines of her face locked together again.

With great determination, she began climbing the stairs. Without looking at each other, Gordon and I followed. At the top, she opened the door to Leslie's room and turned on the light. The room was too frilly for Leslie — a canopy bed, organdy curtains, a fantasy bedroom out of a girlhood that Sarah herself had not had. Two small drawings of cats that Leslie had done in the eighth grade and a group of bright pillows on the bed — these were the only touches of Leslie in the room.

"Did you know that I laid out her clothes every night? It was a ritual between us . . . until this year." She looked over the room closely. "She should put out some photographs. And she should get a new down comforter for winter. She hasn't taken care of this one."

"Let's get you in bed now, Sarah." Gordon folded her into his arms. "And I'm getting you a brandy."

"I'll go fix her bed," I said, leaving the room quickly.

I turned down her covers and drew her bath water. She resisted bed and chose a shower. While she was in the bathroom, the phone rang, but Gordon answered it downstairs. When she came out, she puttered about the room, straightening a drawer of lingerie, repropping the pillows I'd already puffed.

The more take-charge she became, the clumsier I felt. Pretty soon she would be comforting me. But, finally, that restless energy seeped away; she lay down; and I tucked her in.

"Stay awhile," she said, looking the way she must have as a little girl. I sat beside her and held her hand.

"Remember the time at the zoo when Leslie got lost?" she asked. "I was frantic until I found her in the monkey house. And she said — so calmly — 'Of course, I'm here. It's my favorite place.' She looked so darling standing there in her sailor coat and Mary Janes . . . such tiny feet. But wasn't she a solemn little thing?"

"That was before I knew her," I said, patting her hand.

"For years, whenever I left for work, she would stand here at my window; and when I reached the edge of the walk, she'd rap on the pane and blow me a kiss."

"She loved you very much."

"I was her best friend. She told me everything."

I murmured an agreement.

"Everything. All her secrets." She smiled. "In the fourth grade, a boy kissed her on the cheek. She thought I'd be angry, but she told me anyway. Wasn't that cute?" She lay back on the pillow, her back tensed, arched. "Even as a very little girl, you know, she would ask, 'Mommy, are you happy?'"

She lay quietly. I wanted to curve around her emotions, to let her sense my closeness; but she'd leapt into that chasm and I couldn't — or wouldn't — follow. Without warning, she sat upright, her eyes wild, her face twisted.

"Do you think she's found a favorite place? Oh, please, God!" she cried.

I tried to hold her, but she was stiff, unyielding. I wondered what was keeping Gordon. I wished for Madge. She might have known what to do. But, again, she lay back — this time with her arm crooked over her eyes. She looked beyond reach, but once more, she roused herself to speak.

"There is no place for sadness in our lives," she told me in a confidential whisper. "I see to that. When she's unhappy, I feel I've failed, somehow. You know?" Her eyes turned vague. She paused. "I know best, but sometimes she doesn't believe me."

Her eyelids closed for a moment and then opened. Then closed again. This time for longer. With great effort, they opened but closed quickly. Her breathing became regular and deep, but her eyelids continued to flutter, still protesting sleep. And who could blame her? Surely, the worst nightmare of all would be the waking and remembering, all those mornings for all those years.

Gordon came in. She stirred and looked at him. "Don't leave me," she said. I got up to give him my place, but Sarah had fallen back asleep.

In the hall, Gordon suggested I spend the rest of the night in Leslie's room. Was this an overture toward peace or an acknowledgment that he couldn't handle everything himself? Sheepishly, he offered me the brandy he'd brought for Sarah.

"I had one downstairs," he admitted.

"Do the police have any clues at all?" I asked.

"Not one. It appears the only stab wound is Sarah's. Leslie was either choked or drowned. Most probably choked. And Sarah is no help. She can't remember any of it. I've tried to reassure her that once the shock wears off . . . still . . ." He shook his head and left the rest unspoken.

We said goodnight. Then I remembered. "Who was that on the phone?" I called to him.

"Some boy asking for Leslie. I had a hard time making him understand something had happened to her. Would that be her boyfriend? He came over as a rude ass."

"That would be her boyfriend."

I was not sure I could spend the night in Leslie's room. Not only because of memories. I also felt an intruder, an invader of Leslie's closely held privacy. But I was being silly. I had spent plenty of time in here, especially when she was younger. I had even slept here on occasion when Leslie was away, and Sarah and I had work to do, or when Sarah was lonely.

I opened her bottom chest drawer to find a nightgown. I vaguely remembered Leslie keeping her winter nightclothes there. On top were sweat pants, and next was a Laura Ashley gown. I looked farther down, hoping to find a less expensive one, though neither Sarah nor Leslie was given to J. C. Penney flannel, as warm but not as chic.

Slipped between an old sweater and a pair of gym shorts was a small box, a jomo board, I remembered Leslie calling it. She had bought it in a gallery after saving her allowance and birthday money. By a Texas artist, it was filled with wonderful miniatures, a Lilliputian fantasy; and Leslie had responded accordingly. Sarah had been taken with it, too. So taken that she'd bought the others in the exhibition and had written to the artist, David Mc-Manaway, to see if she couldn't get more to give her friends.

Soon after, I noticed Leslie's box missing from her room. She'd gotten rid of it, she'd said with a shrug of her shoulders. She'd grown bored with it. It was nothing special anymore.

Squatting on the floor, I ran my finger down the glass and wondered if later I might ask Sarah for it. For the jomo board was special — too special to become a trendy plaything.

I crawled into Leslie's bed and stared at the ceiling. The knowing of her death, the pain of loss was beginning. Like Sarah, I was afraid to close my eyes. I was frightened of the images — Sarah rocking Leslie; Sarah struggling to hold her; Leslie's eyes, wide open and vacant. Though that was only half my fear, and I didn't want to know the other half.

So I made my lists for morning. Must remember to put Justice Lemon on the thank-you list. But, of course, he would put himself on it, sending flowers or a donation. Must ask Sarah first thing how to handle charitable donations. Must check with Madge about Andrew. And call Gladys. Should already have done it. Gordon must be told not to mention the phone call to Sarah, I thought, as my eyes began to close. How curious that he should care for Leslie and I never noticed.

12

A NOISE at the window woke me; and, even before I knew where I was, I felt afraid to open my eyes. As soon as I remembered I went stiff with fear. "They" had come back. First Leslie, now me. I tried to remember if the window was locked and connected to the alarm system. Could Gordon and Sarah get to me in time? The police would be too late.

Filtering through my fright came shouts from the street — enough commotion out there to keep anyone from breaking in. I opened my eyes. Peering through the window were two men in polo shirts; one, perched on a tree limb; the other, braced on a trellis, camera and window ledge in his clutch. Full of rage, I jumped from bed and ran towards them.

"Get down from there," I hissed. "Get down before I push you down!"

They understood I meant it. They climbed down. Rapidly. I pulled out a robe from Leslie's closet, thought better of it, and put on my dinner dress from the night before.

Judging from the pale sky, it was around six o'clock. Neither Sarah nor Gordon was up. Just as well. Sarah did not need one more violation, and Gordon wasn't the most reliable of emissaries right now. He might actually have the fistfight I wanted to.

Of course, I'd heard the horror stories of reporters hanging from trees, waiting for hapless family members to return from work or school or the grocery store. Of course, I'd heard stories of a press mob massing in front of the house to be the first to tell the spouse of some victim's tragedy. I'd heard and I'd sympathized and been secretly relieved that I wasn't required to make that kind of decision for myself; but until right now I had no idea what it meant.

Armed with my foul humor, I opened the entrance door. On the front sidewalk a half-dozen reporters and camerapersons were arguing with a policewoman and a uniformed security guard. There was lots of jostling, like puppies looking for the supertit, just as blindly and, in this case, without purpose, for the exercise was leading nowhere.

"I told you," the policewoman was saying, "the yard is out of bounds until we've finished checking for clues."

"We're not asking to use the yard. We want to walk down the sidewalk and climb two steps and knock on the front door. Now, there's no law against that, is there?" The voice belonged to a well-known radio reporter, and I vowed never to listen to his show again.

The security guard — someone had obviously hired him to protect Sarah — would have none of it. My first reaction was to go scream at him, too. Let him know his eye wasn't as sharp as it need be. Have the policewoman arrest the two interlopers. Take swings at a couple of camerapersons.

I stepped forward.

"Maybe I can help," I said. "I'm the spokesperson for Ms. Adams."

"Does Ms. Adams know who killed her daughter?" someone shouted.

"No," I answered in my most reasonable tone.

"Could she identify the intruder?"

"Is it someone who knew them?"

"We have no comment on any of that. The police are investigating. It is in their hands," I said.

"When will she make a statement?"

"When can we see her?"

"We want to see the pool."

Some of the faces and voices I recognized, considered co-workers. Whether I liked it or not, we were in the same line of work. If pressed, would I do this? Would Sarah ever have?

"If you'll excuse me now." I started to leave but someone

131

blocked my way. There was general grumbling. The radio voice demanded more information. I felt my neck flushing. "She's in shock," I said, pleased that I was scornful but still controlled. I shoved aside a microphone and did a militant stride toward the house before that control could go all to hell.

"Bull," a female voice piped.

"Fuckers!" I said just out of their hearing and clenched my fists.

Someone was calling to me, but I paid no attention, stopping only long enough to scoop up the morning paper. Whoever it was followed me up the walk. I turned around with a four-letter word on my lips but managed to swallow it when I saw Justice Lemon carrying a breakfast tray. It held starched white linens and Limoges cups and silver, gleaming with the perpetuation of traditions that this city was forever of two minds about keeping.

"Outrageous," he said, motioning with his head toward the press behind us, "but to be expected and ignored." I stood chastened. He was right. I could not wallow in anger, even if it didn't show. Right now we all had to get on with things as best we could. "Here." He handed me the tray. "I thought you could use this."

"And it's so early. I mean, it's so thoughtful of you and even more thoughtful because it's so early." I smiled, ignoring the gang of thugs watching us. I wished he hadn't overheard my outburst. Hadn't he voted against obscenity or something? "It is early."

"I don't sleep much. The English muffins are warm. I looked for croissants but Vivian didn't leave me anything but muffins."

"Muffins suit us fine."

"How is she?"

"It's hard to tell. So far she hasn't let down."

"That's bad. Encourage her to cry. Worst thing in the world is that holding in."

He opened the door for me. "I'll stay in touch," he whispered.

I nodded and closed the door. His own son, I only now recalled Sarah telling me, had been killed in the Korean War.

I tiptoed through the living room and into the dining room, where the sun was already coming in the French doors that led to a cozy bricked terrace. A large mirror attached to the side fence reflected a profusion of ivy and pink geraniums still blooming. A small white wrought-iron table and four matching chairs stood under the large oak that the area had been built around. This spot — tight, contained, lovely within its bounds — suited me better than the rest of the yard, unseen from here. Even in nippy weather, this was a pleasant place to drink fresh coffee and read the papers.

The day was going to be almost as warm as yesterday. We would sit outside. I hoped Sarah would come down before the muffins cooled, but I was also glad to have a few minutes to myself.

As I expected, the story was on the front page. They even had a large picture of Sarah and Leslie linking arms in a fairly formal pose. Where had they gotten that?

"Where are we played this morning?" Sarah asked, coming up behind me.

"Front page, below the fold."

I handed her the paper, but she pushed it away. "Read for accuracy and call them on mistakes."

The doorbell rang, and I heard Gordon getting it. Shortly, he, Detective Brill, and a younger man came into the dining room. I was glad to see Brill again. When he was around, the horror was more externalized, manageable.

He introduced us to his assistant and apologized for bothering us so early. Accepting chairs around the table, he refused the breakfast tray for the two of them. The assistant blinked his eyes a lot and did not inspire confidence, or even ease.

Sarah picked up a muffin but put it down without taking a bite.

"Can't all this wait?" Gordon asked.

"The sooner we get this over, the better for Ms. Adams," James Brill said.

"Gordon, it's all right." Sarah turned toward the detective. "I still don't remember anything about last night."

Sitting there in her silk ice-cream-pink robe, her hair uncombed, her cheeks without a trace of blush, she looked like one of Raphael's madonnas; without guile. Yet I knew better. She would control this interview in the way that the best of the pols did with her, never revealing any more than intended, feigning an openness and frankness that simply were not to be found in the content of the answers.

Brill cleared his throat, hesitated, then began questioning her in the gentle way one might question an easily excitable child who had much to tell.

"Let's begin with yesterday afternoon."

"I've told you. I had a long lunch with Senator Richards, got back to the office at three-thirty, checked my mail. Then I wrote up a memo on my luncheon conversation and took a phone call from my lecture agent." She recited all this in rote fashion.

"After that?"

"I went home."

"And what time did you arrive at your house?"

"Five-ten, possibly five-fifteen. It usually takes me ten minutes but the traffic was worse than usual."

"You asked her all this last night," Gordon said.

James Brill looked at him. "Mr. Simons, I appreciate your concern for Ms. Adams, but we've got to reconstruct this event. Possibly something that Ms. Adams says will trigger her memory. Perhaps you would rather wait in the other room?"

Gordon, chagrined, shook his head.

"Now, Ms. Adams, what did you do when you came in the house?"

"Called to Leslie. I always do."

"Was the door locked when you came in?"

"Yes. I unlocked it, then locked it again."

"Are you sure you locked it?"

"I always lock it."

"Could Leslie have unlocked it later?"

"Why should she?"

"Was your housekeeper here when you got home?"

"No. Leslie let her go early."

"Why?"

"She was preparing dinner and she didn't want Ida looking over her shoulder telling her what to do."

134

"Did Leslie tell you this?"

"In those words."

"Where was Leslie when you came in?"

"The kitchen . . . arranging vegetables on a platter."

"And you went into the kitchen?" James Brill's voice became softer.

"Yes. I asked about Ida. Asked about Leslie's day. We talked a minute more about the menu and when she should serve what. I showed her a more efficient way to chop vegetables, then went up to take my bath."

"Was Leslie behaving normally?"

"Of course. A little excited and nervous, but that was to be expected. She'd never undertaken a party like this before."

"Was she having trouble with anyone?"

"She was pestered from time to time by a boy she was no longer seeing."

"How long since she'd seen him?"

"A while . . . a few months . . . I don't know exactly." Her hand trembled, but her voice remained firm.

"Could he have had a key?"

"No."

"How do you know?"

"Leslie wouldn't do that. He meant nothing to her. I shouldn't have brought him up."

James Brill nodded to his assistant, who wrote something down in his small notebook that he scribbled in from time to time. The questioning could have come out of a detective story, but in a fiction the reader is comforted by the process, like a child playing out fears. That was why mysteries satisfied and soothed. They imposed form, obtained conclusions. Here we had no assurance the puzzle would be solved, and the terrible truth was it didn't matter. Leslie was still dead.

Brill continued the questioning: "As far as you know, was Leslie involved in any way with drugs?"

"I know that she wasn't."

"Not even pot?"

"Never. I've invested too much time and effort in her to have

135

her turn out poorly. This is stupid." Sarah looked close to tears. The detective waited for her to sip some coffee before continuing.

"Let's talk about your enemies for a while."

Sarah laughed. "That's easier. Mine are Presidents, congressmen, cabinet members — hardly candidates for murder."

"Any personal enemies?"

Sarah threw up her hands. "Why do you keep harping on enemies? We don't know people like that. Can't you get that through your heads?"

James Brill's face showed no emotion and his voice remained soft. "You said all the back doors and windows were secured last night, and our men found that to be the case. Ms. Patterson found the front door unlocked; but, if, as you think, the front door was locked earlier, that leads us to someone with a key."

"All right," she said, calm again.

"Just a little longer, Ms. Adams. Now, what did you do after your bath?"

"Went down to check on Leslie, but she was getting dressed herself."

"What time was this?"

"About a quarter to six."

"And after that?"

"I lay down and glanced at the afternoon paper."

"What was Leslie doing then?"

"After she dressed, she came into my room to say that I should take a nap, that she would call me if she needed me. She even brought me a glass of sherry to relax me. Wasn't that charming?"

The detective nodded. "Then what happened?"

"I got back on the bed in order not to spoil Leslie's treat, but dying to know how she was coming in the kitchen."

"And?"

"And I just lay there thumbing through a magazine until I smelled something funny in the kitchen. I immediately jumped up and ran down."

"Was Leslie there?"

"Yes."

"Was anyone with her?"

"No."

"Then?"

"I asked what was burning. She may have answered me. I can't remember."

"Then?"

"I don't remember any more."

"Did she look alarmed?"

"I don't remember."

Gordon jumped up and began massaging Sarah's shoulders. "Only one more question for now, Ms. Adams, then we'll go." She nodded assent.

"What kind of relationship did you and Leslie have with her father?"

"A nonexistent one. He was not part of our lives," she said in a fierce voice. "I kept her away from all the Adamses. Not one of them worth a damn. I took out all the Adams in her. She'd have been miserable as an Adams."

This flurry of words exhausted her. Brill apologized again for bothering Sarah, and I showed him and his assistant out. At the door I started to mention Leslie's involvement with Richard Sanford, but since he had already come up, I would bide my time, see what the police uncovered. It could be a blind alley, and the pain that it would cause Sarah wasn't worth it — yet.

I wished she had been a little more forthcoming, but she couldn't bear the idea of Leslie's carrying on with Rich Sanford or smoking pot occasionally. Though neither had worked for her, she kept romanticizing both childhood and courtship, always trying to make those she loved into storybook images.

I locked the door and looked at my watch. Only eight-thirty and already I was weary. I was curious, though, about the smell of burned food Sarah mentioned. There had been no burned food or smell of any that I remembered. Something sweet maybe. Then I understood. What Sarah had smelled had nothing to do with burned food, but I wouldn't mention it to her for the time being.

13

BY THE TIME I got home to change clothes, rush-hour traffic was over and the early morning streetwalkers were gone until late afternoon trade began. Except for Maxie, who was sitting on my step.

"I haven't seen that dress before," he said. "Maybe you could loan it to me sometime."

"Why don't you give the neighborhood a break and go home."

He looked hurt. "It's my neighborhood, too." From his jacket pocket he pulled two letters. "Mr. Duc said he had an appointment at the Welfare Department, but I think he don't like to be around no unhappiness." The letters were sealed and Mr. Duc's neat script had addressed one for me and one for Sarah. "That's why you gotta stop coming in so late by yourself. Streets are mean places."

"She wasn't on the street," I said, fingering my purse's clutter for the keys.

"Street was in front. Same difference. Even for fat-cat houses."

"I can't argue with that."

Maxie curtsied and left.

Before I closed the door to my apartment, I'd begun undressing. At best, the day was going to be hectic and the sooner I got to the office, the better. That's how I could help Sarah most. Right now she had plenty of good friends offering solace. She was giving as well as receiving, however. As if to provide us a purpose, she had come up with a list of things to do, and mine included dealing with the press as well as handling the office.

Reaching over the tub to turn on the shower, I decided to switch to a bath. A good five-minute soak might do wonders for me. I even poured in Vitabath; and, as the tub filled, I put on water for a cup of tea, the great soother, to sip as I dressed. While I was at it, I dropped the panty hose and silk panties I'd taken off into the tub and threw in another couple of pairs of the silk panties I'd been meaning to wash — not wanting to be idle even during my soak. So long as I acted with purpose I was fine; the minute I let down I went blank, or, worse yet, replayed the scene of Sarah and Leslie by the pool.

Since the tea was ready, I plopped it next to the tub. Might as well sip and soak a minute and think about how I was going to handle the press. No more getting caught off guard. But first I carefully rinsed my stockings and my panties, pushing the suds away from the faucet, letting the clear water run on each pair until all the soap was gone, enjoying the feel of silk on my fingers. Such an indulgence, these silks. Not even a lover to show them to. Cheryl kidded me that if I paid half as much attention to my outer clothes as I did my underwear I'd be the best-dressed woman in Washington.

But the whole point was to have something for myself that had nothing to do with anybody else. To prove to myself — and, in some crazy way, to my parents, who didn't even know of my indulgence — that I was worth nice things. For no special reason.

But what useless ruminating. Now I had to map out a coherent press strategy. My five minutes were up, but I could soak while I thought. I sank back, tasted my tea, felt comforted, and looked vacantly at the ceiling, waiting for inspiration to come.

When the water got too cool, I let some out and replaced it with warm. My sense of urgency had vanished. For the first time I could remember, I could not will myself to act. Only Cheryl's loud knocking finally mobilized me.

She came in with the newspaper, a sack of croissants, and a pot of brewed coffee, not so elegantly turned out as the justice's but with the same spirit. "You poor thing," she said, putting down her offerings and hugging me, "but you've already been mentioned on two radio reports and I didn't know until Dave called — he still wants to go out with you, by the way — to tell me it was on the 'Today Show' — not you there, of course. I came right down but you weren't here. Then I called the office and Gladys said you'd be coming by here so I called in late to work. I'm so upset and I knew croissants would be the only breakfast anybody could entice you with."

"I appreciate it. I appreciate everything. I just don't have time. I needed to be out of here thirty minutes ago."

"That's OK. I'll help you dress. And feed you." She stuffed a croissant in my open mouth. She was right: croissants I could eat.

I rummaged through my closet while Cheryl examined my makeup and questioned me about suspects.

"They haven't a clue," I said, pulling out a charcoal gray suit.

"Don't wear that. You'll look like Queen Elizabeth. Probably organized crime did it." Cheryl started leafing through my clothes.

"I'm not dressing for a fashion show. Why them? I have really comfortable shoes to wear with that suit."

"That's reason enough not to wear it. The shoes belong in a geriatric ward. Here," she said, reaching for a brown pleated skirt and sweater-jacket to match. "Properly subdued but flattering. After all, you are on view to the world today."

"Cheryl, for God's sake!"

"I know this is a nightmare," she said, buttoning the cuffs of my beige blouse. "I'm not minimizing that one bit. But somebody's got to think for you, size up the implications. I'm not in p.r. for nothing." She knotted a burgundy tie under my collar and stepped back to look at me. "Fine. A touch of color, but the tie says no-nonsense. I should dress you every day."

You and Sarah, I thought. "I don't get organized crime," I said.

"Didn't she do a series on the government's incompetence with drug trafficking?"

"That was three years ago." Disappointed, I picked up my purse to leave. I had an unreasonable need for Cheryl to know what she was talking about. "You act like this is some kind of game, Cheryl."

She put her hand on my back, and we walked towards the door. "I know better. I also know Sarah is going to be taken care of as best anyone can. You and her friends will see to that. But don't forget the next few months are going to be tough for you, too." She stopped and waited for me to lock my apartment. "And nobody's going to see about you." She turned and left me in the hall.

Gladys was holding up better than I expected after her early morning visit to Sarah's, where Sarah had ended up consoling her. Now she was too harried to grieve.

"Every news organization in the country is calling here; so are friends, strangers, acquaintances — well-meaning, wonderful people all of them; but I'm overwhelmed. Jean called to say she was coming back from the Cape but won't be in until this afternoon, and I don't know where Jeffrey is."

"He called Sarah's to say he'll be in after an exam this afternoon." Jean was a twenty-five-year-old researcher we had hired last year, and Jeffrey was a college intern for us. The phone had been ringing since I stepped in the office. Gladys just stared at it.

Then tears spilled from her eyes. "Whatever will happen to her?"

"She'll be all right. She's strong, and we've got to help her stay that way." I said this firmly. "I'll be in her office if you need me. Just put through only 'must' calls."

She nodded agreement. This was the first time I'd ever been stern with Gladys. It had always been the other way around. I liked the new way better.

Today was the deadline for Sarah's column, which this week was only half completed and dealt, once more, with Lumb. Following up on my lead, she had found someone at Defense who admitted to putting money for purchase of Stingrays at the bottom of a defense appropriations bill several years ago. This was done at the behest of the State Department and possibly the national security adviser at the time — Anthony Morris. From her notes she planned to finish off with a rehash of Morris's role in the Lumb train wreck and the subsequent U.S. government loan to that Marxist country.

I considered scrapping it for something less provocative. In her reserve file I found backup columns on Christmas, Thanksgiving, Memorial Day, and the Fourth of July. She'd done a couple on the inadequacies of Congress, but they were a little too general, waiting to be filled in with a recent anecdote or a minor scandal. After rummaging through a half-dozen paeans to prominent leaders who might die and one on Washington at cherry blossom time, I decided to stick with what she wanted.

After the decision on the column came the cancellations. The network was less than understanding:

"Gone for a month? Isn't that excessive? We don't have any shows in the can," the voice at the other end of the line said to me.

"Maybe you didn't understand. Her only child is dead. D . . . E . . . A . . ."

"OK, OK, but she has a big following and that's a lotta subs to get."

"I'm sure you'll manage," I said and hung up. The raw-meat theory lived.

Gladys brought in the proofs for Sarah's new book, *The Impotent Presidency*, with a subtitle call in it for a parliamentary system. Nixon, Ford, and Carter had agreed to interviews with Sarah — a real coup. She'd spent a week with each in his home and come back with honest — even self-deprecating, sometimes — answers from them, along with wonderful dinner table conversation for a chosen few about how they now conducted their domestic lives. The rest of the book was mostly political-science rehash researched by Jean.

Sitting at Sarah's desk, I tried to imagine what all this felt like to Sarah, the wonder of it all. Certainly, she wasn't born into a world that expects her kind of achievement, or even imagines it. From her stories I had pieced together a fairly coherent picture of her childhood and teenage years, and I marveled all the more at how she got to this office.

*　　*　　*

She'd grown up in a small town south of Springfield, Illinois. Clement, her father, managed the telephone company, and her mother, Rachel, had taught high school English until she married. Clement and Rachel were considered the town's most handsome couple. Sarah was their second child.

When Sarah was two, her older brother died of pneumonia. Rachel became despondent, left most of Sarah's care to Clement, and remained withdrawn until the birth of another son, Andrew, four years later.

Sarah adored her father and resented it when Rachel began intruding in her life. Since the two of them never got along that well and Rachel was busy with the baby, once again Clement accepted primary care of Sarah. When her mother died, they became even closer.

While her father was gentle and loving, he was not much of a talker, preferring to let Sarah amuse him. She never once remembered his mentioning her mother's death or what it must mean to her.

After her mother's death, Sarah took over the care of eight-year-old Andrew. A woman came in to help once a week; but, essentially, Sarah and her father managed the house and Andrew for the next three years.

Just before her eighteenth birthday, her father met a boisterous woman who tried compensating with makeup and hair dye for all that she lacked in good looks. (So Sarah said.) Three months later he married her. Sarah was appalled. Her father acted like a lovesick adolescent. The two women barely tolerated each other until Sarah left for college. After that, she seldom went home.

Her father, an amiable man who liked his peace, was not as upset by her absence as might be expected, and Sarah knew it. Only now coming of age sexually, he was relieved to be rid of his daughter's watchful eyes. Andrew, who got along well with his stepmother, was less of a problem.

The spring of her senior year in college, Clement Corbin died. The summer after graduation Sarah married a professor in the journalism department. (What I know about the marriage came from Madge, not Sarah.) Her husband was thirty years old, quiet and easygoing. Not long after, they moved to Washington. Sarah brought Andrew to live with them.

Long after she hired me, Sarah told me I had reminded her of her younger self — inadequately prepared and chafing to make up for wasted time. People like us, she'd said, have one real advantage: we're never complacent about what we know or how we got to know it. Sarah, in fact, was never complacent about anything.

She'd considered complacency a real danger of celebrity. "These stories have to matter to you," she'd lectured me when I first arrived, "and you have to assume they're going to matter to others. You'll be seduced into a benign acceptance of things if you aren't careful. You have to believe that what you do counts for something, that you count for something."

The half-finished column stared up at me, mocking me. I, too, had been lulled into moderation. Don't press too hard. Don't be shrill. The *Washington Post* in its Watergate coverage made going out on a limb respectable for a while — so respectable we could conveniently forget most of us managed to avoid limbs. Except Sarah. Misguided or not, she was determined to push on for what she thought right. I set about finishing her column. But what did it matter now?

"So you're Courtney," Andrew Corbin said and leaned over to kiss my cheek with exactly the right amount of intimacy for two people who had been told how well they would get on. Madge had asked me to pick him up at the airport, and I had no trouble identifying him. Weary and shaken, this taller, angular Xerox copy of Sarah looked not at all the spoiled, high-living baby brother. His pictures did not pick up the authority in his eyes — brown eyes, Sarah's eyes. Wearing khakis and a too-heavy sweater that covered his rump, he had brought only a carry-on hanging bag. He hadn't expected it to be so hot, he said when we hit the outside. He hadn't expected to make this trip. His eyes were red as if from crying. In the car I told him what had happened, what I knew of what had happened.

He shook his head. "I've heard everything you've said — the

same things Madge said — but, as soon as you stop talking, I fuzz out. I tell myself, 'Leslie is dead. Leslie was murdered.' I can't go beyond that. I can't think of how it happened. I can't conjure up the how." He strained against his seat belt, turned himself to face me more directly. "You could say it all over again, and I could say it back to you, but I still wouldn't have it in my mind."

"I have it in my mind all right," I answered him. "I see Leslie everytime I close my eyes. Sometimes when I don't. But part of the time I think she isn't dead at all. I'm convinced she isn't dead. I feel a little crazy," I confessed to him.

His face had that earnestness that Sarah's got when she empathized with someone. So familiar were some of his expressions that I could pretend I was talking to Sarah, a more open, calmer Sarah. Though the calm could be fatigue — even as tired as he was, his body was either in motion or preparing to move, muscles always at the ready.

"I wonder if she'll ever accept it," he said.

"The senselessness makes it that much harder."

"Madge told me the police think it could be someone they know."

"It could be anyone. That man over there," I pointed to a man in baggy gray trousers slouching along with his bottle in a brown paper bag. "Or those two lovelies coming out of the drugstore." They had spiked, multicolor hair and wore appropriate heavy-metaled jewelry. "I'm frightened of all of them, including that man with close-cropped hair and the handkerchief in his suit pocket. Any of them could have walked right into Sarah's house. I've never had qualms about going anywhere in this city, but now I'm edgy around anybody I don't know. The randomness . . . ," I said, not finishing my sentence.

"So you think it was definitely a stranger?"

I nodded.

"Then tell me your how," he urged. "Take me through the way you see it." He smiled, and his smile was his own. Easy and wide and full of access. "I won't hold you accountable if you're proved wrong."

"Well, I think Leslie was in the kitchen finishing up the appetizers. I think she decided to smoke a joint. Sarah smelled Leslie's pot and came down — Sarah couldn't stand the idea of Leslie smoking grass."

"I know," he said.

"They probably quarreled. That's when someone slipped in the unlocked door and surprised them. There must have been a scuffle and Sarah was stabbed. Then he chased them towards the pool. Maybe they tried to push him in or he, them. At any rate, he managed to choke Leslie, panicked, and ran away."

"A dripping wet man? Wouldn't someone have noticed him?"

"Maybe he didn't fall in. Or there was more than one. I don't discount that."

"If Sarah ever accepts it, she'll remember," he said. "Though she's always blocked out that she and our mother fussed the morning Mother died. Over Sarah's not eating breakfast, Dad told me later."

"In some ways I hope she never remembers. She'll have to go through that hell all over again."

"She's in it already," he said.

If only Leslie hadn't left the door unlocked. I found myself cursing her for being so careless, but didn't mention my irrational grievance to Andrew. I had confided enough in Andrew for one day. He had made it so easy. He was living up to Sarah's and Leslie's billing. Something I hadn't expected.

Granted, the word on him was always vague. In his late twenties he had hied himself to London, where he'd made himself a small fortune trading in international currencies by the age of thirty-four. While his sister and niece were admiring, I was suspicious. He never bothered to come see them — or write or call all that often. Christmas and birthday gifts were usually lavish, but they showed up weeks or even months after the event and were almost never personal.

For whatever reasons, I was not prepared for his impact. The jab of his hands, the sympathetic face, the intense eyes — these were Sarah's; and I felt a familiarity and pull that astounded me. Still, he was no clone of Sarah; he was most definitely his own person, and here I was opening up to a stranger and feeling only relief for having done so. For the rest of the ride, we watched a rusty sunset and maneuvered our way through traffic in comfortable silence.

Only after we were inside was I aware that the press had vanished from the front of the house. They had moved to the living room; rather, they had been replaced by friends and colleagues of Sarah's, that part of the press that hadn't participated in a vulture-watch in years, if ever.

Madge was directing traffic flow. She looked more tight-lipped than usual. Sarah was holding up well, she reported. Her friends were helping distract her. She was very much wanting to see Andrew. "And Gordon wants to see you as soon as possible," she said to me. "He's in Leslie's bedroom. Hiding out."

Gordon was lying on Leslie's bed, smoking what, from the looks of the nightstand, appeared to be his fiftieth cigarette. When I came in, he swung his feet to the floor and offered me the end of the bed. I moved Leslie's desk chair from across the room to face him.

"Always proper, aren't we?" he asked.

"You called me up for a lecture on bedside manners?"

"You could use one." Suddenly he dropped his head in his hands. "I'm sorry. You are one of the few people who openly acknowledge I'm a bastard, and I take it out on you." He shook his head and looked at me. "I've never seen her like this. At the funeral home, I couldn't get her to make any decisions. When I asked about music, she talked about Leslie's favorite songs. Reverend . . . what's his name?"

"Dalton; Father Dalton."

"He came by, but she was no better with him. About the time we thought she'd agreed, she changed her mind about everything.

"She said Leslie was to be buried in a plain wooden casket, not some vulgar box, that there was to be no music, absolutely no flowers, and no mourners, except us and her brother."

"That seems reasonable."

"Dalton is afraid she's stripping away too much of the service.

She's keeping out all emotion. Each thing she suggests would be fine by itself, but altogether they create a pretty bleak picture."

"It is a bleak picture."

"She has got to accept it."

"Give her time. I told her brother Leslie was choked. Do we know that for sure?"

"Yeah. The instant-death kind of stranglehold."

"Where is Sarah now?"

"Either entertaining her guests or taking a shower. When she can't stand to be charming, she comes up and takes another shower. She can't keep this up."

"I'll see what I can do."

He lay back down and lit another cigarette. "Dream on."

Sarah was in the garden talking to Andrew, a columnist, and his wife. She wore a white silk shirt with full sleeves and a pair of old gray flannel trousers and looked ready for a cozy evening in front of the fire. But she was brittle and unapproachable and not about to be distracted by me or anything that reminded her of what was really going on. After a few words with her, I left.

Madge was in the study taking phone calls.

"Need some relief?" I asked.

"No, thanks. I'm just pinch-hitting until Gladys gets here."

"Then I'm leaving for a while."

"Do. Rest while you can."

"Tell Sarah I'll be back later."

"Sure."

"Do you think she'll mind?"

"She'll call if she wants you. You know that."

"You call if she asks for me." I hesitated at the door. "I don't think I'm doing enough," I said, blinking back tears I hadn't counted on.

Madge took me firmly by the shoulders and walked me to the study door. "Right now she's occupied. When she gets bored with all the others, she'll need you."

In my apartment I was too tired to do more than take off my shoes and stockings. If I could be quiet for an hour or so, I'd be able to go back. Just to rest for a while. I picked up the two letters from Mr. Duc and opened the one to Sarah first. It appeared to be a letter of condolence on a son lost in battle, though Mr. Duc had substituted daughter for son. He was very good at personalizing the originals.

My dear Madam,

In the untimely loss of your noble daughter, our affliction here, is scarecely less than your own. So much of promised usefulness to one's country, and of bright hopes for one's self and friends, have rarely been so suddenly dashed, as in her fall. In size, in years, and in youthful appearance, a girl only, her power to command men, was surpassingly great. This power, combined with a fine intellect, an indomitable energy, and a taste altogether military, constituted in her, as seemed to me, the best natural talent, in that department, I ever knew.

In the hope that it may be no intrusion upon the sacredness of your sorrow, I have ventured to address you this tribute to the memory of my young firend, and your brave and early fallen child.

May God give you that consolation which is beyond all earthly power. Sincerely your friend in a common affliction.

Mr. Duc

But where is that consolation? I put my head down on the couch and cried until I slept.

14

SARAH RELENTED somewhat for the funeral service. In addition to her brother, Gordon, and me, she allowed Gladys, Madge, the Howards, Ida, and Page. We sat huddled together in a small chapel of the National Cathedral, the one where the names of the Vietnam War veterans had been read.

Father Dalton prayed. We followed in the prayer book. The ancient words comforted, but I don't think Sarah heard them. She chose to have no mention made of Leslie. Refused to ascribe meaning, she'd said, to a pointless death. At the end of the service, the cathedral carillon played the lullaby "All Through the Night."

At the graveside she gave one wounded desperate cry, more beast's than human. In the limousine, she put her head on Andrew's shoulder, held his hands in both of hers; and that was all the comforting she accepted.

Her house was brimming with those who, knowing the futility, wanted to provide solace or simply to give witness to endurance. Sarah accepted their efforts as best she could, going from one group to another, testifying to a continuity no longer possible.

For the rest of us in attendance, the goodwill around was suffocating. The Howards left almost immediately. Ida, whose kitchen had been taken over by caterers, went to sit in the basement laundry room, and Gladys went to sit in her car until she'd pulled herself together. After an attempt to play alternate hostess, Madge went upstairs. Andrew had disappeared.

I went up to Leslie's room to close the door for a few minutes and quiet myself, only to find Gordon sitting in the small, stiff desk chair sobbing. Before I could say or do anything, he waved me out. So Madge had been right: Gordon loved Leslie, and how insensitive of me never to notice it. Had I not wanted to know Leslie was capable of being loved by someone other than Sarah or that Gordon was capable of loving? If they were unlovable and unloving, did that somehow make me better? In Sarah's eyes?

A drink suddenly sounded good. At the bottom of the steps Justice Lemon and Senator Ditson were talking. The justice asked about Sarah, about me, and offered to find me a scotch and soda, but I wandered on, not having the energy to appear to care what they were saying.

"All we do anymore is go to Gawler's," I heard some woman say, referring to the funeral home.

In the living room Bob Owens, who was talking to Wilson Kane's wife, caught my eye and waved. He was probably looking for a conversation break, but I didn't want to get stuck with Pat Kane. And tell me, Mrs. Kane, who chooses your husband's sexy underwear? I wondered if Sarah had heard from Mrs. Kane's husband and whose idea it was for Pat Kane to come today. On the face of it, the Kanes weren't close enough to Sarah to be here.

Social amenities were beyond me right now, and I couldn't face the question "How do you think she's doing?" one more time. I would take the drink to Sarah's bedroom and leave if Sarah wanted quiet. For now she was talking to Larry Blake. Larry had sent me a note expressing his concern but also complimenting me on my handling of the situation in the media. He hoped we could see each other as things calmed down for me. In the meantime, I was to keep up the good work; he could tell I was going places.

Inside her bedroom I found huddled together Madeline Owens, Gordon, and Madge. The talk was of Sarah, who could not rest, would not sedate herself, not even with alcohol. "If she could just let go," Madge said. We nodded agreement. "She never lets go," Madeline added; and we knew that was true, too.

We stood with our drinks, settling on a physical closeness for lack of anything more. But I was restless. The talk made me more anxious.

"I'll try to get her up here for a while," I offered. If I could not help her, I could be close to her, reassure myself she was all right. That I was all right.

By nine o'clock the house began clearing out, though for every three that left, one new one came in — just as well since Sarah kept urging everyone to stay. She was still wandering from one cluster to another, sometimes talking, sometimes initiating others' conversations, but mostly just listening, distracting herself, holding back the despair.

Bob Owens took my hand and led me into the back garden. In a quiet spot, the same spot Leslie had told me she was leaving Sarah, he began to talk:

"Something serious has come up. Nothing to bother Sarah with tonight, but Brill has some upsetting news." I stared down at the grass, already turned brown, between my feet. "They found a knife by the pool with Sarah's prints, and hers are the only clear ones at poolside and on the scattered lawn furniture. Also the only clear prints in the kitchen were Sarah's, Leslie's, and Ida's."

"But Sarah was attacked with the knife. She could never have done that to herself. She's too phobic about blood."

"Of course. It's outrageous, but until this is solved, Sarah is a suspect."

"And the cause of death for sure?" I asked.

"Strangulation — as they thought."

"I should have noticed the lawn furniture," I said.

"Noticed?"

"That it was scattered. That day."

"Noticing wouldn't have made any difference," he answered gently, reading my irrational mind.

I stuck my hands into my suit pockets and fastened my attention on a black squirrel poised in the ivy. "Maybe they'll catch him tonight," I said. "Before we have to tell Sarah." He put his arm around me. I shook my head. "It's hard to believe we celebrated Leslie's birthday out here less than a month ago."

15

ABOUT MIDNIGHT Sarah went to sleep, and I felt free to leave. On the sidewalk, I stopped and let out a slow breath. Bob's news had haunted me all evening; but there had been no time to dissect it, analyze it, rationalize it away; and now I was too tired.

Unlocking my car, I became aware of someone watching. A cold sensation slushed through me and my mouth went dry. Nightmarelike, I wanted to call out but couldn't. I hurried into the driver's seat and relocked the door. Hearing a knock on my window, I slowly turned my head. Page Tuttle, Leslie's friend. I wet my pants.

"For God's sake, Page, you scared me," I said when I'd recovered enough to roll down the window.

"I'm sorry. I keep walking by the house. I feel awful." She started to cry.

"It's all right. I'm just edgy."

"I mean, I feel awful about Leslie. It's the most horrible thing that's ever happened to me." She began sobbing. "If only I'd done something."

Reluctantly, I got out and put my arms around her. I was not used to consoling teenage girls, and this one I barely tolerated. She reeked of a false sophistication obtained from the right schools, the right vacations, the right friends, and an alcoholic mother, whose husband, Page's father, was twice her age. In the three years I'd known Page — admittedly, not well — this was the first time I'd seen her show genuine feeling about anything.

Over Sarah's protests, Leslie clung to her, pointing out, and correctly, that Sarah had friends of her own every bit as affected and mixed-up as Page. I asked if she'd like to sit in the car and talk.

In the car she stopped crying and started talking about Leslie. "Did you know that for two years Leslie was the only friend I had? We did everything together — rode bikes, skated, did homework, tried out pot. I've never loved anybody as much as I loved Leslie then."

"When was this?"

"We were twelve . . . thirteen. She was so loyal. She really cared about me. I'd give anything to have it like it was then." She started crying again.

"But you were still close," I tried to comfort, and covered a yawn — not bored, exhausted. We sat there a few minutes while Page got her cry out and I decided how to frame my next question.

"I'm not just being nosy," I said to her, "but were Leslie and Rich Sanford mixed up with drugs in any way? It could be useful to know."

Page answered slowly. "I don't think so. Rich would sometimes do coke or designer drugs, but Leslie stuck to smoking joints. She was pretty levelheaded even when she was down."

"Did Rich get her down?"

"Yeah, almost as much as her mother. And the combination! It's a wonder she wasn't more messed up."

"What did she and Rich fight about?"

"Everything. Her mother. Her moving."

"You mean living with her father?"

"Sure. That's all she could talk about this summer. She was hell-bent to do it. Rich was furious with her. She was a little afraid of him, I think." She must have read my thoughts. She added quickly, "Not that he could . . . you know . . . he could never do that." Abruptly she said she had to go home.

I offered her a ride, but she refused. Halfway out of the car, she paused.

"Sarah tried to break me and Les up. I hate her for that. She was right about Rich, though. Maybe I wasn't so good for her precious daughter, but Rich was awful for her. Really awful. Les and I weren't so close since Rich. He's no murderer, but he sucks." She tossed her long hair and started down the street.

"Be careful," I called out. "It's late to be out here by yourself."

"I'm always out here by myself," she responded.

Damn the police and their slow plodding, I cursed the next morning on my way to Leslie's school. Only a matter of time, Bob had confirmed, before the papers got hold of this development. But the important thing was not to panic. The important thing was to get my own investigation under way. Starting with this interview with John Cahill, Leslie's student adviser.

With some luck, this could get cleared up before the press even smelled it, I reminded myself, walking into the counselor's office. No reason this shouldn't work. After all, I'd been taught to find answers by the best of teachers.

John Cahill, whom I'd called early this morning — with Sarah's permission — was wearing his grief with an air of self-importance. Sometime over the weekend he had been at Sarah's, talking with a group of students, and I remembered seeing his cherubic face, which didn't go with his paunch or balding head. For all this display of intimacy, he had not been invited to Leslie's birthday party. Had he been close, he would have been there. Sarah knew exactly what each teacher's involvement with Leslie was.

Still, he talked about her with insight — not just the usual for-print stuff of being popular and showing potential. He knew she was a good defensive soccer player but too unsure to play offense. He knew she was a talented actress, who could be brilliant when she wasn't self-conscious. He knew she had a sense of humor, though she used it against herself too much. She was, according to Cahill, a real comedian, a quality I'd hardly seen in her.

"You sound as if you knew her well," I said, and sounded more surprised than I meant to.

"Last year we were pretty thick."

I nodded encouragingly.

"I was a great help to her in that cheating episode," he continued.

I agreed. "But what exactly was that all about?" I asked.

He hesitated. I reminded him Sarah had given her permission for this talk. That's all the prodding he needed.

"The kid was flunking pre-calculus and scared to death. I tell you, though, more afraid of her mother finding out about the bad grade than she was of her finding out about the cheating.

"Leslie came in here bawling. Made me and her math teacher promise not to mention the bad grade to Ms. Adams and swore that if we'd give her another chance, she'd get her mark up. We did and she did. She was a real mess until she did, I can tell you."

"Don't most students here feel pressure to pull down good grades?"

"Yeah, but she was about as bad as I've ever seen. The more we talked, the more depressed she got. Here's a girl who's done everything right, and she considers herself a loser. I told her she was giving herself a bum rap, but it didn't do much good.

"I'll tell you the truth: I was plenty worried about her. When I told her mother about the cheating — never did mention the poor grade — I suggested therapy; but Ms. Adams wouldn't hear of it. She said there was nothing wrong with Leslie that a couple of talks with her 'best friend,' meaning herself, couldn't cure. She wasn't too keen on my talking to her, either. I did what I could, but I've got a lot of kids to see. I'm also the college adviser."

"Did she ever mention Rich Sanford to you?" I asked.

"I can tell you, he and Ms. Adams didn't get along. She wouldn't hear of Leslie going with him. I tried to get her to see her mother's point of view, and I think she did. I told her myself that he wasn't any good for her. I don't mince words with these kids.

"Anyway, the problem was moot. She came in a few weeks ago to tell me she was going to live with her father."

"She told you that?"

"Yeah. I asked how her mother felt about it — from what I

know of Ms. Adams, she wouldn't go for it — but all Leslie said was that her mother was having some trouble getting used to the idea."

"Did she mention how Rich felt about it?" I asked.

"He wanted her to stay here. I think she kind of liked the idea that everyone was fussing over her. She liked being the center of all that attention. She'd never had many boyfriends, had she?"

I shook my head no.

"The shape she was in, she was ripe for a boy like Rich Sanford, though, frankly, Leslie's problems were more to do with her mother than with Rich."

A student popped her head in the door, and Cahill indicated he'd be right with her. We stood up and I thanked him for his time and asked one more question: "Was Leslie involved with drugs at all?"

Cahill frowned. "She was not that kind of girl," he said.

"What kind of girl was Leslie? — around her friends, I mean?" I asked Billy Long, Leslie's old school friend.

"She was great . . . funny . . . kind of quiet if too many people were around. She was best with just a few — the ones she trusted."

We were having tea, my suggestion, at the Four Seasons Hotel, a strange choice, he probably thought, but with the advantage of being close to both his house and Sarah's. Also a watercress sandwich and a gooey pastry had suddenly appealed to me as a late afternoon treat.

We sat on a couch close to a vast expanse of window over-looking part of downtown Washington. It afforded a pleasant view. If not cozy, we were comfortable and quiet.

I plunged in and asked if Leslie had ever talked to him about her father. I wasn't sure what it was I was trying to connect, only that Leslie and her father were beginning to seem as important as Leslie and Rich Sanford in terms of getting at the truth.

Billy nodded yes but changed the subject. "I remember once Page telling me that when she was little she wanted to make herself small enough to sit on the rim of a cup, so whenever she got bored or mad she could jump in and float around on the lemon slice. She wished that a lot, she said. She had an awful lot of tea with grown-ups."

"And you feel that way now," I said and we both smiled. "Do you think I'm prying?"

"I guess I think I haven't any right to betray Leslie's confidences. She was about as private as anyone I know. If she talked to you, you knew it meant something." The friendly face reassured me: "It's nothing against you."

"At some point the police might want to question Leslie's friends, and I'm curious about what you might tell them."

"Nothing. I have nothing to tell anybody." He looked for sure like he would jump in the cup. "I mean, she had this thing about her father. Whenever she got mad at her mother, she'd say how much better it would be with her father.

"I tried to tell her that fathers are the same, that if she lived with him, she'd feel the same way. I even pointed out that if he was so great, he'd be coming around, but she thought Sarah kept him from her."

"She told me she was going to her father. Do you think that was wishful thinking or had she really gotten in touch with him?" As I asked the question, I realized just how little stock I'd put in Leslie's story about living with her father. The reason I'd never really thought she would go is that I assumed the thing had to be a fantasy: reconciliation with distant parents — physically or emotionally distant — was, to me, on some almost buried level, an impossibility.

But Billy was contradicting me: "Oh, no, it was real." He pushed the lemon slice with his finger. "I'm not sure she could have done it, though. She was afraid if she hurt her mother too much, Sarah would die."

"Why?"

"Why anything?" he shrugged. "Sometimes they acted more like my parents than like mother-daughter. You know, hurting each other but willing to put up with anything to stay together."

He said all this without self-consciousness; but his friendliness and openness, I was beginning to see, were only a small part of what he was about. The tea crowd had left and the early cocktail

158

drinkers were taking their places. We walked outside together.

"Thanks, Billy. Next time, no tea." I held out my hand to him.

"That's OK. It was good to talk to somebody." He headed for the canal, not towards his home.

The sun was beginning to go down, and once more I had the need to get back to Sarah, to reassure myself that she was the Sarah I knew, not some adolescent's distorted image.

"The President was in a chatty mood this afternoon," she said, kissing both my cheeks. "He promised me a long interview sometime next month. Did I tell you Vice President Burns came by this morning? He's in town for something or other.

"Courtney, you look god-awful. I can tell you've stopped eating, and sleeping, too, from the looks of you. Come to Gordon's with us. He's fixed chili and says I need an outing. Madge and the Howards are coming. Gordon, tell her she must come."

He looked at me closely. "Maybe you should eat."

I assured them both I had just done precisely that and offered to hang around and answer the phones. I looked forward to having the house to myself. I could prowl around some, though I had no idea as to what I might turn up that the police hadn't already. I also wanted to go over the day's conversations. See if some direction would reveal itself. The only way to hold off the panic — over the press, the police, maybe life — was to keep looking for a resolution. Otherwise, I started to feel another catastrophe gaining on me.

When Andrew showed up, Sarah was instructing me, I was to send him over. Or, even better, come with him. He'd had some business to see about, Sarah wasn't sure what, he was always so vague. Finally, they left me alone.

Upstairs I pulled out all Leslie's old school notebooks. She'd kept them back to the third grade. I checked all the pockets in her skirts and jackets and pants. I rummaged through the boxes that held old playbills and football programs and dead flowers. I began on her drawers. When I got to the jomo board, I took it out to take home. Sarah had been touched that I'd asked for it.

Andrew came in and I went down. He expressed relief that

everyone was gone and offered to fix me a drink, which I declined. I had a lot of clearheaded thinking still to do. Shortly he returned with a tray of cheese, two glasses, a bottle of framboise, and an order for me to join him on the sofa. Like his sister, he was sure he knew what was best. "Framboise is medicinal," he said, pouring some for me. "You look like you could use a little boost." Frank like his sister, too.

As it turned out, he had not seen to business at all. Instead he'd walked around most of the afternoon. If he could confine his visit to Sarah, it wouldn't be so bad, but all the small talk . . . He broke off to ask what I'd been up to all day. If he was concerned about Sarah as a suspect, he wasn't showing it.

I decided to tell him precisely what I'd been up to. Let him see my sense of urgency. I began with the morning.

"You knew about Leslie's leaving?" he asked.

"Yes, but isn't that what every child threatens at least once? Leslie was just bluffing." I answered the unspoken question — and didn't tell Sarah?

"I know Leslie." I paused, then blurted out: "I didn't know about last spring's episode with the cheating."

"So?"

"So it surprises me. Sarah usually tells me things."

He picked up my hand on the seat beside him. "Does it hurt your feelings?"

"A little," I conceded. His hand was freckled and the hair on it so blond as to be invisible. I picked up my glass of framboise and began a recitation of my conversations with Page and Billy.

At one point, I stopped long enough for him to start a fire in the fireplace. He listened closely, asked questions at intervals. But when I finished he said, "Don't worry too much. The police aren't as stupid and evil as you think. That Detective Brill knows it's not Sarah, but they've got to follow all their leads."

"You've been talking to the police?"

He acknowledged he had. In an informal way. At his own behest. "She means a lot to me, too, you know," and he began to explain just how much she did mean.

After their mother died, Sarah took on the care of Andrew, as Sarah herself had told me. According to Andrew, she did all the things their mother had done and then some — read him bedtime stories, helped with his homework, took him to the Saturday movies, taught him to kick a football and shoot baskets the way their father had taught her. She did not want him to notice he didn't have a mother, she once told him. He laughed: she had willed his happiness.

I thought he was going to continue, but instead he stared at the fire. We both sat in comfortable silence. For the first time all day I relaxed. I took a sip of the framboise.

Before I could swallow, Andrew leaned over and kissed me, and the framboise shot into his mouth. With great aplomb he managed not to sputter or even break the kiss. He brought it back to my mouth and ever so slowly the sweet liquid disappeared as we continued the kiss. He took the next sip, and we kissed again. I took a sip. We discovered a sip of framboise had a maximum of five passes before it evaporated entirely.

Just as he put our glasses down — our hands having remained chaste until now — we heard a car door slam. I started to jump up, but he brought me close for a proper kiss with his hands, his mouth, his body, until the doorbell rang. Then he stood and pulled me with him.

Bob Owens stood there with a first edition of the *Post*, which he handed me without comment. On the first page was a picture of Sarah and the caption SARAH ADAMS TO APPEAR BEFORE GRAND JURY. The story had not kept twenty-four hours. The gist of it was that Sarah was to be called before the grand jury in the investigation of the death of her daughter. She was under suspicion for murder, though no charges had yet been filed. I read the story over and over. The words made no clear sense to me.

Bob was telling Andrew and me how he planned to handle the legal matters and how I must handle the press. My gaze kept going from the paper to his face, but his words made no sense, either. Andrew called Gordon with the news. To avoid any more scenes with the press Sarah was to spend the night at his place. We were on our way over. I took our framboise tray to the kitchen as Bob put out the fire.

161

16

About the time I got to sleep, the phone started ringing. The press, having lost Sarah, found me. After the third call, this one from a news magazine demanding an interview (with me, not Sarah), I took the receiver off the hook and tried to rest. An impossibility. Too many lists to make. Too many people to talk to. Too many questions to resolve. I turned on my side in the fetal position.

We had talked late into the night. Bob was in touch with lawyers. Gordon wanted to contact the FBI. Everyone had schemes and plans, but no one, solutions. Sarah treated the whole thing as a monstrous joke. "Nobody will believe it. I don't believe it." With that she went to bed and left us with our bad tempers and anxieties and sterile arrangements.

I did not let myself think about Andrew, as if any pleasure deserved only guilt. To wish I had met him under other circumstances was silly. To dwell on him at all, unproductive; also a distraction I could hardly afford right now. To get up and get busy was the only help.

I stepped out of my shower and heard knocking at the door. Through the peephole I recognized Cheryl. Cheryl and Krys. Both had read the papers, and evidently Krys decided the bad news meant she should clean my apartment. We sent her to Cheryl's instead.

Cheryl was wearing electric-pink socks, long johns, and an oversize T-shirt, one of her sleeping costumes. "Sarah had better sue," she said and sniffed. "I think Krys has stopped swimming."

"I know she has. Why don't you explain to her about body odor?"

"First I need to explain to you about image. We've somehow got to distance you from this." Cheryl poured us both a cup of coffee while I towel-dried my hair.

"Why sue?" I asked. "That prolongs everything. Sarah's got to get this behind her. With this uproar she can't even mourn properly."

"Later she can drop the suit, but for now she uses it to express her outrage — as well it should." She put down her coffee cup and folded her arms, her scolding position. "You have to be careful, too. You have your own reputation to worry about."

I slammed my chest drawer. "Cheryl, I don't understand you. A woman's life is falling apart, a woman who is more important to me than anyone else in the world, and you're talking about 'distancing myself.' I don't give a damn about what Washington thinks. I don't give a damn about anything but getting Sarah's life back together."

"Just don't forget her life isn't your life."

"I don't have time for this," I shouted.

Cheryl got out a skirt and sweater.

"I'll burn up in that."

"Yes, but you'll look great doing it."

"You are slightly crazy," I told her as the sweater came down over my head.

Both Mr. Duc and Maxie were sitting on the front steps.

"Don't you sleep anymore?" I asked Maxie.

"I get as much sleep as you," he answered.

I had started on down the steps when Mr. Duc touched my sleeve. He was ready for his last Welfare interview, he reminded me. To help ease the final clearance, we had planned for me to go with him, though I'd begun to doubt if they ever finished interviewing and filling out papers. For months I had been trying to get him a federal welfare payment. The check from the federal government would allow Mr. Duc to move out of the shelter and find a room of his own, a move that couldn't come too soon. He hated the shelter and had practically stopped eating.

I turned on Maxie. "If you dressed like a real person, you could take him yourself."

"If you think you dress like real persons, you're wrong!" Maxie retorted and left.

I tried to explain to Mr. Duc why I couldn't take him today, but he just stood there. I tried again. Again I started down the steps. Then turned.

"Come on," I said in a loud voice, as if deafness were his problem. "But we have to get this over quickly." As if the bureaucracy were his responsibility. No one expected me at the office for another hour, and I'd already lost my race against a news story.

The need to touch base was too strong. I called in anyway. A mistake. Sarah was already at the office. Waiting for me. Gladys put her on. The upshot was that at eleven I was to go to Senator Ditson's office to interview him about Anthony Morris. A week ago Sarah had set it up for herself. Now I was to take her place. Trying to talk her out of it only brought on a stern reminder that we had to get on with life. And did I remember we were going to the auction at Leslie's school tonight? I told her I had canceled the commitment — months ago she had agreed to be master of ceremonies for it — but she had made up her mind to go. "They need me," she said. We could argue about the auction later in the day.

Barney Ditson and I sat in leather armchairs placed in front of his office window. We had a straight shot of the mall and the Washington Monument. A plum office for a powerful senator. Always gracious, he did not act as if it were at all unusual to pursue the Anthony Morris story with all hell — real hell — breaking loose in Sarah's own life. He would do what he could for Sarah, he seemed to be saying; and if it meant becoming a prop in one of her scenarios, so be it.

I decided not to play games. Using Ted London at State as my source (without mentioning his name), I told him what I'd heard: that Morris was virtually running U.S. foreign policy in Lumb because he, Ditson, let him. The bluntness of the charge threw him off guard enough to make him angry.

"That's absurd. The State Department is perfectly capable of handling Lumb without any help from me or Morris."

"Maybe so, but bureaucracies tend to listen to heads of appropriations committees. And knowledgeable heads with the respect and backing of their colleagues have even more clout." He laughed. A man in his late fifties with a small paunch but a full head of hair, he was comfortable enough with himself and his actions not to stay on the defensive.

"All right. It may be a crime, but I do listen to Morris. Not only that, but I listen to the Lumbanese he sends over. For that matter, anybody he sends over. And for two very good reasons: I listen to anybody with a legitimate cause who requests a meeting and a go-between is irrelevant. I will always give weight to someone like Anthony Morris, whose judgment and abilities I trust and admire. Who would you listen to? I can't possibly know everything I need to know about everything I need to know. I've got to rely on others to guide me — doesn't mean I won't try to hear all sides, but it does mean my instinct is to go with the people whose judgment has served this country well in the past.

"Courtney, I would dearly love to have the time to study all the material on all the foreign and domestic policy issues that crosses my desk. I think I do as good a job — maybe better — than most. But I also have constituents to see to; I have to get myself elected every six years; I have to help other members of my party get elected; I even try for a personal life from time to time."

I felt a little like I was getting a lecture in Government 101. Getting my questions back on track wouldn't be easy. Especially since he was still talking.

"If you want to indict me, I can give you a much better case than this. Last week I was visited by three different lobbyists and their clients pushing their claims on the same domestic issue. One of the lobbyists I know well — like him, respect him, and, on occasion, sail with him. After his client left, he came back in to explain the disadvantages of my going with him. I appreciate that kind of help with my homework, and don't think it doesn't go a long way. Another has a solid reputation, though I personally don't know that much about him. The other is strictly sleaze, any way you want to cut him. His bribes aren't even subtle. Know which one I went with? The sleaze. His arguments made the most sense, so I held my nose and voted his client's interest. He'll end up making a bundle off that poor sucker who hired him, and with my help."

As if on cue, his secretary came to the door to announce his next visitor. I had been ever so gracefully outmaneuvered. Yet I was pretty sure of one thing now. Anthony Morris was making foreign policy for Lumb. State had pointed to Ditson, and Ditson hadn't denied Morris. I wasn't sure what we were going to make of it. Certainly having one man decide policy for a small, obscure country wasn't unheard of. Except that this man wasn't accountable to anyone unless you counted Ditson. Neither a politician nor a bureaucrat, he was, nevertheless, exerting an awful lot of influence, albeit on a minuscule territory.

I left with the promise of giving the senator's love to Sarah, though he had to be ambiguous about her right now. The confirmation hearings would be soon. While there was no formal opposition, Senator James had called me about what we had on Morris. The gist of the conversation was that he was prepared to ask Sarah's questions during the hearing. Ditson was too clued in not to be aware of James's proposal.

At the office the interview did not come up. Sarah had already left for a lunch with Andrew, who planned to take her to a place in the Virginia countryside, an hour's drive from Washington. Anything to get her out of the office. She had spent the morning going from one project to another, ordering Gladys to place phone calls, changing her mind, then placing one or two calls herself. Gladys was frantic. Sarah would not discuss the story in the paper, but Gladys also knew that at any moment she could decide to give an interview and, in her mood, who knows what she would say. When Bob Owens had called, Gladys told him what was going on, and within thirty minutes Andrew had whisked her away. Sarah's only word for me was that I was to "rest up" for the auction tonight.

I went to my office, put my head down on my desk, and wished myself back to the third grade. The wish and the rest lasted all of two and a half minutes — until I began going through the first of several stacks of mail.

Gladys interrupted my reading of the AP wire that carried a rehash of the *Post*'s story about Sarah. "Rich Sanford, says he's a friend of Leslie's, is here to see Sarah. What do you think?" she asked.

"Send him in here." Finally a break. A little before I was ready for him, but now the contact would be established.

Except for the mousse holding his black hair in a style more of the fifties than punk, Rich Sanford was unremarkable-looking. Medium height, medium build, and of no particular color. After he took the only extra chair, I came around and leaned against my desk, hoping my looking down on him would give me some authority.

He looked ready to bolt at any minute, and angry. Dispensing with niceties, he began, "Tell Mrs. Adams to lay off me. We'd better live and let live."

"What are you talking about?" I wondered if he was high on something. He had his right foot propped on his left knee, which he kept jiggling up and down. I began to feel as trapped as he obviously did.

"The police. They got real mean. I know she's bad-mouthing me, and you tell her to shut up. Just tell her to shut up."

"You've talked to the police?"

"This morning. I told them I didn't do it, and she knows I didn't do it. It's time for us to live and let live. Tell her that."

"I'll tell her."

He got up to go: "Just tell her what I said."

Was this some kind of threat in case she remembered? I should have tried to keep him, asked more questions, but from the looks of him, the police had pretty well done him over for the time being. I could wait. He was obviously frightened. Probably couldn't give a good accounting of himself. I had been uneasy with him, almost frightened myself. He slouched away, and I wondered why Leslie had found it necessary to choose him to punish Sarah and herself.

I looked down at my Ditson notes. I wasn't sure exactly how to proceed with Rich Sanford, but I had some ideas of how to get to the botton of this Morris mess. No one man should be allowed to run a country. Sarah was right, and I would see to it that everyone damn well understood she was right. She would not be written off. Sarah Adams would stay Sarah Adams, and I would stuff her down the bastards' throats if I had to.

Because I loved her. Because what I said to Cheryl this morning — about her being the most important thing in my life — came out of a place I didn't want to admit to. I liked to think I was too tough to be this vulnerable when all I had done was substitute a fairy godmother for a white knight. But I was, and it was a relief to admit it. She was all those people in my life I'd never had. And she was worth fighting for.

17

SARAH INSISTED on going — a mistake, but there was no changing her mind. I cursed Andrew for letting her talk him into a meeting with some business associates this evening. I cursed Gordon for not staying with her as he had promised this afternoon. If he couldn't talk her out of this auction, he could have come with her himself. He kept assuring me he would do anything to help, but his atonement was somewhat short of perfect, the bastard.

Two couples passed and I heard Sarah's name, could see from the corner of my eye they had turned to stare. I found myself shaking, but if Sarah had any second thoughts she wasn't showing them.

The woman marking off names of guests A–F looked startled to see Sarah bending over her and then relieved to find an envelope with Sarah's name and two tickets. She said she would tell Barbara Foster, the auction's chairperson, that Sarah was here — what a nice surprise; meanwhile, we should look around.

Parents and friends were already beginning to fill up the massive room with its red carpet and glittering chandeliers, for this was one of Washington's most chic fall events. In the middle of the room round tables for ten were covered in white linen and topped by gold mums. Along the sides gold-skirted tables held items to be auctioned, and above the tables signs proclaimed the kind of goods touted in that area — Antiques, Art, Crafts, Housewares, Services, Vacations, Food. With the items were sheets of paper for write-in bids on whatever that table proffered. This was the silent auction, and this was the activity going on now, though not too many bids were yet placed, only a good deal of scouting. Later, when Sarah was to be MC, there would be a live auction having even grander objects to bid on during dinner.

There was a bustle and an air of festivity — urban society's answer to the county fair. And like its counterpart, food plays a large role. You could bid on any number of places to eat, celebrities to eat with (including Sarah, I noticed from the catalogue someone had handed me), ethnic foods delivered to your home, catered dinners in the homes of strangers, even food to be eaten immediately.

All the long night we were damned to browse through the baked goods or get lost in the house of mirrors. Worst yet, we would be a freak show, I realized when the whispers began and the heads turned. There would be no blue ribbons for us. I sensed more than saw a tremor go through Sarah, and I made myself take her arm.

Sarah decided we should start with the Antiques section. She examined an Edwardian muffin stand, a tortoiseshell caviar server, a nineteenth-century crystal inkwell, an old French chocolate pot, and a silk top hat with white kid gloves carefully preserved. She bid on the top hat. We saw an old mahogany lap desk lined in green velvet, and again Sarah wrote her name on the sheet. In the silent auction, the last name (and the largest price) won unless the item was deemed important enough to have a mini-live closing. If that happened then the bidder or the bidder's representative must be around at the silent closing to vie for the treasure. Sometimes the donor, usually a parent, would buy back the article if the last price didn't seem worthy enough for the family's heirloom, which many of the objects were.

"Leslie would like this," Sarah said and bid on a hand-made sterling silver hair barrette. I noticed we had this table to ourselves. She continued bidding and insisted I find something, too. I wrote in $12.50 for a newspaper, the *Aurora General Advertiser*, Philadelphia, July 7, 1796, and wondered if anyone would ever speak to us. I felt enclosed in a glass box where even our words exaggerated the silence. I bid $20 for a small oval Victorian picture frame, slightly damaged.

A man walked over and put his arm around Sarah. "Honey," he said, "I'm so sorry 'bout things." He was the eighty-three-year-old senator from Florida, and the joke was that if he didn't show for an event, nobody else would either, for he was everywhere always. Kept him young, he said; and, in truth, something seemed to. He offered to get us drinks, but I went instead. Some of these people would be forced to speak to the senator; and, if Sarah was under his wing, they would talk with her, too.

At the bar I ran into Frank Carmichael, my great and good friend whom I hadn't seen or heard from since the last British embassy party. He grabbed my arm. "Courtney, it's a disaster," he whispered. "Why did you let her come?"

"Shut up!" I whispered back.

He waited until I had my two wine spritzers and ushered me toward a corner. "I know you're loyal, but don't make a public display of it."

"Have I told you about Mr. Duc?" I asked. "Mr. Duc now has a room he shares with another man. I hope it works. There's a partition down the middle, but only one overhead naked light bulb for both of them, and the other man insists on leaving it on."

"What the hell are you talking about? This is no joke. If you'll use a little common sense, this won't hurt you. If not, you'll find yourself under suspicion, too. She'll suck you down with her."

"He also snores."

"Who?"

"Not Mr. Duc. His roommate." I walked away, but he followed long enough to say, "You know I think the world of her." Then he swooped over to Senator Ditson.

Barbara Foster, the auction's impresario, touched my arm. "May I speak to you?" she asked. I followed her into the hallway.

"This won't do. We've made arrangements with Carl White, and we can't renege on somebody like that." As we both knew, Carl White did not hold a journalistic candle to Sarah, in reputation or performance. She was scolding me like a child. "Doesn't she understand? This is all very awkward. A woman suspected of murder . . ."

She was a large, imposing woman who had got her way from

age three. Maybe sooner. Some kind of accommodation could be made, I insisted. Out of the question, she countered. I threatened to talk with Carl White myself. She backed down. She would arrange something.

"Sarah Adams is doing this school no good with her outlandish behavior," she said, walking away.

I got back to Sarah. She was still talking to the senator, but they had moved to Housewares and had been joined by Phil Larson, a Washington-based columnist for the L.A. *Times*. Sarah pointed to a wicker picnic basket and suggested I bid on it. The price was already over a hundred dollars, and I declined. She put a bid in for me under her name.

Then she turned her most dazzling smile on Phil and told him she had read the galleys of his new book and had sent his publisher a glowing letter, which he was free to use however he liked. Phil thanked her profusely and insincerely — her name would never appear on his book blurbs — and began talking rapidly about his promotional tour and asking her opinion on everything from local interviewers to the best techniques for handling late-night talk show hosts. I saw Barbara Foster headed toward Sarah and stepped out to intercept her.

"To upset her in any way would be grossly inappropriate," I said in a voice just audible to the two of us but with all the anger that had been building since we walked into this place. I managed to erase that smug, all-knowing look on her face. And, whatever her original intentions, she was all maple syrup with Sarah, saying how wonderful it was that Sarah had come and explaining how she was working out a scheme for Sarah to MC with Carl White — if, of course, Sarah was still up to it.

Sarah gave her noblesse oblige smile and declared she was delighted to work with Carl, before dismissing, with a slight turn of her body, Barbara Foster.

Wasn't that Samuel Haverty, the new head of Voice of America, walking this way, Sarah asked Phil. She had heard he was interesting, a former movie producer, a bit exotic for Washington, at least until recently. Phil assured her the man was fascinating — a hard worker, a good politician, something of a jet-setter. As he finished his sentence, Haverty reached us, and the two men shook hands.

"Got a story for you, Larson," Haverty said without preamble, pulling Phil aside. And Phil Larson, everybody's idea of a good guy, allowed himself to be pulled away.

"Want to check the art?" I asked, for Sarah was standing stunned or uncomprehending or both. My own powerlessness to help her was building into a fine rage against this whole gathering.

"We'll find something for your apartment," she replied. She had never been there. Until that moment she had never mentioned it.

We found a print by Lou Stovall that Sarah bid on — for Leslie's room, she said. She began to persuade me (I was getting nervous about all the bids we were making) that I should try for a photograph of an old barn when she interrupted herself to speak to Larry Blake, who was evidently having no trouble persuading himself to bid on every other piece of art, his version of buying books by the yard.

Larry looked startled to see Sarah, but, always playing the politician, recovered quickly. In order to put him, or maybe herself, at ease, Sarah began questioning him on a banking bill before the House. Whether to cover his embarrassment or because he couldn't resist an opportunity to pontificate, he delivered a briefing until Carl White joined us. Carl had come to fetch Sarah for an auction conference whenever she finished her discussion, he told her.

Larry tried to redirect the conversation toward Carl, who firmly kept deferring to Sarah. Standing behind her, his hands on her shoulders, he glared down at Larry Blake and willed him to pay her proper homage. Ponderous old Carl White might understand the futility of this charade, but he would see to it that she got to play it out. For the first time all evening, I felt we were not abandoned.

"Are we prepared to change positions if this policy fails?" Sarah asked amiably, though not uncritically.

Blake's chest swelled ever so slightly. "There are three fundamental things in life," he began in a professorial voice lecturing a rather dim student, "and one is . . ."

Sarah cut in. "Don't ever begin a statement like that to me again."

He continued. "Ships come . . ."

"I'm serious. Don't ever do that again." She said it with the sureness of one who had spent a lifetime practicing goodwill and civilized responses to the most outrageous posturings, under-standing, with the deft instinct of all this town's survivors, their necessity and their limitations. "Shall we go, Carl?"

Spotting Jane Sale, the most outspoken woman in Washing-ton, I walked to Services before she noticed me. She might pos-sibly be the only person here who would actually question me on the indictment. She would never settle for my silence or an official no comment, not even from God.

I positioned myself behind a large poster of the Grand Cay-man Islands, out of harm's way. I wanted another drink but didn't have the energy to deal with the people surrounding the bars. I was not at all sure I had the energy to get through the evening. I wondered if all freaks felt this powerless and out of control. One minute I was furious with Sarah for putting her-self — and me — through this; the next, touched by her game-ness; the next, proud of her courage; until I was furious again.

"What do you want them for, anyway?" I heard a familiar voice ask.

"You know perfectly well."

"No. Tell me."

"The same reason you do."

The questioner was the secretary of state. I wasn't sure about the plaintiff.

"But we have different functions in the Department."

"I still have to eat."

"You need White House mess privileges to eat?" The secretary of state rarely could wrangle White House privileges for anyone.

The voices moved down the table, and I lost the gist of their words.

"Why would she show?" a woman's voice asked.

"Bad form," a man's replied.

I left Vacations for Food. Food was tangible, the substance of the county fair after all. I studied the lists here carefully — I hoped to unstick the knot in my throat. For starters I could bid for a meal at almost any good restaurant in Washington at as much or more than I would have to pay regularly. Or I could buy a bottle of Château Haut-Brion 1961 premier Grand Cru Classe. Or, for $250 (the bidding was already that high) I could have a gourmet dish once a month, including North Texas chili and caviar pie. Out of some kind of misplaced nostalgia, I signed up for a homemade apple cake.

"Think of it," a prominent black city councilman was saying to Judge Sam Bernstein, "if we let women in the Cosmos Club, she would have been a member."

The county fair atmosphere had caught in earnest. Bidding on antiques or on footballs signed by the Redskins was intense, for these were competitive people. Whether it was a day in the Washington Redskins' training camp or a committee assignment or the writing of a brief, it was sought after with the intent to win.

Another counterpoint: "I was too far away. Nobody took care of me." A stammered reply. Then, "Yeah, Johnson was close. Still has a job. I don't."

A close acquaintance waved from across the room but didn't come my way. "She'll suck you down, too." Frank Carmichael's words hit full force. Even at county fairs certain of the community's rules were enforced. One was allowed the peep show. One was allowed to gawk at the Siamese twins. One was not allowed to become part of the attractions. That was only for the outsiders.

The wash of voices, all grays and blacks and no pastels, frightened me. Already the greed had oozed out, staining otherwise sociable transactions. And with greed comes aggression. I wondered where Sarah was and if Carl White was able to look after her and what it took to turn these sophisticates into a mob. We were crazy to be here. A bizarre bazaar, I thought and headed for the bar. And ran into Linda Ditson.

"It's awful. People are saying awful things. I mean really — a mother even suspected of murdering her own daughter," she said. "Why don't you take her home?"

I shrugged my shoulders.

"Some idiots have threatened to walk out if she participates in the auction. A few moral types plan to take their children out of the school. Good riddance, I say. Courtney, you look awful. Are people treating you badly? Probably. It will pass. For Sarah, I'm not so sure. Even when this thing is cleared up. People won't forget. There's a certain amount of glee attached to the tut-tuts. They're closing Antiques now. I've got to help. I hope your friends are supportive. If not, call me." She patted my hand and walked into the crowd.

I went to the Entertainment table, curious to see what was happening with the lunch for two Sarah was offering. Carl White was promising lunch in New York for six, and Donald Bell, a rising right-wing columnist, was hosting lunch for eight.

Bell's lunch had just been bought by a group of psychiatrists, and a woman with short black hair was upset about it. "Outrageous," she was saying. "Joe's lunch should go for more than Donald Bell's."

Joe was Joe Sampson, a moderate on the President's staff, who had been attacked in one of Bell's recent columns. Joe was offering lunch at the White House, mess privileges, obviously. The woman hurried off to round up others as outraged — and willing to pay for it — as she.

I couldn't find the list for Sarah's lunch, and it was only after a second slow look around the table that I realized they hadn't put it out. Too late to take her out of the catalogue; "tasteful" to take her off the table. The woman came back and wrote "one thousand dollars" under Joe Sampson's name.

Over the loudspeaker a local weathercaster announced the closing of the Art section, and I remembered Sarah's request to bid on the Stovall print and hurried over. Gordon Simons was there looking for Sarah. What were we doing here? Was she all right? Why had I let her come?

I assured him she was, so far as I knew, all right; and had he been with her, he might have talked her out of this. Maybe he still could, I added with sudden hope. He assured me he would find her and take us both somewhere for a quiet dinner.

I found Wilson Kane skulking behind a large Robert Motherwell canvas, not far from where Gordon and I had been talking.

"Hiding out?" I asked. We hadn't seen each other since I caught him sitting in Sarah's kitchen sporting his foxy shorts. He had looked only slightly more uncomfortable then than now. He was, he explained quickly, waiting to bid on a painting that his wife wanted, the Motherwell, in fact.

"How is Sarah?" Kane asked me and added, "I'm sorry I haven't made it by to see her."

"Do you have children here?" I asked.

"Our youngest. A son. I really am sorry. You see, she was the most exciting woman. The kind who wouldn't have given me the time of day when I was growing up. I couldn't resist. Not that I'm trying to justify myself."

Gordon came back. "She's talking to Carl White. I don't know where," he said to me, a little apologetic, and acknowledged Kane with a nod. I wondered how much he knew or suspected of Kane's involvement with Sarah.

"Please tell Sarah how sorry I am . . . we are," Kane said as he started to move away. "The papers have really done her an injustice."

"You can tell her yourself. She'll be here any minute. There's a print she plans to bid on." Under other circumstances I would have laughed, he looked so horrified.

"I understand Sarah thinks highly of your work," Gordon said to him.

"That so? I'm flattered," he said with a smile. "If you'll excuse me, I'd better find Pat." He was into his scramble, but Gordon put a hand on his coat sleeve.

"Why not wait to say hello to Sarah?" Gordon asked.

"Excuse me." Kane tried to remove Gordon's hand, now gripping the sleeve.

Gordon did not move his hand.

"Move it," Kane demanded, drawing on all the authority that Wall Street and Washington had invested in him.

Gordon held fast. They feinted, almost perceptibly. Their feet moved rapidly, so rapidly I was not sure what was happening until ten seconds later, when Wilson Kane, apologizing rather loudly for the accident, helped Gordon to his feet.

Later I explained that Gordon lost his balance. Others around us blamed an altercation over economic policy. The *Post* gossip columnist the next day wrote it up as a squabble over a painting, a much more sensible explanation than fighting over the budget.

Wilson and Pat Kane proceeded through the evening as if nothing had happened. Gordon left. I got the print for Sarah.

Then the moment arrived. People began making their way to the center tables, ready for the serious bidding of the live auction that would take place between courses. The room was loud and boisterous, reflecting the alcohol consumption that had been going on for over two hours. All it would take was one drunk, I thought. My stomach ached.

The lights dimmed and Carl White walked onto a portable platform in the middle of the ballroom. The crowd clapped when he introduced himself, but conversations started up again as soon as he began a joke routine and talked up two-thousand-year-old mummy beads and a week at an Irish castle.

It was only when he called Sarah's name that the clamor quieted down. She loved this school, he said. He hoped everyone here could understand the cost and the courage it took for her to come tonight. A good thing we lived in a country where people are presumed innocent until proven guilty, he reminded the audience. That cold blue that always floated through his voice was gone. The plea was there, honest and ragged and from depths I never suspected.

I was relieved and shamed. Relieved that Carl White absolved her and shamed I needed him to do just that. I understood these people better than I wished to, and that understanding made me see with absolute clarity the devastation of the scandal. No matter who the murderer, Sarah would never quite recover, and that was the secret they had known all along.

Then all that was heard was Sarah's slow footsteps to the stage. The spotlight caught the sheen of her short brown curls and the regalness of her carriage. And, whether the makeup or the adrenaline, she did not look bereft. An offense to the crowd. Her eyes remained locked with Carl White's, as if together they could propel her forward, could will the room's cooperation.

Onstage she smiled. The tables remained hushed, one stretched moment of silence that could mean anything. No drunks, please, no drunks, I kept repeating in my head.

"Hello," her voice rushed out to the room.

A smattering of clapping. Linda Ditson rose to her feet. Senator Ditson joined her. Then the couple sitting next to them. Others at different tables got to their feet. Some didn't clap at all. A few left. But quietly and in the dark.

No one yelled. She had done it.

I walked between the tables to Linda Ditson. She watched me approach.

"I'll take you home," she said. "You're sick." I was.

18

AT LEAST, the coffee was good. Already I'd had one cup waiting for Mr. Dobotu to show. I'd scheduled breakfast at this Roy Rogers on Wisconsin Avenue, hardly the place for a clandestine meeting but the one he suggested as on his way to work.

Having arrived a half hour before I was due, I sat and watched the people, an occupation I hadn't had much time for since I'd come to Washington. Quite a few of them seemed to know each other. A sense of camaraderie filled the place. I felt protected sitting here and was almost grateful my early morning phone call had gotten me out. Not by its design but as a result, I had wanted out of my apartment — anything to keep from stewing the same old thoughts over and over. I'd done enough of that last night without Madge Hudson-Marsh this morning to get me started again.

"Linda Ditson told me about the auction," she had come on. "Just how bad was it?"

I described the night before.

"I wish I'd known. I wouldn't have left town."

"You couldn't have stopped her either," I responded defensively.

"Somebody had better stop her; otherwise . . ." She didn't finish her thought. I didn't either.

"Did you know she's sent Gordon away?" she asked. I didn't and said so. She continued: "After Linda phoned last night, I called Sarah, ostensibly to tell her about my weekend; I wanted to hear what she had to say about the auction and to suggest that she and Gordon use my country place for a few days. She told me she didn't have time to get away and she wasn't interested in going anyplace with Gordon."

"He was with her all day yesterday," I noted.

"He says he left yesterday evening only long enough to pick up some clean clothes. When he came back, she accused him of seeing the British woman. He promised her that was over, but her mind was made up. She refused to discuss it with him."

"How is he?" I asked and realized I cared about the bastard.

"I think not well, but who knows about Gordon?"

"Any suggestions?" I asked.

"If she would leave town with Andrew . . . or any of us . . . anything to slow her down until all this is settled."

I agreed to discuss it with Sarah and get back to Madge.

Andrew had answered the phone and was less than optimistic when I broached the idea to him. "Whatever she's doing seems to be working pretty well for her even if it is driving the rest of us crazy. I'll try, though."

Then in a stage whisper he asked me to have lunch with him. Sarah was going to be meeting with Bob Owens and the lawyers. He thought I would be interested in his guest. Philip Adams, elusive father, former husband. I accepted. May all my meals today be productive, I wished as I started on my second cup of coffee just as Mr. Dobotu walked in.

Impeccably dressed down to the white linen handkerchief just so in his pocket, a formality about him that made the Roy Rogers an even stranger choice. He assured me the sausage and biscuits here made for as fine a breakfast as you could get in the city, and from the looks of his stomach, he knew good food. Our discussion of breakfast did not last long. He was nervous, and I was eager to get on with it. The very fact of his coming made me feel he had something else to tell me. I was gambling that this time he would be forthcoming.

"Several weeks ago," I began, "Sarah Adams got a letter in the mail pointing out Anthony Morris's involvement with Lumb.

That's one of the reasons she got so absorbed with this story, and one of the reasons I keep pestering you."

He smiled but continued to avoid my eyes, as he had done since he came in. Unless I was misreading the body signals, he appeared more tense once I'd mentioned the letter.

I plunged on. "After a lot of thought, Mr. Dobotu, I believe you wrote the letter, possibly in a fit of anger after reading the announcement about Morris. Then you . . . for whatever reasons . . . changed your mind." This was stretching it a bit. The letter wasn't his style, but I was more than a little certain he knew who had written it.

His eyes met mine. "I did not write the letter, and I do not frighten easily."

"I didn't mean to imply . . ."

"You meant exactly that, Miss Patterson."

"I certainly understand why you might not want us to pursue this further. Especially once we found you. I'm sorry to implicate you against your wishes — if this is against your wishes.

"As you know, we've uncovered a lot, but the letter — it's hard for me to believe there's not more. Something about that letter makes me feel we're talking about more than an old grievance." I was shooting in the dark and he knew it.

"Don't you and Mrs. Adams have quite enough trouble on your hands at the moment?" His words were like a slap, and my face must have registered that, for he immediately said how sorry he was, what a tragedy, the killer would be caught soon.

I assured him an arrest was imminent. That's why I had time to get back to these other important matters. We both agreed work was an important therapy at a time like this. He must have suffered great loss himself when he chose to stay here, I said and asked how much of his family he had left behind.

As it turned out, his wife and children were already with him and stayed. A cousin and her family stayed, too. His brother came shortly after the coup. Mr. Dobotu had been able to get him and his cousin's husband (also a former embassy official) jobs with Brooks Brothers, one downtown, one at the branch up by Neiman's. The rest were still there.

182

Back to the letter. Did he have some idea of who might have written it? I reminded him of Sarah's reputation for accuracy and fairness, also for covering her sources. "If it's a story you want covered properly, you'd be hard pressed to find anyone to do a better job."

He looked at his watch, as if time might be the deciding factor. Slowly he took me in, appraising my own trustworthiness and competence. Too bad Cheryl hadn't dressed me this morning. She would have known just what promoted confidence. Evidently I hadn't done so badly myself, for he stayed. And he talked.

"I did not know about the letter until after our conversation. When I mentioned to my wife we had talked, she told me about the letter. My cousin wrote it. My cousin thinks it is possible to discredit the present Lumb government internally by pointing out the close ties to the United States, a position not much touted over there, and externally by revealing what my country is up to these days." He stopped only long enough to take a breath.

"She would like to embarrass this country into cutting off aid to Lumb. She is not realistic about the outcome of either maneuver, but then she is a very hardheaded woman determined to go home on her own terms. An impossibility." He shook his head and stared down at his coffee.

I had to hope he did not think it an impossibility.

"And what is going to cause such embarrassment?" I asked.

Almost casually he said, "Terrorists. The present government is harboring a small band of them — anti-American, of course. You understand, neither I nor any of my family can be implicated in this. You would need other sources to confirm this, and that part I will have to leave completely up to you and Mrs. Adams. This is all I am willing to do. You must respect that." He rose. I thanked him and fairly floated out the door of the Roy Rogers.

I had the crux of our story. And in its way so effortlessly delivered that I had trouble believing what had happened. The ramifications now were beyond anything either of us had ever imagined. There were terrorists in a U.S.-subsidized country; and, thanks to Morris, they had Stingrays. I wondered what

Ditson would say to this. While he was far from blameless, I hoped he wouldn't be too hurt by it and knew that he would be. But I couldn't start playing God with the facts. He and Morris had done enough of that themselves.

Although I was disappointed (and relieved) to find Sarah already gone — I'd wanted to have some good news for a change and also, in keeping with a true egotistical nature, get a pat on the head — reality did not completely set in again until lunch. Andrew chose a small restaurant just over Key Bridge into Virginia. He had heard the food was bad, but that cut down on the crowds. We would be able to talk privately.

Philip Adams was waiting for us. A thin man whose jaw had lost definition, he wore jeans, a white shirt unbuttoned two buttons too many, and a once-expensive suede jacket. We discussed the rise of Washington real estate since the sixties, business opportunities in Colorado, Washington weather, Colorado weather, London weather, Iowa weather.

Only after a martini did he appear to relax at all. He sipped his soup with a tentativeness reserved for first tastes in childhood. I could not imagine Sarah ever having been married to him. On reflection he did have one thing in common with the other men she was attracted to: he was another unsuccessful venture — a man who could not stay or should not stay or would not stay. She had won her father and made up for it by never winning again.

"Something was bound to happen," Philip said as the waiter put fried-fish platters in front of us. "She was always too much for me."

"Beg pardon?" I said.

"Sarah. She was always too much, wanted too much."

"Blessed are the meek?" Andrew was holding his fork more like a weapon than a utensil.

"I'm not trying to put her down, and I'm not trying to excuse myself. I know better than anyone what a bastard I was. How do you think I feel having Leslie dead? Knowing I didn't lift a finger to help her.

"I swear, though, Sarah didn't want me to. Those first few years I fell apart — drugs and all. Then, when I got myself together, she refused any help. She let me send Leslie a Christmas present, and Leslie would write me a thank-you note. That was our only form of communication. Until Leslie started writing on her own."

"When was that?" Andrew asked.

"About three years ago. She sent me her annual perfunctory thank-you note and just for the hell of it, I answered. She wrote back. After that we exchanged notes from time to time. I was careful not to say too much — Sarah wouldn't have liked it — but the kid got to where she really opened up with me. Usually after she'd had a fight with Sarah." He stopped eating altogether; his hands clutched the table. "I liked to think I served some purpose in her life."

"Did she write you about Rich Sanford?" I asked.

"Yeah. Sarah didn't like him. For good reason, I guess. He didn't treat Leslie right — I could tell that from the letters. I also got the idea that Leslie either didn't think she could do any better or deserved any better. That damn Sarah, she's to blame for that."

With those words Philip Adams's voice lost its hesitant, almost apologetic tone. Andrew, his jaw twitching, calmly asked Philip to explain himself.

"Andrew, I don't mean to step out of line. We both loved her, and we both know what she can be like. You left before I did."

"Let's stick with the present," Andrew said, his face flushed.

"So, right after Leslie started writing to me, she told me about this great boy she knew, an honor student, a track star, you know, the big-man-on-campus type."

"Jack Kelman," I said.

"That's his name. Anyway, Sarah told Leslie that he was too good for her, or words to that effect. Made the little girl more unsure than she already was and, sure enough, managed to scare Leslie away from him."

"But nothing was too good for Leslie," I said as calmly as I could.

"Nothing was too good for Sarah's daughter, you mean," Philip Adams retorted. "Leslie counted as Sarah's daughter, not Leslie."

"You don't know anything about them!" My voice was high and my hands were shaking.

"Don't I? I know Sarah. And from the letters I knew enough about Leslie, about her weakness, like my own.

"Hell, do you think I enjoyed leaving them? Sarah knew how to produce guilt instantaneously. The only courageous thing I've ever done was to leave her. And that was to save myself. I didn't do a damn thing for Leslie."

"Bastard," Andrew said, "you fucking bastard."

I took Philip Adams's arm. "Let's leave. Andrew, pay the bill. We'll meet you outside."

The sky was overcast and a desultory drizzle had set in. Neither Philip nor I spoke until Andrew, subdued if not chastened, joined us.

"We're not far from the river," I said. "Let's go walk on the bike path, on the D.C. side." For lack of any better ideas, they followed me.

I turned to Philip Adams. "Sarah is in serious trouble over this. Are you willing to help?"

"What can I do?"

"You can tell us everything you know about the last six months of Leslie's life."

Philip looked at both of us — with pity, I think. "It's not what you want to hear."

"Just tell us," Andrew said quietly.

A pause for effect. Sarah's former husband had a few dramatic flourishes in him but, unlike Sarah's, they touched on an artificiality rather than a simple flair for the theatrical. To begin, he gazed out over the water.

"In August I got a letter from Leslie saying she had a new boyfriend and that, of course, Sarah hated him. But she did acknowledge her mother's anger was not without reason. Unfortunately, Sarah overreacted.

"According to what I was told, she threatened to send Leslie to boarding school, but that threat backfired when Leslie said

186

that was fine with her. Then Sarah threatened to kill herself because Leslie was making her so unhappy.

"This news came in a particularly hysterical letter. Leslie was a mess. She wasn't going to see Rich anymore, but she was in a rage. In one sentence she'd say what a bitch Sarah was; in the next she'd be talking about how worthless she herself was and what a disappointment she was to Sarah. Then she'd write how she couldn't bear that much responsibility for someone else's happiness. She blamed me for leaving Sarah and sticking her with the role of husband and child. She said she couldn't stand the burden anymore. She hated Sarah and loved Sarah and wanted to be rid of Sarah and thought she'd die herself if anything did happen to her mother." Tears, real ones, ran down his cheeks. He stopped talking and took a deep breath.

"I tried to call her a couple of times but never reached her," he continued. "Two days later, I got another note. Not to worry about her, she said. She was fine. But then a week later I got the letter saying she wanted to come live with me. I was flabbergasted. The woman I live with now is twenty-three. I couldn't see the three of us together, but I kept thinking of that other letter. The thought crossed my mind that Leslie had learned a few lessons in manipulation herself. I said she could come."

For the next half mile we walked in silence. The rain was harder and the wind was up a little. I was glad of it; I needed something to brace me. That so much went on in their lives I was not aware of made me feel displaced and somewhat foolish. What dream world had I created to keep myself from sensing, if not knowing, what was going on? I had filtered in only as much of the contention as I could allow. Even now I could hardly stand to think that both of them had kept from me so much crucial in their lives. Had I only been given the tip because they knew I didn't want more? Or because, ultimately, I was extraneous to their entanglement?

Philip began again: "The next thing I heard was that Leslie had told Sarah she was working out her plans. She asked if school had already started in Colorado.

"I answered that she could enroll whenever she wanted. I had the idea she planned to come immediately but I didn't hear from her again until last week."

"You never talked? None of you talked to each other?" Andrew asked.

"I was willing to go along, but I wasn't going to encourage it with a phone call. As for Leslie calling me — well, I was part of her dream world. The more removed I was, the better. We both knew, I think, that I would be a disappointment to her in real life."

"And her last note?" I prodded.

He reached into his pocket and pulled out a pale green notecard. "I should give it to the police, I guess," he said, handing it to Andrew.

We stood under a tree to shelter the note written in Leslie's small, tight scribble. With a start, I noticed it was not unlike my own handwriting. Andrew let me read it first and held his hands over it to protect it from the rain.

> Hi, there! Sorry to be so long getting back to you. For reasons that you know, it won't work out for us, but thank you for supporting the myth. You are probably a nice man. Don't worry about me. I will be all right, but you won't be hearing from me again. I wish things had worked out differently. — Leslie

"What does she mean, 'For reasons that you know'?" I asked, handing the note to Andrew.

Philip Adams shrugged his shoulders. "She was a strange kid. At the time, I didn't think too much of it. Now I wonder if she wasn't pretty depressed . . . you know . . . the kind where it's not worth living . . ." He paused and blew his nose.

"The whole note was out of sync. Little things — she always called me Daddy and she'd started signing off with 'affectionately' or 'lots of love' — things like that.

"I enjoyed it. In a way I was kind of disappointed." His voice began to trail. "I was getting used to the idea of having her around for a while."

Andrew took him by the arm. "Where would you like us to drop you off? You're getting soaked."

We left Philip Adams at the Hirshhorn Museum. He gave me the note in case it proved useful to Sarah.

"So many more buildings on the mall since I left," he said as we pulled over to the curb. Tears were in his eyes again, and I was ashamed of my impatience to have him gone.

He leaned over me and whispered to Andrew, "It wasn't her fault — she couldn't help it — but I had to get out. She deballed me. Completely."

Andrew nodded. As we drove off, Philip Adams was standing in front of the Hirshhorn blowing his nose.

19

ALL THE WAY to my apartment I talked about Rich Sanford, not Philip Adams. If anything, Adams's story had confirmed my suspicions about Rich. He was the reason she had decided not to leave. Then she changed her mind again and the two of them quarreled. Maybe Sarah heard them and came down, or Sarah and Leslie were both in the kitchen when Rich appeared. I played out both scenes.

Although he listened carefully, he didn't agree or disagree. His eyes had lost their energy. The lunch with Adams had worn him out, and I sensed he was as desperate as I was.

Once inside my apartment we pretended we were not going to bed with each other. I departed from my usual white wine to have a scotch and soda with him. And because I'd still had no one to share my early morning triumph with, I filled him in on the latest in the Anthony Morris saga.

"How do you confirm such a thing?"

"Sarah has sources in the Defense Intelligence Agency as well as the CIA. If we can't pry anything out of those, there's always the congressional oversight committees."

"It's that easy?"

"No. Not at all that easy. Right now it's going to be especially hard," I said, remembering Mr. Dobotu's reluctance this morning to continue with Sarah.

"I guess I'm naive," he said and stretched out his long legs in front of him, "but I don't understand why a man of his stature would get involved or stay involved. The money's good but not that good."

"Money probably has the least to do with it. I think he did it because it was expedient for everybody — the U.S. government, Grove Systems, the Lumbs in power. Only the victims of the train wreck got screwed on that one. It's possible they didn't even figure into his calculations at all. Once in, why not take money for it? As far as he's concerned, it's business as usual. He's not the first. There have been plenty of other cases."

He took hold of my hand and started playing with my fingers. "So what are you saying? That they see nothing wrong with what they do?"

"I'm saying there's a kind of arrogance that breeds complacency. An assumption of knowing what's best or, at least, workable. You stop questioning. Whether you're a person or a group or a country."

"So we all stand guilty," he said.

"I guess. But certain people or systems claim a kind of power for themselves — or we abdicate it to them to make us feel less lonely. We need heroes. But now I'm sounding like the schoolteacher I once was."

"No. Please go on."

"It's also a matter of degree and even that degree depends upon the ethos of the times. We probably don't put up with as much now as we did thirty, forty years ago."

I leaned into him. He adjusted his arm to accommodate my body. I had not planned to make the first move. Did not calculate it even thirty seconds before I did it. He kissed me and neither of us made any jokes about the framboise. Tonight the playfulness was gone. By the time his hands found my breasts, mine had found his crotch. On the way to my bed we shed our clothes.

This was to be no long stroll, get-acquainted tease; instead, one more form of a desperate cry, a raw need too deep for another body to satisfy it. Yet our bodies did take over and released our minds and, finally, our bodies themselves. We were not gentle or loving or even attentive. Only angry and greedy. And when it was over, stunned by the pleasure received.

191

We lay on our backs, not touching, the emptiness crawling over us again, too soon. For a long time we watched the shadows on the ceiling and continued to after Andrew started talking, softly and steadily.

"When she married, I came to live with her. At first I was excited about it — leaving my father and his wife, having Sarah for a constant companion once again. But I hadn't reckoned on Philip. There had always been boyfriends around, but a husband was different. He took her time and energy. Though he was plenty decent enough to me, I couldn't stand him.

"She started getting on my nerves, too. On the one hand, I wanted all her attention; on the other, I very much resented it when she gave it to me. I felt smothered. I knew I had to get away, so once I left for school I followed Sarah's pattern at our home and never really lived with them again."

He looked over. "When Philip left her, I started to go to her. Give her back a little of what she'd given me. But I couldn't. I joined the air force."

"And ran all the way to London."

"That's all I know to do." He turned on his side toward me. "Things will change now. I'll try to be a better brother. Hang around more. Try to assuage my guilt a little. God, my guilt!"

I didn't say anything, just lay there thinking about my own, until he began again.

"I keep thinking if I'd been around or taken them out of Washington . . ."

"Don't blame Washington. There's no monopoly on Rich Sanfords. Or mothers and daughters. At the most, what you have here are just more of the pressures and ambitions and greed that you have everywhere."

"And unreality?"

"That too, but there's a fairly healthy balance most of the time. You always have the force of grand schemes or project some desired illusion, but you also get a dose of what actually exists out there. Not always as soon as you should, but usually soon enough to keep away real harm." Now I had turned toward him. "Anyway, wanting unreality belongs to human nature and can't be laid to Washington."

He grinned and pulled me closer to him. I cradled my head in his arm.

"I keep thinking about how I saw only what I wanted to see or was forced to see," I said. "I refused to recognize what a mess we were all making. I told myself I was doing what I could for Leslie, but I wasn't about to admit to the seriousness of the problem. I was so determined to keep us a family. Sarah and Leslie were my dream family; and, if the dream turned sour, I would simply shut it off for a while."

"As you just said, that's human nature," he responded.

"Gordon was right about me: I am dependent on Sarah for my being, not just my career. But it's more than Sarah. I realize now how much I needed them both for my sense of belonging. I wanted to belong to a family. I'd never felt that before."

Andrew stroked my hair. "Would you have left?"

"The job? Probably, but only after I felt firmly entrenched in their personal lives. I kidded myself that I was ready to leave now. I wasn't, and I could have justified staying around a few more years. After all, it's a plum job. Everything appears so rational and plausible until you start looking underneath."

The phone rang. I didn't answer, but it served as our signal to get up and get dressed. Without saying so, we both knew it was time to go back to Sarah.

"When I was a little girl — three or four," I said as I buttoned my blouse, "I remember watching my mother on her hands and knees with a mop bucket trying to scrub my scribbles off the wallpaper. She told me she should never have had another child at her age, that she was too old to put up with all this foolishness.

"The water in the bucket got dirtier and dirtier. Her scrubbing was as destructive to the wallpaper as my scribbling had been, but she didn't seem to care." I stopped long enough to brush my hair and put on lip gloss.

"Now, sometimes I dream my mother and I fall into that bucket. She pulls herself out as the bucket turns over but she doesn't pull me. I'm saved only because all the water spills out of the bucket.

"She then tells me she tried to save me. I never contradict her."

"And how do you feel about dirty water?" Andrew asked.

"I panic." I laughed a little too sharply.

"Are you panicked now?"

"I don't know. I can't feel anything."

"Sarah won't save you," he said with great tenderness.

I felt the tears coming. He pulled me to him, rocking us as we stood together. "Do you want to go back in there?" he asked and motioned towards the bed.

I took his hand and led him to the front door. "If we start using sex as a tranquilizer, we'll never get out of this place."

20

MADGE WAS waiting at Sarah's door for us. "She's closed herself in her study and is writing a column on the inanity of the stock market," she said, glancing from one to the other of us. Earlier in the afternoon she had asked Gladys to put in calls to the producer of the "Morning Show," to Senator Packer for an interview, and to an editor at *Atlantic* about a piece on Anthony Morris. Gladys was able to stall, but something had to be done about her. "Unfortunately, we were at my house when a reporter called asking me what kind of mother she'd been. Since then, she's been on this rampage."

Madge kept clasping and unclasping her hands. Andrew suggested she go home and rest awhile, persuaded her we would get the situation under control. I wondered if he really thought we could. Without discussion he and I walked in her study together.

Sarah was sitting behind her desk typing. "Don't you work anymore now that you've met my brother?" She did not look up from her typewriter. "I think we're going to put in word processors after all."

"Sarah . . . ," Andrew started.

She interrupted, never looking up: "Tell me, Courtney, is Andrew as good a lover as he used to boast he was? Such tales from such an innocent-looking lad!"

"Could we talk a minute?" I asked.

"Talk," she said, but she continued typing, an old master at carrying on a conversation and composing at the same time.

Andrew leaned down and unplugged the typewriter. Sarah recovered quickly.

"Damn you!" she screamed, jumping up. "You've broken my train of thought."

Andrew, visibly shaken, put his arms on her shoulders. "Sarah, you're not being smart. Come talk to us."

"I have work to do."

"Later. It's not a good time now," he coaxed.

"I'm sick of all you fools yapping at me." She looked at me. "You're too vulnerable for him. He's much too restless. He will break your heart, for he always leaves, don't you, Andrew? I was his first desertion; I ought to know."

"Sarah," he said, grabbing her wrists.

Andrew stared down at the floor, refused to look at her. But once again she switched roles. "Courtney, you look awful," she said. "Come upstairs with me and we'll try to do something about you. Andrew, go in the kitchen and put something together for dinner. Ida has left enough food in there to feed all the homeless in Washington."

Upstairs she focused her attention on me — a way of making up for the earlier remarks downstairs. Better to feel my way slowly through this, I decided.

"Sit down here and I'll think of something," she ordered. She reached for a brush and pulled one side of my hair up, then the other. "We'll give you a European look, something very sophisticated. We should have tried this long ago." She continued to work.

"When Leslie was young, I would play with her hair by the hour. It helped when I was down." She handed me a hand mirror to see the results. "She was very patient with me. Your hair reminds me of hers — straight, fine, but good color."

She sat down on the side of her bed, smoothing her duvet over and over with her hand. "Now she gets exasperated if I even try to brush it."

"That was bound to happen sometime," I said when the silence got too long.

196

"That stupid counselor said Leslie had low self-esteem. He's crazy. How could she as my daughter? Anyway, after that I did try to build her up. You know something? Underneath all this, I still get scared myself that they'll all know I'm not so smart or clever. My life was made up of fairy tales." She paused and finished in a flat, dead voice. "Well, it was, wasn't it?"

Before I answered, she began again. "In August I brought home a new school wardrobe . . . hand-picked it myself. I wanted to be sure everything flattered her. I took off a whole afternoon. Sometimes you and Gladys would let her talk you into . . . well, she threw those new things down the stairs. Told me she was old enough to choose her own clothes." Sarah's hands had stopped moving, and she was staring at them.

"She was just going through a phase," I said. "She always loved what you bought her."

"She did, didn't she?" She appeared to be losing interest in the conversation.

"I have some big news on the Anthony Morris front if you want to talk about it," I said.

"Of course, I want to talk about it. What's wrong with you?" Immediately her posture changed. She was all attention. I told her about my meeting with Mr. Dobotu and about the terrorists in Lumb and asked her which sources I should check in the intelligence community.

"Let's not start with American intelligence. If they knew, the chances are Ditson would know — he's on their oversight committee — and if he knew, he wouldn't be so casual about our role there." Now she was the old Sarah — alert, savvy, considering her options.

"I think we'd do better with the Israelis. They've had operatives in those African countries for years."

"But if they knew, wouldn't they tell the CIA?" I asked.

"Of course not. They don't trust the CIA or the politicians who watch them. The leaks aren't what they once were, but they're still there."

"So how come they'll tell us?" Especially the two of us, I thought.

"Intelligence won't tell us anything. I've used government of-

ficials before — they like to stay in good with the American media."
She must have realized that staying in good with Sarah was no
longer the equivalent of staying in good with the media, for she
quickly went on: "I think this one calls for someone with a cause,
someone out to embarrass the Likud wing of the government."
She got out her Rolodex and started leafing through it for a
"true Zionist." Someone who believed Israel's spiritual and moral
integrity was paramount, she said, and would scoff at the idea
of Israel aligning itself with certain countries simply in the name
of security.

"How about Chaim Stern? He's a retired agent. East European
background, so socialism, not religion, is the guiding principle.
He considers most of the Israeli cabinet theological fascists and
still burns with his original fire." She had stopped before his
name in the Rolodex and looked extremely pleased with herself.
"At one time he helped train terrorist agents, including Idi Amin,
by the way. And more to the point, he happens to be in the
States now on a lecture tour. I just received a note from him
about . . . this . . . this . . . about Leslie."

The reminder was too abrupt. Anthony Morris and terrorists
and Israeli agents were not enough. She slumped, her energy
gone. "Tell Andrew I'm not hungry. I'm going to bed." She
laughed. "Much to everyone's relief. You go eat with him. I will
not be responsible for turning you into a waif."

Instead, I left. On an impulse I had decided to go by Rich
Sanford's, for I knew that no story in the world would make any
difference until we put Leslie's ghost to rest.

His rented room was in the basement of a turn-of-the-century
townhouse in the Mt. Pleasant section of Washington, a transitional neighborhood with comfortable homes and gracious trees.
As often as not, the old homes contained as many families as
rooms. This particular house, however, had been spruced up
and looked to be occupied by one young family, judging by the
tricycle and wind-up baby swing on the front porch.

The steps approaching Rich Sanford's door had been swept,
but inside, two McDonald's sacks and a dozen empty beer cans
littered the bare floor. A stained mattress only half covered by

a sheet and a moth-eaten army blanket occupied the center of the room. An electric guitar and two large amplifiers stood in one corner; in another, an expensive stereo. In another corner we sat cross-legged.

Rich on his own turf was almost at ease. He offered me a joint that I refused, started to light up anyway, but changed his mind.

"So what can I do for you?" he asked.

I decided to stick with the direct approach. "Why did Leslie change her mind about going to her father's?"

"Take that up with Mrs. Adams," he answered.

I started over, my voice low and agreeable: "I wonder what the police would say if they knew you burglarized Sarah's house." This was a wild shot that had just occurred to me; the stereo looked like Leslie's. He looked startled.

"I didn't have anything to do with that. Leslie did it herself."

"The police will find that interesting," I said.

"Listen, she took the stuff to pay for her ticket to Colorado, but the silver covered it. She made me pawn it for her over in Baltimore. I was holding onto the stereo until she left for her father's."

"But she changed her mind about going. Why? Did you threaten her?"

He jumped up and glared down at me. Did I really think he would confess; or, if he did, he would let me go? I don't know. I was running strictly on instinct. In this instance, a reliable guide.

"Don't try putting this on me. Ask her bitch mother what happened. She fucked Leslie up. Not me."

I looked over at the stereo. "It's all going to come out, anyway," I said.

"Sarah shouldn't have done it to her," he moaned. "It's the one thing she shouldn't have done. I was there and it made me sick." He was pacing around the room, holding his face in his hands. I waited. He came back and sat down. I stretched my legs and leaned against the wall to listen.

"A couple of days before that party Leslie was giving for her mother, I'd come over. Their maid was off and we'd decided to take advantage of the empty house — Leslie saw it as another way to 'get' Sarah. She'd left school early, and we were in the kitchen fixing sandwiches when Sarah came home, already mad. Finding me just made it worse.

"She told me to get out. I started to put my sandwich down and oblige her, but she slapped it out of my hand and started hassling me. She threatened to have me busted on drug charges if I ever saw Leslie again.

"Then she turned on Leslie. That morning she'd found the plane ticket to Colorado. Wanted to know what that was all about. Accused Leslie of trying to ruin her life.

"Leslie stayed cool. Reminded Sarah that she had told her what she was going to do and she'd meant it. Said she was planning to tell her again after the party. Asked why she'd been snooping in her things. How else had she found the ticket?

"Sarah started crying. Went on about giving up everything for Leslie. Blamed Leslie because she'd never remarried — hadn't wanted to bring in someone who didn't love Leslie as much as she did. She asked how Leslie could live with a man who'd never done anything for them, not even sent money when they were broke.

"I kind of felt sorry for her. She looked old and hurt — like anybody's mother would — but Leslie got mad. Said she couldn't live with a bitch anymore, and, whatever else, her father wouldn't smother her to death. Sarah laughed and said he'd never have her.

"Leslie told her they'd been writing. That seemed to hit her mother harder than anything. Leslie noticed, too — all of a sudden she started trying to reason with Sarah, telling her she'd be leaving home soon for college and she was a lot more grown-up and responsible than Sarah thought she was. The distance would stop their fighting and then they could be friends again.

"Sarah didn't say anything to that. She poured herself a glass of orange juice and we stood there and watched." He paused and took a breath. He'd been talking rapidly but he began again slowly, more deliberately.

"Something about the way she fixed her shoulders and her

mouth — like a good pitcher winding up — made me want to warn Leslie to watch out.

" 'Well,' she said to Leslie, 'Philip Adams is a more generous man than I ever suspected. Too bad he's not your father.'

"Leslie looked stunned but came to enough to call Sarah a liar. Her mother kept on smiling. 'He was good enough to marry me and give you his name, but he's not your father.'

"Leslie yelled, 'Liar! Bitch!' She was really crazy.

"But Sarah, now all cool herself, just said, 'Bitch, yes. Liar, no.'

"Leslie started crying. I got the hell out of there."

"And?" I asked.

"She told Leslie she'd slept around a lot the winter she conceived her." His voice cracked. "She had no idea which one was Leslie's father."

My legs were paralyzed. I couldn't get up. Rich asked if I wanted a drink of water, the private-school boy coming out from all those layers of toughness. I shook my head no.

"Leslie said she didn't believe her mother, but everything about her was different. She told me she wasn't going to live with her father, she'd changed her mind. At first she kept going over and over what had happened — we must have had twenty conversations. Then she wouldn't talk about any of it anymore. Or much of anything."

Clearly now I would have to leave. I wished I hadn't come alone. I wished I didn't have to be the one to tell Andrew. I wished about a thousand things one after the other, for I knew that night I would go home to nothing.

21

THE NOISE wasn't part of any dream, I knew instantly. A less than ethereal creature was at my window, and this time I would attack. I jumped up, grabbed my lamp, and began shouting. He scrambled away. But more noise was coming from my living room window, and someone else at the door. I yelled and charged in with my lamp. The window noise stopped. However, at the door someone yelled back. Cheryl. Still holding my lamp, I opened the door.

"This place is crawling with hookers," she said. "Two just came through my window. The police are raiding the neighborhood cathouse. What have you got to smoke?" She was walking around the room, this time wearing a turquoise mini-length T-shirt with sequins on it and white lace anklets.

I shook my head and said, "I thought you were the press."

"Same difference. What about a line for morning?"

"Don't you read the papers? That stuff kills people. What happens in the morning?"

"Just a boring meeting. Where is your new friend Andrew?"

"Listen to that," I said. One of the women was shrieking as two policemen tried to force her into a van. "They should be out looking for murderers."

Cheryl shuddered. "They scared the shit out of me. Speaking of which, my friend Dave still wants to take you out. The notoriety attracts him. You should go. It will send out the right signals."

"I thought you just said he's a shit."

"But a respectable one," she countered.

"So what? Why can't we do it on our own? Why a super-achieving duo? Why not concentrate on our own skills?"

"Two generate more power than one. Besides, that is part of our skill."

"You mean using other people? You make us sound like complete frauds — getting by on who we know, dependent on the goodwill of others. And why am I having this conversation with you right now? I have too much else on my mind for this."

But Cheryl ignored the last bit. "We all consume other people's energies, but some do it more than others. Think how you got where you are now. Sure, there are the Sarahs and the Senator Ditsons, who have power based on hard intellect and homework, but those are damn few. That's why they stand out so. For the rest . . ."

"Everybody works hard here."

"They work hard at not getting found out."

"I'm doing it the other way."

She looked at me with her even gray eyes. "If you were doing it the other way, you would be able to distinguish your life from Sarah's." She went to look out the window. "Quiet out there," she said. "Maxie may even be grateful to me. I'll bet I saved him from the sweep."

"Hasn't he been back yet?" A couple of days ago, he had unlocked the back door of Cheryl's car to sleep in it, awakening and scaring Cheryl as she drove to work the next morning. Whereupon she told him, among other things, to get the hell away from our steps.

"He'll be back soon enough," she answered and yawned.

I handed her a letter addressed to her that Mr. Duc had given me when I got home. "Since when have you become his pen pal?"

"Since yesterday. I've found him a room with the family of our office janitor."

"Why didn't you tell me? You did that? I mean, it's such a nice thing." When she pointed out she was capable of a nice thing, I blushed.

The room had a hot plate and they were going to get a mini-refrigerator for him. That way he could fix his Vietnamese food. Cheryl, of course, had not been overcome by modesty at all, but had simply been saving this for the propitious moment. I, in turn, applauded loudly as was expected and as was her due. She was not through.

"Before we both get carried away with my sainthood, I should confess to firing Krys. The good deed for Mr. Duc was partly compensatory." She held up her hand to stop my protest. "We should have done it a long time ago. With winter coming, we could never have gotten rid of that smell in here."

"We can't just let her go. We've got to see about her. Help her."

"Courtney, she never wanted our help. Remember when we fixed her up to look after a church youth house? And when you tried to get her to apply for welfare? She's smart. When she wants another job, she'll start swimming again."

"You can't walk away from people like . . . like . . . they were . . . dogs." I was crying again, this time out of anger. I hated Cheryl.

"You've got this fantasy about life," Cheryl said. "You think you're going to save everybody. Well, you're not. You'll be doing well to save yourself."

I picked up the lamp and threw it just to the right of her head. Without a word she went to my kitchen. Without a word she returned with the broom and dustpan. Without a word she began sweeping.

"I'm sorry," I mumbled.

She went back into the kitchen; then opened my front door. "You have more trouble with change than anyone I know. But you'd better learn to accept it. You better give up some of those myths, the first one being Sarah, before you destroy yourself." She left with a dramatically quiet closing of my door.

I sat in the middle of my floor and continued to cry. She was right about one thing: I couldn't let go. Change came hard for everybody. Any fool knew that. Sarah couldn't accept the change in Leslie, couldn't let go of some crazy mother-daughter image. And Leslie herself was stuck with some father dream that had nothing to do with the truth.

I made myself think about Leslie. Not Sarah and Leslie. Leslie and me. Was part of my anger with her because we were more alike than I wanted to admit? She had felt not good enough and had come to rely on magic — the father who would rescue her. I had done the same; only Sarah was to be my savior. We both nourished ourselves too much on unfulfilled expectations, twanged out unreasonable yearnings for some alien force to protect us. And if the magic went away, panic set in and anything was possible.

"Anything is possible," I said aloud as I got up to go into the bedroom. But instead of bed, I dressed. If Cheryl as the messenger could make me violent, then what was Leslie capable of when Sarah destroyed her daughter's one sustaining promise? Rich Sanford might know the answer.

Two phone calls interrupted my leaving. The first was from Chaim Stern in California. He knew it was late, but Sarah had insisted he call. He could corroborate my story. He gave me times and places and two incidents. Also, he said, Mr. Morris was aware of the group. He paused.

This certainly was not the way he preferred to handle a matter of this magnitude, but Sarah had told him it was vital I get the story today. He did not understand the urgency but took Sarah's word for it. He wished me success with my endeavor and congratulated me. I started to tell him it was not my endeavor, it was our endeavor; but he was gone. I was annoyed with Sarah's maneuvering. This was not the way I would have handled it either. Surely this called for a face-to-face meeting. The next call — minutes later — cleared it up.

Andrew's voice was strained. The prosecutor was almost ready to make his case for probable cause. Sarah was to be arrested within forty-eight hours. Bob Owens had come to tell them. Sarah's message to me was to contact Morris and get the story out immediately. Sarah's column but my byline. Andrew's voice choked. It was to be my story now. We didn't even say good-bye.

I stood there clutching the telephone waiting for a voice to rescind Andrew's message. Sarah's arrest now seemed inevitable, and I was scared — for her and for myself. And I didn't want to hurt Anthony Morris. I didn't want that kind of responsibility.

Anthony Morris, shaved and fully dressed, received me in his living room at six in the morning. He was polite enough to offer me coffee. Other amenities were gone from his demeanor, his authority collapsed in the heap of scandal soon to surround him.

He did not deny knowledge of terrorists in Lumb. Only, if there were, the Lumbanese contained them better than most countries. For that part of the world, they ran an efficient government. He had no apologies to make for supporting them. At any rate, hindsight was useless.

The talk didn't last long. We had little to say to each other. By the time my story ran, he would have withdrawn his nomination for U.S. trade representative.

As I was leaving, Sheila Morris came down. "I hope you and Sarah Adams know you have ruined the best man in Washington. I hope you are proud of yourselves. You have destroyed our lives."

"Sheila," her husband said.

"It's true. She should know what it is she does."

"And so should your husband," I answered. But the nagging doubt remained: were Sarah and I the upscale equivalent of the press mob in front of her house? He was, I knew, of that breed of public servant not much in evidence these days. He was not wantonly greedy, nor had he, like so many others, debased the offices he held. He cared. Though he had been too casual in his caring.

Then Anthony Morris did an extraordinary thing — he took my arm and walked me all the way to my car. He opened the car door for me and said, "To the best of my ability, I have tried to serve my country. That involves making judgment calls, and some of them are wrong. I acknowledge them. This one was beyond the accepted limits and I tried to ignore it. I chose to work beyond the system and made a mistake. Excesses are not to be condoned. You have nothing to be ashamed of." His hands were as sure and graceful as ever.

By the end of the day, I would have written my story. A coup handed to me by Sarah. Her way of saving me. I had expected a feeling of accomplishment — I had worked hard, brought it all together. Yet a feeling of sadness stuck with me. He was right. He had exceeded the limits and ignored the consequence. A result of pride and arrogance rather than avarice. But that didn't make it better, just more ambiguous, and I was sick of ambiguity.

Which didn't get me out of my next house call. Rich Sanford. Confronting him was to accept another truth, too hideous in its dimensions.

Finally he came to his door. With bare feet and no gel on his hair he could have been taken for an ordinary twenty-year-old. We both stood there shivering, but he did not ask me in until I told him I knew — Leslie had planned to kill her mother.

"You're nuts," he answered, but pushed the door open for me.

"You said yourself Leslie wanted to get her. She planned it beautifully, even provided herself an audience — a little after the fact, but we would be a nice backdrop for later."

"Nuts," he repeated.

"Why else would Leslie wear rubber gloves to chop vegetables? That never made sense to me. And why smoke pot in her own house, knowing it would provoke Sarah?

"She wanted Sarah to come in that kitchen furious. They could have a fight. Sarah's anger would make it easier for Leslie to kill her. Later she could blame it on an intruder. The burglar, for instance, who had come back for another go. She even left the front door unlocked to accommodate him."

He folded himself down to the floor and kept shaking his head. I had to control an impulse to kick him. Instead, I went on: "Sarah came into the kitchen furious. Leslie turned on her with the knife, a clever tool since Sarah panics at the sight of blood. But there was only a glancing wound."

"You don't know that," he said.

"Then," I went on, raising my voice. By now I could not stop my body from trembling. "Leslie kept going after Sarah and Sarah must have fought back hard. Finally, Leslie chased Sarah to the pool — if she couldn't stab her, she'd drown her. Sarah defended herself and in the struggle Leslie was strangled. Instantly. Before Sarah could know what she had done."

"I don't know," he mumbled, not looking up. He was right. I had gone far beyond what he could possibly know. But I had to say it. To explain it all as far as possible. I could not say only a part and not say it all.

"From the beginning you knew what happened, but you didn't want to get involved because that would implicate you, too." I got on my knees next to him. "You would let a woman's life be destroyed because you have no guts. Isn't one life enough?"

He did not look at me, but he started talking.

"She hated Sarah," he began. "All the time she felt guilty. All the time. Then when Sarah said she didn't have a father, she went a little berserk. The past few weeks she'd been acting crazy, but after that she flipped out.

"She said she didn't believe Sarah. Kept saying what a liar she was, like I told you. But when she canceled her plans to live with her father, she said it didn't matter anymore. She kind of gave up.

"By then I thought maybe she should go ahead and go and I told her so. After I said that, she told me — and this is the only time she acted like she believed her mother — she told me she could never know for sure if Sarah had told the truth. 'She took my father and my certainty,' she said." He slowly raised his eyes to me.

"She never spelled out what she was going to do, but she'd say that Sarah was going to pay. She told me how her mother got hysterical over blood and how she'd get an opportunity to see blood again. That's when she was still talking. I didn't really believe she could do anything."

I stood up. "What should I do?" he asked.

"I'll let you know."

Outside the sky was still dark. A lone bird signaled the beginning of morning.

22

ANDREW ANSWERED Sarah's phone. I was on my way over and was Bob still there? To my relief he said yes. I wanted Bob to be around when I told Andrew, for the proof of self-defense was an admission of Sarah's culpability. No matter how justified, she was responsible for Leslie's death. Whether the blow happened as Sarah warded off the attack or as she struck out in rage and panic — Sarah herself might not even know — she killed her daughter. And (to face the worst) was that moment's extra strength completely accidental or born out of fury? That, I was sure, no one would ever know. We knew too much already. Sarah had murdered Leslie.

I didn't have to think about that. No time to. I had to think of how to help. Now she had to be helped. And after the trial, we would go away — Sarah, Andrew, and I. Then she could start rebuilding her professional life because, I might as well face it, a certain amount of mending was going to be necessary. But she was such a fighter. A good fight would be the best antidote possible. The Morris story, of course, would come out under her name as well as mine. We had shared a few bylines before. I would tell her that this morning. In fact, with a story like that and the strong case for self-defense, this town would be hard pressed to hold her reputation hostage for too long.

Wisps of pink mixed in the gray sky and a real chilliness was in the air. The season was changing. A cool autumn morning was in the making. And with Andrew's help, for it would take Andrew, too, we could all have a new beginning.

*   *   *

Andrew was standing outside, hands thrust in his pockets, hair tousled. He came to me, pressed my head hard to his chest. Wordlessly we swayed back and forth. As we entered the house, he held my hand.

Bob Owens was there, as were Madeline, Gordon, and Madge. Andrew shook his head to let me know he had not told them anything. Madge motioned toward a chair. I leaned back in it and tried to shut out the silence. Gordon bent over me, his hands on the chair arms.

"You are going to snap," he said. I didn't say anything. "Frantic. You look frantic."

"Hush, Gordon," Madge said. "Let's talk about what's to be done for Sarah."

"Nothing can be done for Sarah," Madeline said. "For God's sake, can't any of you see that? Nothing can be done for her," she repeated, looking straight at her husband.

"You wouldn't mind her rotting in jail, would you, Madeline?" Gordon asked.

Madeline got up, stood directly in front of him, slapped him hard on his face, and sat back down. The rest of us watched in silence; sat in silence. After the tensions eased, Bob took Andrew and me into the study and closed the door.

Bob told us he had extracted a promise, or something close to one, that the police would hold off for another forty-eight hours. The warrant was being kept under such tight wraps that he doubted the press would get hold of it. All this because Sarah very much wanted the delay until I had run the Anthony Morris story. She was obsessed with getting that story in print. I assured him it would be.

They looked so mournful, suddenly I was eager for them to know what Rich had told me. Maybe also eager to share the burden. I began talking and, as I talked, I looked only at Bob, not wanting to see the pain on Andrew's face.

To my surprise he told me he had already started preparing a case of self-defense. For quite a while, he had suspected the truth; the police, almost from the beginning. They had gone this slowly only because of the celebrities involved. Now the circumstantial evidence had piled up: Sarah's fingerprints; a clear lack of motive by anybody else; and the latest — Rich Sanford's testimony that Sarah and Leslie had been quarreling. The bastard, I thought; Rich hadn't told me that. No wonder he was feeling guilty.

We agreed that I would talk to Sarah first and tell her what Rich had said. There was some discussion of having a doctor on hand in case Rich's confession triggered her memory. (We all agreed the chances were her amnesia was real.) Andrew was reluctant to involve anyone else at this point if it wasn't absolutely necessary.

As I knocked on Sarah's bedroom door, all that was necessary, I reminded myself, was to get through the next few hours and days. To face the worst and begin to heal.

She was sitting on her chaise longue drinking coffee. The morning paper lay in front of her, the rubber band still around it.

"So the lover returns once more," she said. Wearing her pink silk robe only loosely caught at the waist, she made an effort to cover those high breasts, which she could draw up the way other people raised eyebrows. In the pale morning light, she could pass for twenty-five in spite of circles and no makeup.

"If you can tear yourself away from my brother, you are welcome to join Bob and me for lunch with his hotshot trial lawyer. Bob insists that I see him, but he's so dull. I know he's a brilliant lawyer but boring as sin. I told Bob that. Do you believe in sin?"

"As well as I can understand it."

She brought her hand down on her leg. "God! Don't take everything so seriously. Where's your sense of humor?" She sat up straighter. "This place is turning into a mausoleum. Leslie would absolutely not believe what is happening here."

Then she laid her head back and shut her eyes. "She was the only constant in my life, and it's as bad without her as I always knew it would be."

"Sarah," I began, "I've talked with Rich Sanford."

Before I could say more she pulled me over and examined my clothes. "This jacket looks like a used Band-Aid. It's one thing to be sloppy; another, to be unimaginative. You must work on that. Imagination is the key ingredient to any success I've achieved."

I tried again: "He said some things that could be helpful for your defense."

"Hard work helped, but imagination provided the impetus." She got up and began pacing, her arms crossed over her chest. "It kept me from the ugliness of limitations."

"You've always lectured me about cutting through the bull, and that's what I'm trying to do . . ."

"That's other people's," she interrupted. "I surround myself with as much illusion as possible, and I advise you to do the same. You will die without it."

"Even though our business is to strip it away?"

"That doesn't happen to be what I'm talking about." Abruptly she sat back down.

"But suppose the truth really does set free?"

"A myth promulgated by a sadist."

"Rich Sanford says Leslie was very angry with you."

She placed her hand to the back of her head in the most casual of gestures. "Daughters are always getting angry with their mothers, or didn't you know? We were the best of friends — you know that."

"Yes, but things happen. Nobody means them to . . ."

She interrupted. "What are you doing here? Have you written that story yet? It's got to come out tomorrow. It could mean a book contract. At the least, the job of your choice. It's too soon for a column of your own, but I don't rule it out entirely. Just don't count on Andrew. You're too ambitious to take him on. He's still looking for someone to take care of him, though he doesn't know it."

"Please, listen." My voice shook. So did my hands.

Sarah jumped back up. "No. You listen. I want you to leave me alone. I want everyone to. This is a wonderful opportunity for you. You'll be launched. If you want to do something for me, do this."

I clutched her dressing table for support. "I know what happened. We can get you out of this mess. You can write your own book."

Her body became still with that taut, nervous grace associated with opening moments when any mistake is treachery. "You're hallucinating," she said in an even voice. "I am the only one who can possibly know what happened, and I don't remember. Your prying is disruptive. I want you to keep your thoughts to yourself. And I mean to yourself."

She was no longer looking at me but somewhere to the left of my shoulder, and her voice had lost its resonance. "You are confusing truth with piddling facts. I've taught you better."

At that moment a child's terror of separation exploded inside me. Sarah could not be saved. Her hell, neither dissolved nor lightened — only made worse. She was right: we had all been snatching after facts, running aimlessly.

The only thing to do for Sarah was to abandon her. If I really cared about her, I would let go. The search had been for me, not for her. Since Leslie's death, she had been doomed, and only I could be saved. I had always known, and now I knew I had always known. Now I needed the strength to act in her interest. For once, to think about someone other than myself.

I moved to her side and put my arms around her for what would turn out to be the last time. She caressed my head, the way she used to Leslie's.

"I can't see you anymore," she said softly. I nodded.

As I left, she called to me, "Don't make your story lead too sensational. You want to establish a measured tone." Then, almost as an afterthought — "Without me, she couldn't have survived."

23

BOB AND ANDREW were waiting in the hallway. I told them what
had happened. Andrew protested. "She's in no state to decide
this for herself."

"Yes, she is," I argued. "To acknowledge that Leslie could kill
her is worse than death or prison. She's been trying to tell us
that."

Already Bob understood. And finally Andrew accepted. We
agreed Bob would explain to everyone downstairs. For the world's
consumption, there would be a plea of not guilty. It probably
would not work, but the sentence would be light. Bob could
almost guarantee that. His eyes had become as old as the rest of
his face. I wished he were my father.

I watched him as he entered her bedroom. "Sarah, darling,"
he said as he put his arm around her before closing the door. I
wondered how many lifetimes I would have to live before I could
find that kind of friend. If only it had worked out between them,
maybe . . . but the "ifs" and "maybes" were over.

Could he drop me somewhere, Andrew wanted to know. I
reminded him I had my car. Then there was the story to write.
But could he drop me? he insisted. He would pick me up later.
For the present, he was useless around here. Just to be together
a little while.

As we left the house, Gordon grabbed my arm. "Where do
you think you're going?" he asked.

"Too late," I said.

"You a quitter? I didn't know you were a quitter. She's not, and I'm not going to let you turn her into one." He shook his finger in my face. "That was the thing about us. The thing that kept us together. We weren't quitters. I always came back, didn't I? I'm not too proud to admit I needed to come back. She gave me life. The only real life I ever had. She gave you life, too; only you're running out on her."

"Let up," Andrew said. "She can't do anything. Madeline was right. None of us can." Andrew was gentle, as to a child. Gordon's body began to move with silent heaves. Madge covered her mouth as a cry escaped. She ran from the room. Andrew propelled me out the door.

We sat in front of my place and watched Maxie get out of a car down the block. Before strolling off, he pocketed his money under the streetlight. Leaves banked the curb, awaiting a truck sweep. No new ones were left to fall.

I felt diminished. From now on I would toss up my thoughts with nobody there to catch and embellish them, to send them back polished and shining just for being shared. Already I knew of the mornings when nothing would matter to me. Of the mornings when I would wish her dead so as to forget. Of the mornings when, looking for transcendence, I would try once again to invest her with mythic qualities. So long as I did not accept the limits of her perfectibility, I eluded the limits of my own. Now I had lost forever the ephemeral state of magic that was hers to give.

Andrew picked up my hand, the way he'd come to do when we were talking. "Have you ever been to Cancún?" he asked.

"Never."

"It's lovely — quiet, beautiful. When we get through this nightmare, I want to take you there." I didn't answer. "You'll love it. I promise."

I put his hand to my lips. "Andrew, it won't work for us. Not now."

"I need you."

"You need Sarah. I'd make a lousy substitute."

"You underestimate yourself."

"No. Sarah is going to have us for a long time. We both deserve better than each of us is now."

"Are you sure you know what the hell you're doing?" His voice went husky, and I felt myself getting wet. I touched his cheek with my fingers and resisted moving them downward. Then I opened the car door and got out.

"If Sarah should change her mind about seeing me . . . I'm . . . I'll be here," I said to him.

He nodded but turned his head away from me. "I'll have your car dropped off," he said. He drove away. I stood there watching.

After he was out of sight, I looked around me and concentrated on the crunchy sharp flavors of the street. A prostitute carefully crawled out a boarded-up window of what was supposed to be — since the raid — the abandoned whorehouse. A couple of early-morning risers were already starting their cars for work. An elderly man was putting out his trash for pickup.

Standing there I began to feel a strength, the promise of completeness — a state exact and unceasing and not to be equated with peace. Maxie turned to me and waved. I smiled and raised an arm to wave back.